The Book
of John

First published by O Books, 2010
O Books is an imprint of John Hunt Publishing Ltd., The Bothy, Deershot Lodge, Park Lane, Ropley,
Hants, SO24 0BE, UK
office1@o-books.net
www.o-books.net

Distribution in:

UK and Europe
Orca Book Services
orders@orcabookservices.co.uk
Tel: 01202 665432 Fax: 01202 666219
Int. code (44)

USA and Canada
NBN
custserv@nbnbooks.com
Tel: 1 800 462 6420 Fax: 1 800 338 4550

Australia and New Zealand
Brumby Books
sales@brumbybooks.com.au
Tel: 61 3 9761 5535 Fax: 61 3 9761 7095

Far East (offices in Singapore, Thailand,
Hong Kong, Taiwan)
Pansing Distribution Pte Ltd
kemal@pansing.com
Tel: 65 6319 9939 Fax: 65 6462 5761

South Africa
Stephan Phillips (pty) Ltd
Email: orders@stephanphillips.com
Tel: 27 21 4489839 Telefax: 27 21 4479879

Text copyright Kate Niles 2009

Design: Stuart Davies

ISBN: 978 1 84694 291 4

A CIP catalogue record for this book is available
from the British Library.

Printed by Digital Book Print

O Books operates a distinctive and ethical publishing philosophy in
all areas of its business, from its global network of authors to
production and worldwide distribution.

The Book
of John

Kate Niles

BOOKS

Winchester, UK
Washington, USA

The Book of John is a revelation—a wise, deeply observant book about nature, about regret, about love. Kate Niles has given us an unforgettable cast of characters, each on their own complicated journey toward healing. The past, she reminds us, breathes right along with the present when we excavate the bones of our memory, dig through the ruins of our heart. **Gayle Brandeis,** author of *The Book of Dead Birds* and *Self Storage*

As both artist and archaeologist, Kate Niles conjoins crafts to illustrate the buried truths of the Southwest's prehistoric people—a colorful history that pulses even now with both passion and savagery. Like ancient Clovis points unearthed from the Four Corners' desert catacombs, her prose is at once brutish and elegant, her characters flintknapped to perfection. Together they deliver fatal blows to the illusion that, in our attempts at progress and civility, we have not lost something utterly vital. In Book of John, Niles has performed the most difficult of excavations—that of the howling human heart. **Amy Irvine,** Author of *Trespass: Living at the Edge of the Promised Land* and winner of the 2008 Orion Award for Best Nature Writing

Kate Niles has given us a fascinating, multi-layered novel. With prodigious knowledge and lyrical prose she takes us on a journey through the myriad landscapes of the American west, from the red rock canyons of the Four Corners and the sere deserts of the Great Basin to the lush, verdant coastline of the Pacific Northwest. With powerful imagery she takes us into a place of ancient atrocity and into the modern halls of academe where archaeologists attempt to understand that atrocity. Niles maps all these territories with authority. But as we follow her compelling protagonist, John, on his often painful journey of self-discovery, we find that Niles is equally at home in the complex terrain of the human heart. **Paula Huntley,** Author of bestseller *The Hemingway Bookclub of Kosovo*

The Book of John does for archeology what The Secret Garden did for inconspicuous little doors—changed forever how we see our world. **Christopher Noel**, author of *In the Unlikely Event of a Water Landing* and *Impossible Visits*

Kate Niles sees more than most. Sees deeper. Farther. And what she observes she transforms into story and scene woven through language that both simmers with beauty and pierces with untempered insight and honesty into the human — and more-than-human — condition. In THE BOOK OF JOHN, Niles again has such a vision to share. This time the story is about one man's long journey to a home — to several homes — he had forgotten, and sometimes didn't realize he had. It is a lovely and difficult path and vision. And once again, Niles' clear-sighted prose conjures in each of us visions of our own forgotten homes. **Ken Wright**, Author of THE MONKEY WRENCH DAD and WHY I'M AGAINST IT ALL

Other Books by Kate Niles

Geographies of the Heart (poetry)

The Basket Maker (novel)

For Jonathan,
with gratitude and love

Acknowledgements

To P.W.A., who lives on in my heart always, and to many of my students, who have taught me a great deal about learning disabilities.

To Karen, Andy Sue, Dan, Rusty, Dave, Ray, Martha, Ken and everyone else from the University of New Mexico archeology program in the late great 80s; you kept me alive.

To Lew Binford, whose ability to piece together the human story from what remains in the dust is my bedrock, my muse, my framework through which I understand the world. Thank you is a woefully inadequate set of words.

Apologies but much delight to Brian Billman, Richard Marlar, and everyone even remotely involved with Cowboy Wash and its Famous Turd. I've pillaged your site's story mercilessly and with great respect for the quality of your research. I will buy you beers to make up for mussing up your scientific reputations any day.

Special thanks to Jerrold Levy's superb study of community disharmony at Hopi (*Orayvi Revisited*) and to the work of Mark Varien, Linda Cordell, Jim Judge, Chip Wills, Fred Eggan, Alfonso Ortiz, and Ramon Gutierrez. More personally, Mike Hoffman, the late Bruce Anderson, Bob Powers, Charlie Haecker, Liz Oster, my colleagues and rangers at Mesa Verde National Park, et al ad nauseum; I owe you all that I know of southwest archeology and ethnography, field work, bones.

Many thanks to Chris Noel and Gretchen Treadwell for reading and editing earlier versions, and for their enthusiasm regarding this novel. Much gratitude to Joan Schweighardt, who continues to believe in me and my writing beyond all of my wildest hopes, and to John Hunt and the good people at O Books for believing in it too. Many thanks to the ongoing support of Jan Nesset, Ken Wright, the deeply thoughtful, funny, and talented poets and writers of my home region, as well as Joe Foster and Maria's Bookshop.

In the desert
I saw a creature, naked, bestial,
who, squatting upon the ground,
held his heart in his hands,
and ate of it.
I said, "is it good, friend?"
"It is bitter – bitter," he answered;
"but I like it
"because it is bitter
"and because it is my heart."
- Stephen Crane

I am the voice of one crying in the wilderness.
- John 1:23

PART ONE

CHAPTER 1

I.

The Makah, who live at the extreme northwest tip of this country, where the seas swell in the rain and everything is green-gray, green-gray, hunt whales in spare and beautiful canoes made of cedar. When the whale is finally dead, which may take three days or longer, one of the fishermen dives into the ocean and sews its mouth shut. He does this so the water will not enter the whale, making it too heavy to drag home. This is John, the story of John Thompson. He is the whale, lips sealed so he can bob along with the crowd, where they cannot tell he has lost his heart to the bottom of the sea, all along.

He has come to Neah Bay because it is green-gray, green-gray, and to "get over" the last nine months, which have left him depleted. He doesn't look depleted; he looks fat. But here's a secret: the fatter he is, the more depleted inside. Another way he is like the dead, bloating whale. Down the block from him is a tiny silver trailer that will never again be without the smell of salmon; salmon, and smoke, and fish grease. His "landlord," if you can call him that – he rents a shack from him for fifty a week – is a man his age named George who, on days when he feels like it and days when he feels there might be a tourist to sell to, smokes salmon in a 55-gallon drum with a pipe for a chimney. He's actually got a fire inside the trailer, at the bottom of the drum, and when he sees John coming he smiles his round-faced smile, and says, "John. John Wayne Gregory-boy. Got somethin' for you." And anymore John doesn't tell him it's John Gregory Wayne Thompson, not the other way around, because it keeps some small flicker of happiness alive in him, to make George happy, to have a joke at his expense. John can't help his name. Sometimes what George has is a chocolate bar, or an illegal six of beer, carefully disguised in a bulky tote bag so the Rez cops won't see it, or even some cedar strips for John's attempts at Makah basketry. But today he pulls up a Kerr jar full of salmon packed in oil.

"Open it," he says. "Smell." He takes a deep breath in his smoky trailer as if heaven itself could be expected.

John unscrews the lid cautiously, gives it a quick whiff. It's not awful, but it's unfamiliar. He's puzzled.

"It's salmon preserved in seal oil, buddy. For you. My auntie makes it. Salmon confit!" George cackles. "Just like that duck shit I used to use cooking in that restaurant in Seattle! It'll survive Armageddon." He grins and stokes the fire.

John's touched. He's always touched when it's something made from the ground, from hard work, from knowledge that means a damn. But it's when he's touched that he is especially glad for his tinted glasses, which are supposed to lighten up indoors but never fully do. He digs in his pocket for his own contribution. He finds the Folsom, his perfect Folsom point channeled directly from the Pleistocene, the only one in the last ten he has attempted that hasn't snapped at the last minute, when he tried to put the flute in.

"Here," he says. "Thanks for the salmon."

George looks at the point. He has encountered John flintknapping many times. Sometimes John flintknaps till he's bloody and the rain is sagging the tarp that comprises his covered front porch, and his fingers ache from the cold and the damp.

George's eyes go wide. He knew John, intensely, for six months five years ago, when they both worked on a dig south of here along the Pacific coast, a hitherto unexcavated trash mound associated with a well-preserved and now-famous long house archeologists originally dug in 1970. A mudslide hit the long house and buried it for posterity, till somebody found it and the Makah got interested and called the "experts." They recognized that did not know how to extract, as thoroughly as possible, all the culture they wanted back from the ground. They did not care a whit for the archeologists' theories or posturings, but the extraction was so effective at retrieving their culture that when, thirty years later, they found money to excavate an associated trash mound, they called the "experts" again. John came with that crew.

George is like John, overweight, not prone to speech. He has stick-straight Indian hair that will look as though someone hacked it with a knife no matter who cuts it, a slow, squinty smile, getting toward middle age. That middle-aged part is also like John. He rolls his lips against one another.

"That took a lot of work," he says, about the point. "You keep it."

But John thrusts it at him, shaking his head. He's no good at this. "No," he says. "No." And slaps it on the counter next to George's cash box. What he wants to do is grab George by his ragged smelly t-shirt neck and tell him all kinds of things, about what a shit he, John Gregory Wayne Thompson, is, and how the Folsom is the only way to feel good about himself right now. But he is a whale with his mouth sewn shut. Cedar twine and bone awl puncturing, the cold grease of the sea cutting into the fisherman as he works. At least he sings for the whale as he does this, the roil of water sighing him up and down, up and down, as he breathes on the whale's snout. John tucks the jar of salmon under his arm, ducks out. George will forgive, understand. They are both autistic, really, which is why they like each other and why, when John showed up a month ago, George nodded toward the shack, gave him wood and extra blankets, and started bringing him goodies now and then, whenever he emerged from his isolation.

* * * *

John has felt autistic since grade school. When he reads the definitions of autism, the associated behaviors, he thinks: surely we are all autistic at some level, in some place in our hearts? Living in this country, with its glamour and malls, its stream of cars, its TV and competitions, is like battering yourself against a sea wall, time and again. How do you not retreat into a world of your own in the face of that?

He'd love to stay in those questions, where all blame can be put on forces outside himself and the refuge of what he knows is cynicism beckons. But that ended, that refuge. And so he has sent himself here, to Neah Bay, where he once took his lover (another refuge, rearing up heartburn the more he tries to ignore her influence) and she said: I could spend a year here just writing. It has a shrouded feel, as he imagines the islands in the North Sea must – Scotland, Ireland, the Hebrides. Sweaters and tea, endless rain, his ancestry and her ancestry tugging in some pale-skinned echo of genetic memory. His lover, Meghan, who is long-ago by now, or nearly so, but feels, especially recently, like yesterday. Meghan, Southwesterner by childhood rights and memories, and by adult careers and explorations, then admitted that the rain, after a while, might pull her down. Rain in the southwest is an entirely different matter, a rupture of lightning and downpour, or teasing strands that almost reach the ground but instead splatter two drops on your windshield and dry up. Same with green; the relief of a cottonwood so brilliantly emerald against a red cliff face is sometimes indescribable, a kind of Oh-Thank-*God* when you come around a bend and see it. Here, green is a given, and a red cliff would be the surprise.

Of course, he is not really autistic, not by any diagnostician's set of rules. But what do they know? He is just cripplingly inarticulate out in the world, and so what is the difference? He scribbles in his head all day long, running commentary in his deliberate way, this beast full of pull and desire and thick, thick failure. He supposes he has come to reckon with that, or that he ought to. He should have reckoned with it since fourth grade, when Sister Theresa of Saint Luke's of the San Diego diocese finally caught on that he could not read. Until then he had night-mares where big letters, Bs and Cs and Ss and Js, upside down or sideways, sometimes three-dimensional, some not, but all of them black and huge, danced around his classroom, cutting into him as he ran. He of course was naked, and the other children were laughing at him, and he felt like jelly, nothing but a mass of jelly. He still has those nightmares now and then; he had them three weeks in a row before he left his house for here.

Sometimes he thinks he has come not only for the rain, though, which keeps him looking inward all the time – maybe too much. He wants to be Too Busy and cut bad jokes with his colleagues but whenever he envisions the situation where he might do that he is drawn up against his inadequacy, his impostership. *Archeologist, hah! You can't put thoughts together on a page to save your life.* Which is not entirely true, but such are the vermin swimming in his mind. And because he has gotten away with scanning far horizons in the way only an interior westerner can, a place of no horizon is a good thing right now. But, too, in scratching his head at his return to the sea, he remembers the first book he was able to read, cover to cover, of any substance. *Island of the Blue Dolphins.* Neah Bay reminds him of that, too, even as the island in that book is off the coast of California, and not the Pacific Northwest. He has kept the book, brought it with him to this exile of rain and waves and forest. He picks it up often, reads the back cover. "In the Pacific there is an island that looks like a big fish sunning itself in the sea." His copy is wrinkled and starting to fray at the edges, the paper gone brown with age. The front cover has the Indian girl who is its heroine, and a bear, and a hut made of saplings. The island is in the shape of a dolphin, canoes tucked into one corner of it, seals in the underside of one flipper. He can't see any island like that here, nor did Catalina or other the islands off the southern California coast look like that. But they *were* that, somehow, anyway, and that island is here, wherever it takes him and wherever he takes it.

CHAPTER 1

* * * *

How could last summer's prehistoric site, of an ilk with which he has much experience, wreak so much havoc? A good "dirt archeologist," his colleagues in the Southwest have called him. That means he can run string in perfect one-meter squares at level heights. He can follow research designs and dig trenches where those designs dictate they be dug. He can do survey work, walking the desert plateaus and basins in perfect north-south lines, looking for signs of human habitation. And he has dug quite a few of the Ancestral Puebloan roomblocks like the one whose secrets he has just run from. "Dirt archeologist" as opposed to a "Theory Man," or a Big Picture Dude, a writer of fine-thinking articles about the nature of it all. Sweeney, his wife, can be relied on to help with what write-ups he must do – mostly cut-and-paste contract reports – and the years of struggle with school have at long last passed. But here he is, up against ten again. When he was ten he thought archeology an impossible career. He sat straight up in his chair watching Louis Leakey on a *National Geographic* special, because until then it never occurred to him that a person might make a living studying the past. *Island of the Blue Dolphins* had peeled back a prior world, revealed what was under the surface of his daily life of strip malls and asphalt, providing a pulse to something older and simultaneously simpler and more meaningful. Once he began noticing this world, his dad noticed him. Because of *Island of the Blue Dolphins* John began fishing for sea urchins and mussels in the tide pools at La Jolla, or even Laguna, where his Aunt Kris lived and they visited on weekends. He crouched, humming, in the lap-lap of low tide, by these pools. He wore what he wore most summers – a swimsuit, his hair dried and salted from the ocean. He was tan, and at ten, between fourth and fifth grade, elongating suddenly, becoming lank.

"Ate that way in the Pacific sometimes," his dad said, when he

9

saw him poking to remove a mussel one Saturday. The sun caught the water and winked blinding stars at him.

John peered up against the sun at this adult-sized shadow. "You did?" "The Pacific" meant World War II, not the calm beaches of southern California.

"Yep. Japs had us pinned down without rations, so we did what we could."

His dad, the Ultimate Marine. World War II, then Korea. Decorated a million times over. Now he ran a VA hospital. He fathered three children, two girls and then him.

His dad bent down and actually tousled his hair. He had never tousled his hair before. "Take you to the desert sometime. Teach you to eat out there." John looked after his father's silhouette in disbelief as it moseyed past him that day on the beach. Then he looked back at his tide pool, not knowing what to do, seeing only the gentle lap of sea water in it, clear and revealing.

The pivotal parent-teacher conference six months prior came back to him. "You never noticed his trouble with reading before?" Sister Theresa asked. John sat slumped and sullen off to one side. His parents looked at each other in acts of appalled surprise. "No," they said. "Never." "Well, then," she said, pursing her lips, "I recommend a specialist for him."

He poked tentatively at a sea urchin, shame making his hand weak. That he and his family should be the source of a nun pursing her lips...

* * * *

At thirteen, post-Leakey and *National Geographic,* he went to the library. This was something not as strange as it sounds for a kid like him. Libraries had always felt like churches, cathedrals full of books, spandrels of words he would know, like secret codes that nobody had to know he knew. He could know them there with no one looking over his shoulder. They could think he was slow, dumb, "disabled." But really, in the belly of that whale, would be words, words earned on his own terms, and someday he would surprise them.

He looked up Archeology, Careers In, and the impossibility of the world closed in again. Too much education, a Master's or a PhD, preferably, required, said the reference books, which he read as the specialist taught him to do, with a ruler under the lines to keep them straight in his mind. It was dizzying, the thought of that many years of struggle. How many term papers would he need to write? At the beach with his oldest sister that Saturday, he purchased tamales from a man up from Tijuana, and gazed out to the sea.

"Aren't you going to surf?" Lindsay asked. He was a champion body surfer, especially in the last two months. For the first time he could keep up with Lindsay. That summer he had started to grow. If he was lank at ten, he began to fill out at thirteen. He was a big thirteen-year-old. A big thirteen-year-old with glasses.

"You go on. I'll be there." He chewed the tamale like cud. The only thing he felt a passion to do and he could not do it. A PhD!

He finished the tamale. He surfed. But as he came back to his towel he saw a shaggy man sitting on a blanket not far away, doing something with rocks. He went to watch him with a prerogative left over from a younger time, when small children felt free to ogle anyone. The shaggy man was making an arrowhead, and he started talking to John. "See here," he said, holding up a smooth rock the color of orange cream. "This flat part? That's the platform. You need to hit there to peel off a good knife base, or whatever you are making, from below it. But the angle has to be right." John slid to his knees and watched him work. Lindsay came and went, twice, before she finally said it was time to go. The mountain man handed John a sandstone hammerstone, a piece of the orange cream rock ("good chert, that"), and a flyer for a Mountain Man rendezvous happening in two weeks. Flintknapping, the man called what he was doing. He winked at John. "Practice with the rocks I gave you. See you at the rendezvous." John was hooked. If nothing else, he thought, remembering Leakey's palms closing in on a chopper almost a million years old, he could do this. He was fantastic with his hands.

II.

("John! We need to go public with this! The tests came back positive! We've got it, John, we've got it.") Shut up, Dr. Mellars, he thinks, Mr-Biochem-Genius. The mere glee in the man's voice makes him cringe, because the assumption behind it is that John would be as happy as Mellars; John would now write it all up, as if he had been waiting, eagerly, for the past eight or nine months, for just that moment when Mellars' data were complete. Instead, he has fled. He has given his crew three weeks, now, of silence. They have no idea that he has come to Neah Bay. Not even his wife Sweeney knows that.

To avoid falling into guilt, he goes out to his stoop, and begins knapping an obsidian core such that he peels off smaller and smaller blades. He has prepared it perfectly, the core, with a flat platform off of which he strikes the blades. Each blade creates, on the original rock, a backbone, a crease falling down the side of the core, on either side of the hollow groove that is the ghost, now, of the blade that once was a part of the rock. He hits the next blade, then, on the platform over the crease, ensuring, if he hits it right, a long skinny flake, smooth on the side that had been inner to the core, ridged in the center on the outer surface. Eye surgeons use the blades now. (Meghan's poetry: *And we wonder why it would astonish/ Everyone but ophthalmologists to know/ That 2000 years of Christian Improvements/ Still do not cut as clean/ As a heathen blade of obsidian.*) He nods, those words coming back not in one big visual – he has no movie screen in his mind's eye like most people, or only an odd, fragmented one – but with the rhythm of his hammerstone on black rock. *And we WON-der* (whack), *WHY* (whack) *it would ASTON-ish* (whack)...A cut from obsidian makes those from a steel scalpel look like a chain saw's when you examine the effects of both under a microscope. He shuts his eyes against Mellars' glee, against the sudden flash of the site that produced the thing that Mellars, the biochemist and MD, tested for human blood protein. He shuts his eyes against its accompanying bones, its kiva full of rot and atrocity, Meghan's verse mixing in. *Whack*, done in that confused and blind denial, and he opens eyes to a sliced finger.

"Shit," he mutters, bringing his forefinger to his mouth and sucking in the metallic taste of his own blood. He fishes in his tool kit bag for a Band-Aid.

He hears the ocean breathe a block away and thinks that unlike here, the sea in the Southwest has turned to rock. Water shadows everywhere, if you know what you are looking at. At Wupatki National Monument, north of Flagstaff, where he worked for a time, Moenkopi sandstone forms in rippled slabs that break off into patio-sized pieces, the shallowed landing of water on sand so evident in the frozen ripples. What stopped time in that trap of sand fused together, then oxidized it to a bright orange-red? Movement caught and juggernauted, such an enigma, a contradiction in its plaster-of-Paris casing. Or more recently, out at the site that has stymied him, has sent him flying here, thick layers of Dakota sandstone crease with Mancos shale, making for roads that undulate as they sag into the shale bands. The shale and coal seams are the products too of water, water-logged plants and animals, quagmired dinosaurs whose energy humanity now releases and destroys the planet with.

From his site, if you stretched your neck around the bend, the glint of the San Juan River, sliding by like a brown snake, can be seen. It's rare for a crew to be so close to water. A Southwesternist spends most of his or her time in desert territories where water is a secret to be deciphered. If that can occur, you might just get a handle on how the ancient peoples lived here, how the Ancestral Puebloan navigated, in their ships of corn and adobe and pots, this desiccated place. At Mesa Verde, east of the site by twenty miles as the crow flies, the secret is behind the rock shelters that housed the people for their last hundred years – there the shale interrupts the slow drip of rain-time through sandstone, and the water is forced to come out, breaking the rock as it freezes and thaws, freezes and thaws, eventually forming the shelters themselves, and seep springs in the back of them. The rest is just human manipulation, age-old tricks of check dams and a few feeble reservoirs, and perhaps, when John is dreaming up stories at the onset of storms, the hurried footsteps of women with enormous ollas putting them out at the pour-over line, where a good rain will curtain off the top of the mesa and over the rim of the rock shelter.

At Wupatki, cradled in the shadow of Sunset Crater, the secret was the volcanic soil. Things could look bone-dry on the surface, but scratch the knobby cinders and the color of wet would greet you less than an inch down. At the site he has run from, with the bones and residues of blood, two miles down the drainage lies the San Juan. An easy source. A place where, when conditions are just right, say, in early August when the light switches ever so subtly to autumn, the water and the sun do a dance of a thousand winks, and he thinks: *So this is joy.*

What happened at that site, then, the one called Tin Cup Wash? It took two months to excavate the whole of the kiva, those underground stone circles of buildings the Pueblo still use for ceremony, for clan life. A kiva is by its very construction sacred; it is underground because the ancestors come up from beneath, through a series of worlds. The Pueblo will go out of their way to make sure their kivas are therefore also beneath, sometimes building up the soil around it, sometimes mauling into every-thing from soft sediments to volcanic tuff with stone axes and digging sticks. On the floor north of the hearth, usually, a smaller hole is dug – this is the sipapu, the Place of Emergence, the literal belly button through which the people arise into the next universe. Mostly they are small, these kivas, maybe eight or ten feet in diameter; sometimes they are huge, fifty feet or more, like the great kivas at Chaco Canyon or Aztec. You don't plant a kernel of corn without consulting with your gods and your fellow clansmen in the kiva first; you don't get married, weave a blanket, or do much else, either. That's what the kivas were, and are, to the Pueblo.

To John, in that summer dig at Tin Cup that began nearly a year ago, a kiva was a kiva was a kiva. He'd excavated a few before. Sometimes you found the remnants of murals, peeling off the walls. Sometimes a kiva pot, lid still on, a single cob left inside. Sometimes weaving spindles, a bead or two if you were lucky. Marvels, artifacts, things to catalog and add to the general pattern of knowledge. This was cool because you were the first one to see these things in 800 or 900 years; it was cool at Tin Cup especially because you were the scientist at last, the bumbling school kid with the odd mind who after thirty years of scraping along, finally landed a job as a project director. You thought it would be easy. A simple report, rote descriptions of geology, plant life, what was found. Other people would analyze faunal remains and pots; you would do the stone tools. A small site, a typical unit pueblo with a nice set of rooms on top, the kiva below and discernable on the surface by the telltale circular depression. This project was for the Utes who wanted to make irrigated fields, after all, not Harvard University. Easy.

Fat lot he knew, he thinks now, giving up on his flintknapping. He hears a shuffle.

He looks up. George is silhouetted against the misty morning light.

"Low tide," he says.

"I know."

"Go with me and Nina to find crabs?" Nina's his niece. John looks to a girl with messy braids whose loose strands form a kind of wiry halo around her shadowed face.

For one brief slice of angled light, as steam curls off of him, George looks like his father as he saw him when he was ten at the beach.

John nods. Puts the blade core and tools away. Takes his coffee cup and walks, looping over the same tracks, with his friend George and a nine-year-old girl on a beach rimming the ancient Pacific.

III.

George and Nina and he find remnants of things, clams and mussels, but not much crab, a bald eagle soaring overhead doing exactly the same thing they are. Nina, her hair long and black against determined shoulders, moves ahead by herself, humming, and tucks a piece of driftwood under her arm. Coming off the beach and crossing the road to the museum not far from his salmon trailer, George stops, his hand on the nape of Nina's neck. They're near to the building, narrow windows open at the top under the eaves. He puts a finger to his mouth and they are still. Low laughter comes out from the windows, then an old woman starts talking in the staccato q's and c's that the Makah language sounds like to an English ear.

"She's telling a story," Nina whispers.

George smiles down at her. "Want to go listen?"

She nods.

George looks at him. "Sorry, bro. Time to go."

"You understand Makah?" John asks.

"Naw," George smiles. "Not that way." Then he sobers. "But I get the stories, bro. Don't know how, but I do. And Nina here is learning in school."

"What kind of stories do they tell?" They are talking in low tones, so those inside do not hear them.

"All kinds," Nina says. "That's a woman telling, so it will be about somebody's bad marriage or how they made seal blubber or something." She giggles and shifts the driftwood to the other arm.

"Okay," John says. He can't help smiling back at her. "See you around." But as they walk into the museum, John stands, a riveted gorilla, under the eaves. Syllable after syllable rolls over him, stories of whaling and seal hunting and smoking fish he will never understand. The mist clears on the bay for a bit, and he sees a fishing boat moving out to sea.

Then someone inside the museum lets out a sharp retort, in English, after a ripple of laughter has gone through: "Not funny, Dennis. It only took a generation to lose everything. To lose the culture. We got it back, thanks to that long house dig. Thanks to us, here, rounding up the elders. You got to be careful."

You got to be careful, and he's falling back to his kiva, the one he feigned such tiredness for at first, the one reeking very soon after that of conflict, of loud voices and then far more. Kivas have flat roofs when intact, a square hole cut for the smoke to go out and the ladder to go in. To make the smoke go out, you need a convection current, which you achieve by constructing a ventilator shaft down into the bricks of the kiva wall. A reverse chimney, ingenious engineering, using nothing but a stone axe, plumb bob, and digging stick. Warren, his colleague from Wupatki days, had been cleaning around the shaft of this kiva for a day or two, moving closer to defining its boundaries from the rock and rodent holes around it. It was another sunny day, hot, thunderheads off to the north over Sleeping Ute Mountain. They couldn't see those from down in the kiva, though. Warren was whistling, low, as he usually did, old like John and therefore eschewing the iPods of the younger set comprising the rest of the crew, who were working on the rooms up top. He brushed the ventilator shaft free of some dirt and then his whistling abruptly stopped. John looked up.

"What is it?"

"Come here," he said.

John went. Stood with him as he continued to brush gently. Bones began to appear among the dirt. They both stared. They realized at the same time that the entire ventilator shaft was full of bones, and that they were human bones. The small skull of a child dislodged and fell at their feet, making a sickening hollow noise. John bent down to pick it up. He didn't want to look at it but already he could tell it was caramel-colored in the way of roasted animals. Crap.

Warren wiped his forehead with a dusty forearm and looked at the skull. "We're in deep shit, man."

* * * *

They didn't need to say much else. They knew what they had to do next. John hauled himself out of the kiva and left a message on the cell phone for the head honcho, one Mark King, of their little contract archeology outfit, because this meant they would have to call the Native American crowd for legal purposes. Somewhere in the back of his mind was a niggle that said this would no longer be the easy site report to write, but for now that was a distant itch. He was more immediately dismayed by the anticipation of the looks on Hopi elders' faces, of being told to rebury the bones quickly, of all that they might or might not be able to do with them. When it came to human Native American remains, the archeologists did not have final say.

He told Warren he was going to eat lunch, and walked off, where the sun shone strongly and the heat of the day promised no shadows, no hidden secrets, no bones among the low rocks baking in the arroyos at noon. He found a lone juniper, pulled out his sandwich and water bottle and ate, not particularly tasting anything. Out in the field he tried to have a treat to look forward to, and that week it was a bag of honey Dijon rice chips from the natural foods store in Dolores. So much of his life has been measured in these kinds of doses: how lunch becomes precious in the field, how you notice clouds and whether or not they will cool you down or zap you with lightning or do nothing at all. He doesn't eat much when it's hot and he knows Warren always wonders why he's fat, though they've had a couple steak dinners together and then John thinks he has seen his face flicker.

His juniper was up on a rise and he could see most directions save north, where Sleeping Ute Mountain blocked his view. Sleeping Ute is a giant who will rise up one day and kill all the white people, heh-heh, said the man, Stan House, who was their liaison with the Ute tribe. "You stay off it, eh? Not for white folks." They nodded; anyone who worked in the Four Corners had known that for years.

· Four Corners, four states. His rear end was barely in Colorado, his view composed of the river to the south, then above it on the other side, New Mexico and Arizona. He couldn't see Utah. This was tough terrain, lover terrain, Meghan-land. The bones reminded him of her too. Meghan knew her bones.

He began absent-mindedly to take his hand and Braille it along the slickrock he had been sitting on, a low, blonde Dakota sandstone full of little knobs, whorls of differential erosion. He closed his eyes, the hand caressing the way Mrs. Carrington, his fourth-grade reading specialist, taught him so long ago to do on a typewriter. M-E-G-H-A-N, first finger of right hand for M, third of left hand for E, first of left hand for G, first finger of the right hand for H, left pinkie for A, first of right hand for N. A bump on the rock corresponding to each letter. The light was no longer sharp with shadows, the way it became in the morning and at night. Then the light made you do different things. After work the day before, sun-showered and relaxed, the entire crew hiked up out of the wash to overlook the River. There were eight of them, five men, three women. The women and one man were at a later Pueblo site a hundred yards from theirs. They hiked out because a canyon wren trilled up wash from them and Nan, the crew chief of the other site, said, "Hey," of a sudden in the defined silence, and Preston, the one man on the other team, said, "Wow, look at the sun on the cliff across the river," what little bit of it they could see, and then Warren (it was always Warren, that little Leprechaun of a man who nonetheless could lead armies) said, "Well, let's go," and they took their beers and water bottles and remnants of potato chips up to the overlook.

Speechlessness there too. How do you get your tongue around what feels like love, the cliff face vermillion in the low evening sun? But in the hot bake of the desert noon, his mouth full of rice chips, the world was merely gelatinous, and usually he could talk then. Practicalities, the loose adolescent jokes of field work, inane conversations about whether Miracle Whip or mayonnaise was better. His heart was a soundless thing, quite still, in noonday heat, and if no bones awaited him, he could eat lunch with the others. But today he needed to stay away from the shock of the shaft full of what looked like mass murder, and his suspicion, the feel of the child's skull in his hand returning to him, that it wasn't just murder, but deliberate butchery, one of "those sites" where, over lunch, even with just Warren, the word cannibalism would sneak in while chewing bites of ham sandwich. He didn't want that. He wanted the hot, saturated air, the ticking desert, the hibernation of rodents until nightfall. The low light of evening would be enough to loosen him, and then Meghan's hip (that bone!) or sometimes, still, Sweeney's smile, would come back to him. He balled up his fist in shame then, from writing her name, as if caught at something. He finished his sandwich hurriedly, and returned to his job.

* * * *

After Nina and George have gone inside the museum, he

swallows under its eaves in the same kind of shame he felt that day in the desert – always this boy, peering into other people's lives, or wishing for one different from his own. Quickly he moves on, lest anyone see him. Later, in the shack, he thinks again of that day when they found the bones, the ticking here that of small rain on rooftops, not the sleeping noonday desert. In his bed now, ten o'clock at night with the rain picking up to beat steadily on the roof, he fumbles for his wallet on the little crate by his bedside. He takes from it one of the poems Meghan wrote when she visited Sweeney and him ten years ago. He made a great pretense of friendship with both of them, most of the time, so much so that he had Sweeney bearing her occasional visits. And of course, no physical loving took place then. In the low light of a small lamp, he reads.

I am reminded that you once set my poems
out to sea, past the seals on one raft
made with the deft of your fingers
and a single bough of willow…

He rolls on his back and puts his arm over his eyes. Did he do that? Set her poems out to sea? What an idiot. He should have clung to them for dear life. Because she is completely gone now. His own doing. And nine years after the fact, he is still crashing into that stupidity, that self-imposed slaying of a love affair, Sweeney intact and waiting for him at home, in Salt Lake City, but what's left of him – well, that he could not say.

CHAPTER 2

I.

His second love, the love of desert, began when his dad made good on his promise there by his first love, the sea. When fall came and it got cooler he took John out to the Mojave. John thought his dad had forgotten all about his summertime tidepool comments, but on a weekend when the girls were off camping with Scouts or some such, he woke John up with a thud of an old Marine day pack against his bedroom floor. "Pack up. Long underwear for the nights, because they get cold. Hat, sunscreen, good shoes. Okay?"

John nodded. He didn't think he meant it, his father, but he never ceased to sound like a military man. He collected history books, and about that time seemed excessively interested in conversations with Lindsay's high school history teacher. This continued as John's second sister, Syd, entered high school, and he would get into long disputations with one nun in particular, a Sister Callahan, who seemed fascinated by his war service but with definitive theories as to the why's and how's of World War II that conflicted amiably and sharply with his own. But he helped run a VA hospital. He had a high school education and three children and it was 1968 and as the world cracked open around him – Viet Nam was particularly painful – his wistfulness grew by the hour. Once, in the trash, John found a San Diego State catalog, dog-eared to the requirements for a history degree.

Packed, breakfasted, and driven four hours, they started walking. Even in October it was hot, and his dad did not recommend walking in the afternoon under normal circumstances. "But today we only have so much time," he said, an odd dryness to his voice, and he did not look at John when he spoke. Here, he said, looking down after they had walked for twenty minutes or so in silence, this is a banana yucca – fruit is like a

22

sweet potato when you bake it. And here – he pointed to a mound of dirt and a hole under a bush – some critter lives here you could club if you had to. When they got to what John would learn to call a deflated area later on, a flat pancake of land devoid of vegetation, his dad stooped and pulled up John's first stone tool, taking it in his hand, fascinated, while John watched.

"You can go to college and study this stuff, if you want," his dad said, peering at the tool as if it possessed some knowledge he craved.

Time stood very still. The shadow of a craggy mountain yawned over them, keeping things a little cooler. John thought of Mrs. Carrington. He thought of his father's long conversations with Sister Callahan. He wished he could talk to his dad like that. What, after all, did a nun have in common with his father?

"Do you – do you know much about the Indians out here?" he asked.

"Little bit. Tough bunch. You stay small. Not much water for growth out here," he guffawed, standing up and flinging an arm out to the dry, shimmering horizons.

John remembered seeing fields down by the river at Needles. "You could grow corn next to the Colorado," he said, his heart pounding, straws grasped as his flailing mind wandered for topics.

"So you could. So you could. But not much anywhere else. And that's a long way from here. It's a big desert."

John was not sure he and his father had ever talked this much. "So, did the Indians by the river – I mean, did they grow corn?"

"Think so. Yuma. Maybe some bands of the Chemehuevi. But out here –" he shook his head. "It's all hunting and gathering."

"Gathering what?" What was "gathering"?

"Plants, seeds, roots."

"Oh." Why didn't he know this? His unbearable inadequacy felt like someone sitting on his chest. Why wasn't he like Sister Callahan, or his own sisters? He groped to both keep the conversation going and to get rid of the pressure. "Lindsay wants to be a history teacher," he squeaked out.

"I know," his father said. *But you are his only son* then squashed John's chest, the next unspoken piece of torture. His attempt at shunting off responsibility onto Lindsay had failed utterly, though God knew what his father really thought. It was awful enough that he believed John was college material. How badly would he, John, his spitting image save for his mother's eyes, let his father down? And his dad was Marines and he loved John Wayne and that's why he was named that but could he not see he would never be a man, standing on his own, the way John Wayne did? That he would need a Mrs. Carrington all his life?

He looked at his father's profile, the late afternoon breeze whiffling his hair. John said nothing and the man walked on, oblivious to the hard walnut growing in his son's throat. But he did find him another tool, and pretty soon John was scavenging the whole hardpan, into the creosote and greasewood. He learned, there, that if the ocean was a curl of water that would tumble you clean, then the desert was the site of revelation, of nakedness, of things stripped bare and scoured out of the soil after centuries. They walked, bent, looking for small clues, and when John looked up the vast space all around him was appalling.

Finally his father moved them toward an alluvial fan that ran up to a tuck in the mountain, a place where the geology changed, and there he brought them up against a spring.

"We'll camp here," he said, the only words they'd shared for well over an hour by that time. "Look around. Springs are good places to find things."

John tried one last time to talk. "Right. Because we're not the first to camp here."

His father tousled his hair for the second and last time. "You bet. Dead on, there. A spring in the desert is home over and over to a lot of things."

24

John blushed in this tiny spotlight, joy leaping. He sat down, fingering the soil next to him, proving his father right by pulling up tiny, thin flakes he would later learn were the product of the final stages of making knives, arrowheads, spear points. "See?" he said, holding them out.

His father nodded, but he did not look. He was too busy gathering sticks to start a fire.

II.

Improbable men. Salt-lip men, pack rat men, men who hoard the desert on their skin, men who love space and stars so sharp they crackle, men who grew up alone and found a perfect match for their solitude in the desert's sighs, its isolated cacti, its baked shit-eating grin, sloppy and limp at 4 pm. Time to find a tree skimpy shade rattlesnake hangout. Close your eyes like the snakes do. Never come home. Marry your cactus girl, your saguaro mistress, your buxom mountain lover. Bare hills like bones. Skeletal. Fault-lines, uplifts, ruptures, places where the earth splits open –

Precipice. Lose my heart over the precipice. Your wife out at Zuni Pueblo, two and a half hours away, while you finish your B.A. A B.A. for a man who knows more archeology than anyone alive. A B.A. "Learning Disabled." The labels that stick and bind and make a man at thirty-six fall for a twenty-nine year-old incest survivor, needed her to feel good John goddamn you John I took your encouragement at its word and fled into health. Why would you never go with, especially with your hands as they would be on my hips, the proverbial sense all soulmates possess of having known each other in eons before this one, the love the great love: why, why, why – ?

He hasn't dared read that passage for a long time. He only read it once before, when she sent it to him at the end of everything, and then he couldn't finish it. Meghan lasted nine years in real life and has been gone nine years hence, but the passing of what the outside world understands as time never seemed to matter. He remembers he shoved that piece of writing into the box he kept full of her poetry, letters, photos, a hammerstone, buckskin, a small buckskin doll she made, and put the whole thing on the top shelf of his closet, behind his winter sweaters. He was angry.

But when he fled Salt Lake (*I have an M.A. now, dammit*) he grabbed the box at the last minute, along with all his notes from Tin Cup, his flintknapping kit, and some clothes. He has pulled it out this morning because he awoke thinking about the desert and his father, and how Meghan's father too had loved the same desert, and then he remembered she'd written something. He had wanted to understand his father, but he found, by the end, that he was reading about himself. He gets up, disgruntled, puts on his tinted glasses that make the shack almost too dark, and gropes around for coffee.

Accountability. *Why would you never go with – ?* He hates her words because they bring up that one word – the word of right-wing politicians and Jesus freaks, used along with "personal responsibility" – and he snorts as he bangs the coffee pot down on top of the wood stove. But that's still the word that floats up now. Accountability. Be accountable. To Meghan, to Sweeney, to himself. Is that possible, he thinks, pouring grains in the bottom of the pot, without hypocrisy? *I'm a good enough human specimen, aren't I?* All kinds of defense rush to his aid. He saved Meghan as she crawled out from her cruel childhood. He worked well with Sweeney and laughed with her. He agreed to work for Warren and do the job at Tin Cup. *So why these questions?* Is he as callous and fake as those preachers with their big hair and big cars, screaming "personal responsibility" while hiring gay guys to blow them in the off-hours? While they fight hard against any sort of social welfare, any vision of the greater good that doesn't include their personal version of Jesus? That was not the Jesus he grew up with.

He shakes his head. He can't believe he's thinking in favorable terms about his Jesuit high school teachers, those monks left wide-eyed by the 60s and teaching them Marcuse along with Western Civ. The coffee boils, true cowboy dirt. He picks up a hot pad, pours himself some, finds pure cream in the small fridge that hums in the corner under a table with a hot plate on it. Because here he is, after all, like the preachers caught with their hands in the till, or the priests who had secret male lovers, or just even Jimmy Swaggart, seducing whores so long ago. An ordinary coward, someone not who people think he is. They *think* he is capable of writing scientific articles. They have never paid attention to his junior author status, that articles of any consequence with his name on it are few and far between, and Sweeney is invariably the senior author, the first name on the masthead. Mostly he writes four, five, six page sections on the lithics for odd contract projects. Paint-by-number, fill-in-the-blank stuff. Nothing taking larger vision, or more importantly, with his agonizing dancing letters and rulers, too much time.

He sips his coffee. *Face it.* He has *run away* to Neah Bay, to a rainy country with shrouds for horizons and rotting organic matter for soil. You can't see anything here, for god's sake, except for the sideways glances of Makah elders, who make him squirm too. One of them even asked, one day, "What are you doing here?" He had no answer.

The crossed arms and barrel chests and steady gaze of Hopi elders also make him squirm whenever he thinks of Tin Cup. Navajo old women, too, who can tell you what to do with every plant on the rez and then say, lookee here, that coal company you doing archeology for? And they point to a dead sheep, a poisoned water tank, the fine black dust that settles on their kitchen tables every day. Two crew members quit that job because they developed asthma.

He remembers that he *ran away* to lunch the day the bones were found, too. Because when you find bones anymore, you must be accountable there as well. You might as well put a police light on top of your car and whiz around the countryside blaring "Human remains! Human remains!" because that's what finding bones is like these days. It doesn't matter if they are politely buried or thrown into a pit or a ventilator shaft, hacked up and clearly disrespected in their final moments. You must "notify" the office. Then they "notify" the pertinent tribes. The next thing you know you have Hopi and Zuni and Ute and Navajo bureaucrats out at your site all staring down at you with long disapproving looks. The Ute and Navajo do not think any sane person should hang around places where people have died (so that rules out all archeologists by definition) and the Hopi and Zuni really don't like you messing with their ancestors, especially if their ancestors might not have treated each other that nicely. Then they make the decision about what you can do with the bones.

* * * *

Warren and John spent the afternoon brushing the bones clean and mapping every one of them in situ. He got back from lunch and shut his mind down and just worked. They got the map done and by four had begun wrapping the bones up, individually, their provenance written on the plastic shrouding them. It would take a full day or two to do the rest of them. They worked in silence. Craig and Steve, in their late 20s and full of grad school conversations in the off-hours around dying campfires, occasionally hummed a tune up top and their voices wafted down in unintelligible motes. When John was done wrapping the bones, he climbed out of the kiva in the same mood that he had sought lunch. He could feel Warren looking after him, wondering about companionship at dinner, but did not turn around. After washing his hands and face, he made a salad out of baby greens and cold roasted chicken extracted from a cooler well tended with ice. Someone made a run to Aneth, over in Utah, or the Ute casino and truck stop mid-week to pick up more ice if need be, and they had all become experts at maintaining functioning coolers. Even so, it was best to eat vegetables and other delicate goods earlier in the week, rather than later.

Steve, John's youngest crew member, with a lanky build and a ruddiness John tended to associate with Scottish people, had erected a chaise lounge under a juniper tree thirty yards from the site. A low cliff behind the chair defined the western edge of the wash, and his little spot had become a removed reading-and-drinking-beer locale away from the rest of the camp. Camp lay in full view from the juniper, tents sagging in the sun on the far side of the two sites, a fire pit roughly in the middle of the flotilla of bright nylon. Beyond the tents, their cars, parked haphazardly in rabbitbrush, snakeweed, apache plume, but mostly the beige dust of extreme southwestern Colorado. Light blinded in chrome stars off of fenders and side windows, the cars mostly pickup trucks in various degrees of dilapidation.

At the lounge, where John took his salad and a cold beer, Steve had left a book lying in the dirt, and John gazed at it. He still didn't want to talk to people much and if they asked him why he would not be able to tell them. Steve's book was on Hopi, the ancient village of Orayvi in particular. The front picture had the compelling stillness of a certain kind of good photograph, sepia-toned, kiva ladder poles reaching into a bleached and sand-born sky. Hung horizontally on the poles lay a bow with what looked like horse hair fringe hanging off of it, as if to say, *We are down in our kiva and no one else shall enter.* In the foreground, on the kiva roof, sat haphazard collections of branches for firewood; in the background, the sandstone brick-and-mud apartment-style houses of which John's site was a small precursor. No living plant could be seen anywhere, and if he didn't know it was America and if he hadn't spent so much time traipsing the Painted Desert surrounding Hopi, or the rest of the Colorado Plateau for that matter, he would think it was Afghanistan, Iraq, northern Africa, some stricken country

National Geographic took pictures of so that you would think, "Good God. How does anyone make a living out there?"

His mouth full of chicken, he flipped to the back flap to find information on the photograph. *Entrance to the kiva during the Hopi Snake Dance, Orayvi Pueblo, ca. 1900.* Photographer unknown, curated at the Huntington Library near Pasadena. He shook his head at that incongruity. The Huntington reeked of 19th century notions of beauty and art, gardens full of roses and Japanese bridges, the Library saturated with oil paintings in ornate frames. He went once, in high school, as part of a class field trip. The Jesuits again. But how odd that a picture such as this, of a desert world where taking a bath would be considered a rather phenomenal waste of water most of the time, with a bow hung ominously from a kiva ladder while the men below prepared to dance with rattlesnakes in their mouths, ended up in the Huntington. The invasion of the unmanicured, the earthly, Conrad's natives sneaking into the pantry when no one was looking – yet here he himself was, feasting on that past clarity, squinting at the bow to see if he could discern its construction.

The Hopi would not like the bones, the Tin Cup bones. Out of all of the Pueblos, the Hopi would defend against their implications the most fiercely. Funny, that, he thought, because he knew they were guilty of a notorious massacre of one of their own villages in 1700, and some would argue cannibalism was involved.

He turned back to the front of the book. *Oravyi Revisited: Social stratification in an "egalitarian" society.* Huh. In other words, Who wins? Who loses? A book against the flatness of the usual interpretation of Ancestral Puebloan history. Intriguing. He took a swig of beer. The flat interpretation dictated that the Pueblo were one unified tribe, and that they all loved each other equally, and that there had been no factions. That, he knew, had never been right. Modern Pueblo alone spoke eight different languages, yet if you just had their archeology to go by, you'd never guess that.

Same kivas, same stone masonry, same way of making a living on the planet. Oh, there were small variations. Square kivas versus round ones, really nice masonry versus cruddy stuff. But overall? To a Euro-American people, with a tradition of finding the differential minutiae of cathedrals meaningful, the Pueblo manifestation seemed simple.

Noble savagery, too, scowled John, as he stabbed lettuce. That played a role. Noble Savagery, version 6.2 for the Ancestral Puebloan, meant they got to be earthy-crunchy peace-loving farmers, even in this day and age. Even after someone finally broke open the possibility that they were a little more brutal with each other sometimes. Pueblo massacres were hard for some people because then you had to say, *dammit, they're just like us.* Not pristine. Not infallible. Human. Accountable! And then here was this book, suggesting something other than total egalitarian peacefulness in an ethnographic context. He had never heard of it.

III.

Out of his shack, claustrophobic, John walks to the gas station in his yellow slicker, though the rain has let up. He buys a Dr. Pepper, heads for the beach. Nina is sitting on the pier, her legs dangling over the edge, her head bent with her hair draped around something he cannot see. She's wearing a rain poncho and wet jeans stick out from underneath.

"Shouldn't you be in school?" he asks, settling beside her and popping his Dr. Pepper can open.

"Shouldn't you be back in wherever you came from?" she retorts, not looking up.

Startled and hurt, he asks, "Should I leave?"

She swings her hair around to face him. In her lap is the driftwood piece she picked up the other day when they went walking at low tide. A swatch of sandpaper rests in her far hand.

She says nothing.

"What's the matter?" he asks her.

She shrugs. "I dunno. Yeah, I should be in school. But I woke up with a little fever and my auntie said I could stay home and since I was hot I came out here."

The air is, as usual, gray and cool, the rain reduced to a spit.

"You live with your aunt?"

"And my dad, sometimes. But he has to work construction off the rez a lot, to find a job."

"Where's your mom?"

She swings back to her driftwood at that question. "Don't know," she mumbles.

He sighs. The smoke drifts from George's trailer. "We could go visit your uncle."

"Naw," she says. "George is okay, but I don't feel like it. He can be moody, you know. And I don't want to get stinky from salmon. My tummy's off."

John gives up and looks at the driftwood piece. "What are you working on?"

This tack works better. She sits up, hands it to him. It is a gnarl, a cedar hunk with a knot to its core, a place where the tree burled up and got fat before falling apart and eventually washing up in the sea. It must be a foot long and about eight inches wide. She has sanded it smooth, so the grain and the shape of it form waves, streaks of remnant cedar red interspersed with weathered gray curving through the shape of the wood. A little tail of it swoops up to a rounded point; the body reminds him of a seal belly; the other end is a swirl of sanded knobs, like little flippers.

"This is beautiful," he says. He's surprised at how beautiful it is.

"I have more. I put a clear coat on them when I'm done sanding it to what I like."

"You should sell them."

"Really?" She peers at John for the first time as though he

might just be a good guy. *Don't get your hopes up*, he wants to say to her. Instead he says, "Sure. People would buy this in the museum," and turns the wood over in his hands.

"Do you sell your arrowheads that you make?" she asks shyly, blushing.

He has to smile behind his tinted glasses. "You know about those?"

"George showed me the point you gave him. And you were making something when we stopped by to walk the beach the other day."

"I can show you more," he says, feeling useful for the first time in a while.

"Really? Like how to make them?"

"Sure," he says. He nods to the driftwood as he hands it back to her. "You're good with your hands, I can tell."

The rain has picked up again. They stand and walk the block or two back to his shack. She holds up her driftwood piece. "It's like the knee bone of a tree, isn't it?"

"Maybe, yes."

"That's why I like driftwood. It's like the bones of trees."

IV.

He and Nina flintknap until her flu bug catches up with her and she gets too queasy. She stands up then, wobbly, takes a sip of water, and heads for home. She promises she'll come back some other time, and John hopes she does. Her handling of hammer-stone and core is as he has suspected – strong and competent – and he registers a certain delight in finding another soul so impelled by the ability of the human hand. The aftermath of her disappearance leaves the air heavier than he likes, though. He picks up the knapping tools and in the process finds she has left her driftwood piece. He caresses the piece, admiring it further. But in the silence Tin Cup beckons once again, a phantom he can never entirely shed. He sits down, resigned, in front of his two boxes of data, books, site forms, and photos. The top photo is the shaft in its entirety, before the bones were extracted from it. He snorts. If only the bones were all of it! After breakfast the day after his chaise lounge chicken salad book browsing, Warren looked at him. "What's on our plate for today?" Warren was his friend, and usually the leader, so it was hard to reverse the roles. But he tried.

"Well," he said, "Craig and Steve can keep mapping the stratigraphy of the trench up top. Let's you and I do the hearth."

They had left the hearth for last, mapping the floor and noting all the rocks and fallen roof beams in their proper location lest they had to move them while excavating into storage cysts, post holes, loom anchors, further down. The hearth sat as all kiva hearths do, in the middle of the circle, a deflector between it and the ventilator shaft. This was toothbrush and small trowel work. Hearth dirt they saved in Ziplocs for ethnobotanical analysis, as it revealed not only what they were cooking but what wood they burned, and what stray pollen might have blown in during the time it was in use. John smiled doing that; it reminded him of working with Sweeney one time, at a pretty little Fremont site near Moab. They also saved out some hunks of charcoal for possible C-14 dating, though they had beams from the roof that would give a more accurate reading via tree rings. So they began this process, finding quickly that they had to work around a funny lump, black and hard, in the middle of the hearth. They brushed and picked and eventually created a mound of this black lump, a pedestal of three or so tubular darknesses on top of the remaining hearth dirt.

"If I didn't know better," Warren said softly, peering around all of its sides on his knees, "I'd say that was a turd."

"Fossilized? A fossilized turd?" John blinked. "What's the word for that again?"

Warren grinned. "A coprolite! Yes, my dear Watson." He

wormed up even closer to it. "A fossilized turd. And if I didn't know better, I'd say it was human."

John looked at it too, in a squat with his arms crossed. "What else would it be? Mr. Bear isn't going to take a dump in here, is he?"

"Nor Mr. Coyote."

"It doesn't look like either of those, anyway, to tell the truth," John said. They looked at each other and John pushed his tinted glasses up his nose. "I mean, somebody took a shit in a kiva hearth. Huh."

Warren made a face, a sour face, the only kind of face to make in that situation. "Not very nice, that," he said.

"Nope."

"Bag it," they both said more or less at the same time. And quickly, before the bone people got there to discuss legalities, before anyone else figured out they had the Smoking Gun of all archeological sites related to possible cannibalism, that C-word of the Southwest that people have been in an uproar about for the past ten years. The nay-sayers all screech: But you don't have PROOF they ATE them! The Meghans of the world, who are good at bone and what it tells them, say: The inferences are pretty strong; if these bones were deer there would be no question. But both sides agree that to go beyond the circumstantial, you need exactly what they might very well have had before them: a coprolite with human blood protein in it. Warren and John had a moment of staring reverently at their find.

"What if King says we don't have money for that kind of analysis?" John asked, after a minute, thinking of his boss.

"King would be an idiot. He'll get an *American Antiquity* article out of us for this for sure. Maybe even a panel at the archeology meetings this year. Good advertising for his business."

John froze, save for his gut, which tumbled southward. If he were a horse he'd have gone colicky. The unease of the past few days, ever since finding the bones, fell full-fledged upon him, his intestines pinching. This site had been odd from the beginning. Odd abandonment habits, odd sequence of apparent events, odd absence of corn cobs, then the bones, then this. *American Antiquity!* He must have looked ashen because Warren asked, "What's the matter? This is great! Maybe we'll get real jobs out of this."

"Real jobs" meant permanent positions, either in contract archeology or in academia. For Warren, very nearly complete on a doctorate, a Real Job was academia. For John, it would be anything, anything not on Sweeney's coattails (Sweeney, who had a Real Job and a PhD), anything not temporary, hopscotching from one field experience to the next, holing up in winter to do stone tool analysis or to flounder in panicked unemployment. He had been crew chief a million times over, analyst some, even assistant director – but to write more than the stone tool analysis, to be in charge of the report, to squeeze out of himself something that involved scientific theory and speculation and worst of all, uproar, had been something he'd studiously worked around most of his life. But Project Directors were directly responsible for site write-ups. For making sure appropriate research and laboratory analysis occurred. He was Project Director here because Warren was already Director on three other smaller projects that were wrapping up and King didn't want him overextending himself. Project Director because Warren trusted John in the field, because he loved his flintknapping, because he liked him, though God knew why. It was he who had recommended John to King.

John's mouth went to paste. "Nothing's wrong. I just, uh, this project is metastasizing."

Warren smiled. "Ah, welcome to the life of the Project Director. Come on, let's take care of our turd here."

They tried to improvise the best way of wrapping up the three pieces of coprolite, as neither one of them had ever encountered one in the field before. "Warren?" John asked, the pressure on his chest back as it had been in the desert with his dad, or during his graduate exams, or even in freshman composition so many times until he learned to pass it.

"What?"

"Does NAGPRA cover coprolites? I mean, it's a human remain." NAGRPA stood for Native American Graves Protection and Repatriation Act, the legal muscle behind decisions about human remains and sacred artifacts.

"Oh for god's sake Johnny Tommy-cakes, will you shut up? We're fine. What are you so worried about?"

Warren held the last coprolite, bagged and ready, in his hands. They caught each other's eyes for a brief five seconds, John's lenses not nearly tinted enough for his taste at that moment. For he found in Warren a look of genuine sympathy that rooted him to the spot, that took a nutcracker to the walnut of him, and in surprise he thought he was about to admit something, about to say, Warren, *I can't write very well*, like a screaming child. But from up above came a wail. "C'mon and SQUEEEE-EZE my lemon till the juice run-down-my-leg! Bamp bumpbampbede badeba." This was Steve, singing at high volume to his iPod.

"Jesus," John said, cracking into what he knew looked like laughter but was half-tears.

"Led Zeppelin at ten in the morning." Warren rolled his eyes.

"Too bad it's not Hendrix," John managed to say, waves of relief over him now that the moment had past – and Warren and he crawled out, took a break, hiding their coprolite in John's little lunch cooler first.

V.

"King? John Thompson here." He gripped the cell phone to his ear, reception crisp in the unobstructed desert air.

"What's up? Did the NAGPRA people make it out to the site?"

"Not yet. We, uh, found something else."

"Oh?"

"A, uh, human turd in the hearth. I mean, we think it's human."

John could hear him sitting up in his chair in Salt Lake. "A what?"

"A human –"

But then he was hooting ecstatically on the line. "No WAY! This is EXACTLY what we need! Sweet!"

John's colicky stomach came back in full force and he sat down on his car seat, bending double over it. "We, uh, are going to need money for analysis."

"We got a little in the budget. Plus I can pull some strings. Let me go talk to a friend of mine at the U." The U, the U of Utah, site of John's last inglorious attempt at education. The Master's he barely pulled off, after five years and Sweeney's help and a whole lot of shame. No thesis for him, the exam option modified and modified and modified in a process he would never, ever repeat. The PhD dream, one he'd dared to harbor now and then as an adult after meeting Sweeney, left for good. He let out a gasp that King of course heard. "You okay, John?"

"My stomach's acting up, is all."

"Take care of yourself. But, whee. We might get a good couple of papers out of this." *You fucking imposter, you finally got caught* belched out of some gargoyle place in his brain. Papers! *Research* papers? The awkward life of his hands on keyboards, the sheer time it took to organize his thoughts amidst twisting letters, backwards d's and b's, line blurrings – no. He wanted Sweeney hopelessly. *Can you write this, sweetie Sweeney?? Because I don't know how.*

You worthless piece of shit.

"John? You still there?"

"Yeah."

"Well, keep me posted when the NAGRPA people come up. I'll call you when I know something from the U."

"Okay," and John hung up, fist over his stomach, staring straight ahead over the dash of his truck, seeing nothing.

CHAPTER 3

I.

The rain is back, a medium steadiness on the roof, what the Navajo call a female rain. It is dark, the fire in his wood stove dying in glowing red, and he is buried under a sleeping bag in a coma of memory and paralysis, thinking back to that sickening phone call with King. He recalls hanging up and spending a great deal of time at the camp's designated latrine, all the nervousness expelling itself in instant shit. You'd think he was about to compete in the Olympics. Well, that *was* his Olympics, that ringing death knell-disguised-as-happy-endorsement from his boss. After the latrine all he could think of was Meghan, a kind of ravenous craving for someone who loved him in what seemed to him a worshipful way. He could use some worshipping. How did he find her? How did he track her? How did they know – in that uncanny way people who have soulmate business with one another – always know? He scrunches into a fetal position and watches the fire, going back to the beginning of her.

She was presiding over an Albuquerque classroom, the archeology lab in the basement of the small building that housed most of the archeology profs at the University of New Mexico, as well as a few classrooms. You could skim through in the back even if a class was in session because the two entrances – one an interior door, the other exterior, leading to the rest of campus – were both in the back and the back was also full of spare black-topped lab tables, crammed up against each other, so no students sat there. John had a class upstairs, a graduate-level course in spite of the fact that he was still struggling for his Bachelor's, and usually went out upstairs. But one day he did not; one day he must have followed a prof downstairs, or gone to the bathroom, because he found himself investigating the possibility of slipping out of the building through the lab classroom.

He'd seen her before, knew her the way you know many people in archeology – by summer projects, by fly-by-night meetings at end-of-the-summer professional get-togethers, by needing some bit of information that one person's contract firm or state archeology office or Park Service research center has and that you, the errand boy, must go get. He knew she was a graduate student and did bones, faunal analysis, human osteology. He didn't know she could teach.

The fire pops a spark onto the brick apron his stove sits on. He watches it glow, then slowly go out. Sleep isn't coming, but this flow of thought and remembrance is not unpleasant. He talked to Sweeney earlier today and she was crying. *When are you coming home, John? Why are you doing this? Warren wants to know when you and he can get together to write "the article." What article, John? You've never written an article without me…*and so he goes to his refuge, his chest of memories of the one woman who might have saved his life. That possibility ached in him immediately upon seeing her, in the way in which she held attention in the class, in the little shoe box lids full of what she termed "field kits" placed in front of each of her students, who were mostly freshmen possessed with the basset hound look of the hung-over, or the disheveled quality of puppies with large feet whose bodies were awkwardly trying to catch up. It was the second week of classes, and he was arrested by those kits. They held, each, a dozen artifacts of various sorts. She held up a potsherd from her own kit and asked them to find a similar thing in theirs. Then a bone, then a chert or quartzite or basalt flake. The students had to feel them, look, lick, taste. No writing, no boring textbooks full of description. Hands-on. John would have died for a teacher such as this one.

"Now," she said, "you each have two bones in your kit. What animals do you think they're from?"

So the scrutiny began, and John could tell some of them felt as he did. The hangover look erased itself, the baggy pants were hoisted as they stood up and bent over their bones.

"What do you notice about them?" she persisted.

John craned his neck to see over the backs of the last row of students. The bones were of the same size, one perhaps a jackrabbit tibia, the other he wasn't sure.

"One's really light," said a girl with a punk haircut.

Meghan lit up. She just lit up. "Right. So what kind of creature would benefit from light bones?"

Another sullen youth reached up his hand. "I know. Birds."

Now she was grinning. "Excellent. How'd you arrive at that?"

Sullen Youth shrugged, then admitted to building balsa model airplanes for Boy Scouts. John would never have guessed he was a boy scout.

"Cool," she said. "Now what do you think the other bone is?"

And so it went. Rabbit versus turkey; corrugated greyware potsherds versus Santa Fe black-on-white versus Rio Grande glazewares; obsidian flakes versus chert versus basalt; biface versus scraper, then each student having a "rare find" in each kit – a bead of turquoise, a small cord of woven yucca, a basket fragment, a gizzard stone from a turkey.

"I hope you'll consider field school in the summer," she said, as she ended class. John could not imagine any of them wouldn't sign up. "Your homework is to go to the Museum and find out as much as you can about one artifact on display." She distributed a sheet for them to fill out regarding the artifact. "I'll see you next week."

He had to wait in line to talk to her. Students four deep were wanting to share with her, about what they found on their uncle's property, about Auntie Bess's medicine bag (this from a Navajo girl!), about an arrowhead they spotted after a good rain. Finally, they were gone. She looked at him. "John, right?"

He smiled like an eighth grader at a pretty teacher.

"That was phenomenal," he said.

"Really?"

She blushed. She actually blushed. The blushing brought her crashing to him, put her on his same plane. She was not some goddess of teaching who had no shame of her own. No, somewhere, somehow, brown hair, blue eyes, she was like him. So began conversations on archeology – field work, theory, various professors, her ideas, his ideas. She was married, he was married. What was there to worry about? He had many female peers.

But when he started teaching her to flintknap, her sitting between his legs on the ground as his arms traced hers and his hands held her hands to direct hammerstone to core, to teach heft and degree of force and angle of strike, electricity eeled through him. He had taught dozens of people how to flintknap, sometimes in this very position. He never held that position long, but there he was with Meghan on the back stoop of his shabby Albuquerque apartment that he rented during the week while Sweeney brought home the money working out at Zuni Pueblo. There he was and the shudder, the flood went through, and he said, before he could think, "I hope no one sees us like this." He was actually laughing. She said nothing then. But when she came back from a summer in Europe, her marriage in shambles, ugliness from her past rising to the surface, it was he she fell apart to, on a bench in front of the anthropology building.

"I can't go on with this. I have to quit archeology. I have to quit my marriage. I have to quit everything." Tears streaming, her lip trembling, her hair in her face.

"Come on," he said. "Let's go get a beer."

"But you have class!"

"Screw class."

She looked at him like someone for whom nobody had ever offered even that small kindness. A softness flowed through him, a melted butter feeling, a complete rightness with the world because if no one had ever offered her that kindness, no one had ever remotely assumed, either, that he could seriously be of use to other people. He put his arm around her as she sniffed her way to the bar on Central, where Patsy Cline played on the juke box in the dark and long-time drunks hunkered benignly over the counter. It was three in the afternoon and the butter feeling lasted as she stumbled her way through the story of the summer – a love affair, a wake-up call because she hadn't married to have a love affair, an uneasy dream of her father stealing her pocketbook on the steps of the Art Institute of Chicago: "John, I want to write and paint. I don't want to do academics." He sat there and held her with his ears, with his intense listening, the way an elk might hold the air on a moonlit night. A pool of warmth spread like nothing he'd ever felt before, not sex not mother-love but both together, an atomic dissolution of all the scaffolding that separated him from the rest of the universe until he hardly needed to touch her or anyone, his fingertips so alive and his heart calm and full at the same time. He would not, he vowed, move away from this ever again.

* * * *

But he did, didn't he? He stands up. He must have slept some because it is near dawn, the light gray and pale. He puts on sweats, a rain jacket. Out in the gray world he heads for the beach. The harbor boats list slightly in the morning breeze. No Nina on the pier, but he sees a familiar lump sitting on the sand, dark and shrouded, like those women in RC Gorman prints.

"George," he says, lightly, coming to stand next to him.

George looks up. Tear streaks are running down his face.

John steps back. "What are you doing? Are you all right?"

George turns to face the sea again. "I was listening," he says. "Did you know, John-Wayne-Gregory-bro, that the ancestors could tell just by listening to the waves if it was safe to go fishing?" The words fall out in gulps, something broken inside of him.

"I didn't know that."

"Can you imagine knowing that? Imagine knowing that, John!"

John swallows. Imagines. Imagines knowing exactly who he is and being good at it. The swish and pull back of the ocean is gentle this morning, the fog low and thick. John sits on the wet sand next to George, and listens too. George puts his head between his knees and a wild, private keening admits from between them. John hesitates, then puts a hand to the back of his neck as if to say, *Don't*. Don't. Because I'll start too, George, just as much a failure as you at reading the sea, the way to navigate, the bone blood knowledge of how to live on the earth, intact, when you've spent your life split apart.

PART TWO

CHAPTER 4

I.

Two days later John hears school kids go by in the morning, and watches for Nina. He hasn't seen George since he left him keening on the beach, though later that day he could see smoke from the salmon trailer. Time seems to go by in the same manner that the fog does here. Slowly, drippingly, not cognizant of clocks or alarms.

"Here I am," Nina says, coming along with a knobby bag. "I brought my three best."

"Are you feeling better?" he asks.

She nods. John takes out her pieces. The driftwood is sanded and buffed and lacquered. One seems a kind of abstract seal like the piece she was working on at the pier, another clearly a salmon, the other the wing, almost, of an eagle. He smiles. "These are great."

"So you'll take them to the museum while I'm in class?"

"I'll see what they think, if they'll take them on consignment."

She grins. "Awesome! How much you think I should ask for them?"

"I don't know. I'm going to look at how much they sell other stuff for first."

"Okay." She pats his hand, this usually scowling Nina does, and skips off to catch up to her friends. "Maybe," he hears her say to them, her voice a fading echo in the gravel, rain-pocked street, "my daddy won't have to work away from us so much!"

Shit. Such expectation. And he forgot to hand back the piece of driftwood she left the other morning. The museum doesn't open till ten, so he wiles away the hours reading a science fiction book, half expecting George to show up for another beachcombing exercise at any moment, sheepish after his tears two nights before. But he doesn't, and when John peers out of the small shack windows he doesn't see him or smoke out of his trailer either. At eleven, John resigns himself to getting out of his chair. He stokes the fire, makes his customary coffee, puts the book down. With certain types of popular fiction, he can skim and doesn't need rulers anymore. But waiting for George, or for the museum to open, has just been the excuse. What he is really doing is avoiding "the article," as Sweeney puts it. Why can't he just tell Warren he needs help? Why not go to Sweeney, who would talk him through, in bed in the morning, or over coffee on the weekend, the various ways to present the data?

But he has always gone to Sweeney. He went to Sweeney when he was twenty-five, a flunk-out from school twice over, a Marines Corps discharge for blowing out his knee, hired thank God for a summer season in the Sierra Nevada foothills by a friend of a friend of his flintknapping instructor. Sweeney has always been called Sweeney, though her first name is Patricia. John picked her up for the first day of work and as he came around the bend, she was sitting by a mailbox, flintknapping. He still likes to say it was love at first sight, this strawberry blonde, big-boned woman with obsidian in her hands and a piece of buckskin for protection over her knee. She was a PhD candidate, five years older than him. Fellow Californians, they were also lovers of desert archeology, primitive technologists who spent weekends going to Mountain Man rendezvous and learned how to make their own buckskins, willow baskets, flint knives, and the like. Wasn't that who he *was?* Someone who did those things? Who shunned malls and suburban ease? The two of them had done, in their youth, several weeks-long trips where no one had anything an Archaic Indian didn't have, living off of caught mice and brackish waterholes, sleeping huddled up against one another at night for warmth. Sweeney and he have years and years of this, and their backyard is full of obsidian piles and frames for stretching buckskin.

He bangs the screen door and faces his current pile of rock, spread out on the blue tarp. He walks to the edge of the covered area, more like a carport that a porch, save that it extends out over the entire front of the shack. He sticks his neck out into the drizzle. One car moseys down the street, its tires splashing through puddles. Not much else moves. He goes back to his stump, picks up the blade core he has been working on, and has a moment of constriction, of missing Sweeney. The core drops from his hand as his stomach curls in on itself once again. He is surprised, sideswiped. He wants to cry, of all things. He thinks to call her. But she is at work and he just talked to her not long ago and Meghan swirls and lingers and this makes him feel guilty.

The Great Unraveling began with the bones and the turd, he thinks. The man Mark King talked to at the U about the turd was one Dr. Samuel Mellars, who was an MD and a biochemist and apparently extremely excited about the coprolite. He said, according to King, who called John Thursday morning of the week they found it, to get it up there as soon as possible. They were to keep it dry above all else. ("Believe me," John said, "I don't want it reconstituting on my watch." "You mean under your nose," King laughed. "Not all has turned to rock in there, my man.") Mellars even said he might be able to get away with doing some of the analysis for free, or at least not telling the rightful authorities at the medical center. King was hopeful.

John left Thursday about four, getting home by eleven that night. Past Moab, the shadows began to grow long, and as he turned on to I-70 the Book Cliffs to the north deepened to red hues of neon in the last rays of the sun. Long shadows stretched hands out across the land, and the great sweep of the San Rafael Swell in front of him winked out into one massive edifice of shade, a rock dinosaur of enormous proportions. The Swell was his favorite geological phenomenon. A series of sandstone fins ruptured out of the earth at sharp angles, and it seemed monolithic from far away. But it was really down-cut by dramatically narrow canyons that trickled water and revealed, if you felt safe enough to sneak up to them, amphitheatres of pictographs, petroglyphs, the drip of ferns in secret wet places. It was a series of women, Meghan said once, her eyes full of smile. A series of what? He'd asked, nearly gulping. Because it was true, wasn't it? Those slits in the rock, the wet revelation in between...Gad. Keep your eyes on the road, boy.

By the time he coasted into Price it had gone dark. Price Canyon played tricks because the road wound between mountainside and sharp canyon, and big semis bore down on his left and the coal mine, still going, glittered with its strings of lights off to the right. Train tracks nested between the road and the coal mine, down in the canyon, and when the diesel locomotives came opposite with their fat headlights and loud rumble, the spray of industry surrounded him in the dark and if he were a child he would have presumed himself doomed.

Sweeney was asleep by the time he made it home. He gingerly placed the coprolite on the kitchen counter, still in its little cooler, which had been meticulously washed and dried for this purpose. Three baggies with the turd segments wrapped in plastic and cotton, not much changed in appearance from when it was first deposited. He'd eaten nothing but a bag of chips and two Dr. Peppers for dinner, so he grazed for leftovers and found shrimp scampi lingering in a bowl on the top shelf. Sweeney was a pasta addict in her culinary tastes. He took the bowl out, putting it on the counter while he dug for some parmesan to melt on it. Coco the cat, Sweeney's cat, her best friend in all the world, jumped up on the counter, even though he was expressly told not to about twenty times a day. "Coco," John said, stroking his head. His fur was soft, as ever. "How old are you?" He purred. "Six now?" He still purred. John continued, his head cocked. "How long is it going to take to sink into your little pinto bean of a brain that you are not supposed to be on the counter?" He picked him up from underneath and put him on the floor.

"Meow," he said. And less than a minute later was back up

again, watching while John grated the cheese onto the pasta.

"Coco." Scooped up again.

"Meow."

Grated the cheese.

Thud of cat on counter.

"Down!"

John put the pasta in the microwave. Back turned, a fantastical crash emanated from behind him. "You little – !" But Coco was, of course, a blur of tail and stripe, whipping out of the kitchen. Broken glass – John's glass – and ice water glinted all over the counter. "Shit," he hissed, hoping Sweeney had not woken up with the ruckus. He picked up the cooler, whose bottom remained impermeable but nonetheless shiny with water, and moved it to the middle of the dining room table. He wiped up the mess. The microwave beeped at him. He got a new glass, the bowl of pasta, and sat down, rumpled, at his own table.

Sweeney had a bird clock that he found obnoxious beyond parallel, and since it was parked far away in the spare bedroom he could usually barely hear it, but there it went that night, a raven marking midnight. You'd think the manufacturers would do a nice soft bird, like a dove, at that hour. But no, someone had a sense of humor, an Edgar Allen Poe fan, they both figured. Black as night, black bird, raven. "Caw caw caw," it said, his pasta half in his mouth. At least it didn't say Nevermore. He dove into more of his pasta, exhausted. How did people with kids do it? And all of a sudden, like the train blinding him as it showed up from around a corner in the canyon, the second-to-last time he saw Meghan shined in front of him, when he took her to the airport and the concourse seemed overly littered with young families, strollers, car seats, children in knapsacks, slings, hands being held. It was as if he had fallen into another realm where all of that seemed possible for him for the first time in his life. It had never been possible with Sweeney.

Meghan was a month pregnant with her son by then. John

knew this. He tried to put his awareness of the overabundance of families down to Mormon demographics, to the simple fact that she herself was with child. But it was more than that. He kissed her goodbye and watched as she boarded her flight, her brown hair falling past her shoulders. Almost to the gate, she turned back for one last look at him. He was not expecting it. He wished she hadn't. He knew what his face looked like, felt her looking at an arc of pain he had never meant her to see and had only allowed himself because her turquoise gaze was no longer upon him. He flushed and looked down. A child squealed to his right. The child was a beautiful, brown-haired, blue-eyed, girl. He looked up again to the line of passengers boarding the plane, but Meghan had gone.

II.

John watched Sweeney as she dressed in the morning, sluggish after his drive. He had an appointment at ten with Dr. Mellars, and he lay there thinking about bones and death and what would make a person shit in a kiva hearth. Sweeney smiled at him from the mirror. "How was the trip up?"

"Fine, but Coco broke a glass."

She made a face. "I thought I might have heard something."

"What do you have at work today?"

She made another face. "An 8:30 meeting with Marion Natural Gas."

Sweeney, like Warren, has a permanent job in the contract archeology world. She has always done well in finding jobs. It took her five years to finish her PhD after John met her, but even the first field season after they met, she saved him. "Look," she'd said, at its end, as he faced unemployment, the thought of a return to school or some work as a bouncer or some such, "I think I could persuade the boss to let you do the lithic analysis."

"Really?"

She nodded. "I'll help you write it up."

She knew his struggles by then. And she got him to stay on. She "overwintered" him, as they joked later. He can write lithic reports pretty well on his own by now. He can plug in measurements and talk about bifaces and thinning flakes and platform reduction and fire-cracking, because he has re-created all these things himself and so he finds he does not care about fighting with the keyboard as much. Until now he has still run everything by her, though. What has been so wrong in this strategy?

* * * *

It seems to be raining only lightly so he puts on his slicker and wanders to the strand. He holds Nina's bag in his hands. The tide had been high two nights ago, and odd things lie strewn in the crevices between rocks. More seaweed than usual, a tiny squid, the shells of several crabs, the half-decayed leg of what he guesses was a seagull. He picks up the leg, still held together at the knee by bits of sinew, the few remaining feathers waterlogged and ragged. In the end he leaves it draped on a rock, and goes off to the museum.

Little carved canoe replicas, earrings and bracelets and pendants of totem animals, postcards of the Straits of Juan de Fuca, of whales, of the long house in the museum, a scarf of red and black with raven or wolf motifs, cedar chests with the same – some of it well-done, others not so much – line the museum's gift shop shelves. He has no idea what to ask for Nina's pieces. They look like nothing else here.

The man behind the counter looks at him. "Can I help you?"

"Uh, yeah," John says, laying the canvas bag gently on the counter top. "These are made by a local girl. Nina Ward. You know, George's niece."

Something dark flutters over the man's face for a moment, like a shadow in the lens of a camera. It passes before John has time to wonder about it, but it makes him extract the driftwood pieces a little more quickly, as if their beauty will wipe away any negative associations the man might have with the Ward family.

"They, uh, look like animals," John says as he unveils them. "Sort of. Abstract in a way, in a way not."

The man puts his hand to one. John has been hoping for just this; Nina has sanded so smoothly and stained them so lightly that they look like satin. They are meant to be touched.

"Huh," says the man, his fingers not stopping, as if they cannot help themselves. "These are pretty neat."

"Would you take them on consignment?"

"Sure. How much?"

John swallows. He wants to ask how much the man thinks Nina can get, but that has to be a sure way to leave Nina's goods under-priced. "Let's start with a hundred for the bigger seal piece. Seventy-five for the wing and the salmon."

The man nods as if that is entirely reasonable. "That's not too bad. Okay." He lines them up in a neat display. "I'll put 'em over by the little toy canoes. Does she have a name for them? For what she does?"

"A name?" John shakes his head, still getting over the fact that the man has taken him up on his offer. "No," he says, smiling. "She just says they look like bones, the bones of trees, these driftwood pieces. Then she takes them and turns them into something else."

"That's kinda nice. But I don't know if people would get that."

"No, probably not," John says. "But they'll get what they are just by looking at them. Put a sign up. Brag that it's a nine-year-old Indian girl who makes them. White people love that shit. I can speak with authority on that one."

The man's face breaks into a grin. "You that friend of George's, eh? In the shack?"

"Yes."

He extends a meaty paw. "Terrence Williams. I run the

museum store here."

John takes his hand. "Nice to meet you."

Terrence laughs a little as John makes to leave. "'White people love that shit!' Man, that's perfect. That's just perfect."

* * * *

At the beach, he finds the seagull leg again. He pulls at the knee joint, watching the bones seesaw against each other in the late morning light. Meghan's specialty when she was still doing archeology had been bones, animal and human. Animals were eaten, or intruded into a site later on, and so a good faunal analyst looked for signs of either. Were there butchering marks, the cut of stone blades? Had the bone been cracked green, or not-so-green after cooking, in order to extract marrow? Did the animal simply burrow into the site and die there, completely oblivious to its deposition in former human abodes? He turns his seagull leg over, squinting for hairline fractures, for gnaw marks of other animals, anything. Was an animal butchered on site, or brought in at least partially butchered from somewhere else? If the latter, perhaps the less meat-yielding parts would be left behind at the kill. Perhaps toe bones and vertebrae would not be as present in the site. At the trash mound he dug with George five years ago, seal bones were their main faunal find. Tons and tons of seal bones. He hangs onto his seagull leg and walks more of the beach, as if a seal bone might materialize if he just looks hard enough. But in the Southwest, deer and rabbit and turkey comprised the remains. How many turkeys? How many deer? Did the type of rabbit change through time, cottontails more prone to woodlands, jacks to the open plains? Did a shift to more jacks indicate they had cleared a lot of the woodland over time for more crops? What happened when squirrels and other smaller meat showed up? Did that pattern coincide with drought or hard times? He turns up to toward his shack and away from the sand. Still no sign of George.

Age, sex, diseases – these were important in animals but took on whole new meanings when doing human analysis. In an early visit to Meghan in the lab at UNM, before the summer she went to Europe and the giant egg of herself cracked open, she had laid out nine femurs, seven upper arm bones, eight skulls, various skull parts, four tibias and a few ulnas. She had gone to the bathroom a moment after John had walked in, smiling shyly and saying she would be right back. He'd come in deliberately, propelled by the memory of her teaching her lab class, by the feel of his arms teaching hers to flintknap. He idly tattooed her assemblage with his fingers, dimly aware that these were fractures of people, shattered skeletons, and not whole citizens. On a legal pad, she'd written:

FROM TAD:
Some things to look for:
1) A single, short depositional episode. Minimal bone weathering and animal scavenging. So:
2) Bone preservation good to excellent.
3) Almost all body parts disarticulated.
4) Vertebrae are normally missing. More meat yielding parts present than non-meat yielding parts.
5) Massive perimortem breakage in about half to all of the remains.
6) Breakage is by percussion hammering against some form of anvil, with spiral and compact fracturing very common. Reaming of marrow cavity evident in a majority of long bones.
7) Head, face, and long bone breakage is almost universal.
8) Burning, pot polishing, cut marks/skinning all possible, though in lesser amounts than 1-7 above.

YOU GET THE IDEA. Key Q: How is this "cannibalism"

versus run-of-the-mill violence?

John winced. Meghan returned from the bathroom.

"Who's Tad?" he asked.

"My osteology prof in college."

"What's pot polishing?"

"You know, if you boil up a critter the ends of the bones rub against the side of the stew pot."

"That's what I thought."

"I don't have that with these bones here, but Earl Morris has some wild descriptions of that from a shelter up the valley from where these were found. In fact, that was pretty much his 'site.' A couple of ollas with human bones inside."

"Earl Morris found stuff like that?" Morris was digging in the 1930s, if not earlier. "How come nobody talks about it until now?"

She snorted. "Even now they aren't talking about it. I had to dig around in the lit quite a bit to find out my bones were not a complete anomaly."

"Oh." He fingered a femur and then picked it up. Two cuts had been made at the distal, or knee end, one from either side, creating a near-vee toward the center where it would have articulated with the tibia at one time, the little patella floating above the two bones like a fossilized apple slice.

"They're all cut like that," she said. "Look."

She picked up another femur. Same pattern. All nine of them had this.

"Are there other femurs in this lot?"

"No."

John looked at her. "So they were all disarticulated at the knee." *Disarticulated.* Such dispassionate speech. So easy to objectify, to not feel, with words like that. The fact that he did made him feel bad, as if he were less than a scientist, as if the defeat that crept in him upon looking at the bones – a kind of universal despair for the human fate – was some fault of his learning-disabled mind. *Noble scientist, noble savage. Keep your head up, don't let them see you cry.*

"Looks that way," she said.

"How were they buried?"

"They weren't. They were thrown in a pit and covered up. These are from a site in the San Juan Basin, near Farmington." She moved to a skull, picking one up and holding it to the light. "All these are cracked and roasted."

John's stomach, never a strong suit, coagulated and he felt faintly nauseous. "How do you stand looking at this?"

"Well, it's pretty interesting." She smiled, and then a flicker crossed her eyes. "I stand it because I want truth, John. If this is what the truth looks like, so be it. No pussy-footing. I can't stand lies." She said this so strongly, and in that moment he brushed up against a deeper Meghan, the substance itself of her being. It was like glimpsing a deep blue hole, a bottomless swirl of perfect water.

They sat on lab stools, very still, the hairs on his arm touching hers as they rested side by side on the lab counter top, each of them with a bone in their hands. The week before had been the back stoop lesson in flintknapping, and for a millisecond all of the burning he felt then came back.

"If these were deer, I'd say they were being eaten," she said.

"If these were deer," he echoed. He removed his arm. The analysis of animals – "faunal analysis" – and the analysis of humans – "human osteology" – were merging here, the purposes of their deaths determining the slant by which science would treat them.

"Heisenberg," he said softly. "Uncertainty Principle."

She knew. She nodded. "The lens through which you view something determines what you see."

He flashed on Aztecs, Mayans, virgins thrown down limestone cenotes or the hearts of enemy warriors extracted, alive, on specially carved tables of stone. "A Mesoamericanist would say this was human sacrifice."

"Yes."

And what has stuck with him, besides chaotic flashes of the feel of hacked-apart femurs or spirally cracked tibias in his hands, is the small feminine hairs of her arm, the perfect way they talked to one another, how one solid woman who possessed all the skills he lacked seamed her attention to his, so that he loved her, right then and there, in a lab sick with some ancient human misery.

III.

He went to the medical center, looking for Dr. Mellars. Mellars turned out to be a petite man, about 5′5″, with a pointy little brown beard and impish eyes. He reminds John, now, of one of the scientists in his sci fi tale, or that he could audition for the role of Santa's chief elf. He looks past the sand toward town for any sign of smoke from George's trailer, and anticipates Nina's return from school when he can tell her about his trip to the museum. He remembers feeling like a buffoon around Mellars' birdlike grace, his paunch and height covered by a plaid button-down shirt and his nice pair of jeans newly washed for this meeting. This would be dressed up by archeological standards, and he'd also cleaned his boxy, 1980s glasses, as well as combed his hair.

Mellars took this all in as he shook John's hand. "Let me guess," he chuckled. "You are into lithics and Paleo-Indian time periods."

John gave him a look. "How do you know?"

He laughed. "I did forensics for a while, you know, CSI stuff, sometimes prehistoric skeletons. Every Paleo guy I ever met was, uh, overweight, and looked like he really wanted to be on the set of *Easy Rider* but had settled down to a fine career of dust and dead people. Oh, and the fashion sense was completely outdated."

John tried to hide a smile but failed. "What fashion sense?"

He grinned back. "Right. And how come there aren't any Paleo women?"

"Women go for ceramics, which is always later in time. Though there are a few bone women."

Mellars nodded. "Some fine ones. We have a woman here, Type I diabetic. Completely blind. But she can do bones better than anybody I've ever seen."

"Well, we might have some for her." John wished he could say he had Meghan in tow, Meghan waiting in some fictional background he always kept her in his mind. He pinched the bridge of his nose from under his glasses to reset the image. Reality was that Meghan lived in Santa Fe, taught freshman comp, wrote poetry, painted, was married, and had a child.

Mellars was looking expectantly at him. John told him about the shaft full of bodies to clarify their need for a bone analyst. Mellars' eyes widened. "God. That will cause a stir."

"Yeah, I know."

John followed him to a well-lit lab. Mellars had taken possession of his cooler and removed the coprolite to put it under a microscope. "Sweet," he said, his neck buzzard-like as he peered through the eye piece. "It's amazing how much it looks like someone just took a dump yesterday."

"Yeah," John snorted. "So we need to isolate human blood protein," he said nervously, spouting Warren who seemed to know something about this.

"Okay..." He peered at it again. "First, don't get your hopes up."

"What do you mean?"

"You know. Just because someone craps in a kiva full of bones doesn't mean the poop is full of meat."

"Right." John let out air. Duh. How could he overlook that idea? "So test for contents first."

"Yes. Your average Anasazi poo – actually, your average New World poo below Lake Huron – is filled with starch, corn being the mainstay of the diet."

"Ok. That will be easy, right?"

"And cheap."

"Then what?"

"Well, if it tests for meat, then we have to find out what kind. And if it's human, how do I separate out proteins found in quotidian rectal bleeding versus proteins that come from actually eating someone else?"

"'Quotidian rectal bleeding?'" John grimaced. Medicine had never been his cup of tea, and he vowed never to make another shit joke again.

Mellars laughed. "We doctors are sick, I know."

"Well," John sighed. "How long till you can test for starch?"

"Oh, I'll do that today. Then I need to think about the other stuff."

John felt himself sag and Mellars patted his shoulder, reaching up to do it. "Don't worry. There will be an answer."

Something about Mellars was superbly funny. John smiled again. "Always trust science."

"Back off, man, I'm a scientist!"

They both grinned. John looked on in amazement. "You said that too, in med school?"

"You bet. Actually, more when I was getting my biochem degree, but still."

John chewed his lip, more at ease with this man of multiple degrees than he had thought he might be. He allowed for a molecule of the kind of thought that made butterflies somersault in my stomach. "You know, in archeology, they're going to argue endlessly about whether this was cannibalism or witchcraft."

"Witchcraft?" Mellars looked baffled. He was not an anthropologist.

"Socially sanctioned persecution of people."

"Excellent." He looked at John. "And you find this – ?"

Something in John drooped even more. He thought archeology would answer all his questions about the human race but the longer he stayed in it the less he saw that it accomplished. "I find this idiotic. I mean, maybe it matters to the Hopi or some such. Gad, so much of my field is politics anymore. We stake out our turf and then lose – lose the big picture." He smirked at himself inside as he said this, since he had never gained the big picture himself, since his mind worked in shards and slivers and with hands and ears. But he went on. "All of us lose. Injuns and white guys. But really, what's the difference? Either way, you're brutalizing people. Isn't *that* the big picture? The one that matters?"

"Ah. Morals and science. Always an excellent combination." It was Mellars' turn to smirk. "Did you know science was brought about to 'control' and 'conquer' nature? Sir Francis Bacon said that, the pig!" He started laughing. "Get it? Bacon? Pig? Sorry. What I'm trying to say is that we're fucked from the get-go if that's the case and any more these days I have to go over and over why I am still practicing science." He sighs. "Has to do with being such a good method, in the end, for slapping you in the face with your own bullshit, if only you let it. But back to you. You are asking what's the difference between socially sanctioned terror versus 'crime,' in other words."

"Right."

They settled to silence again. Holy Communion, of all things, wafted over John, the taste of bread and wine in his mouth on endless Sundays. *This is my body, take, eat, do this for the remembrance of me.* What was that? Socially sanctioned cannibalism? He drew his sleeve across his mouth.

Mellars clapped his shoulder again. "Well, for now, let's not worry about the entire intellectual house of cards that is probably Western Thought. Let's just figure out how to tell rectal bleeding from ingestion of little people parts."

John smiled wanly. "I leave that to you, my good man. Send King the bill." And he exited into the bright summer Utah morning, the thunderheads building over the Wasatch Range already.

* * * *

At home an unearthly silence prevailed. He hated it. What was this place in him? Did just anyone have this? A wound that wouldn't ever quite heal, it tended to re-open – *suppurate* was the word, another one of those secret library words he'd captured for himself – when he had unexpected time to himself. He should be working in Colorado, but thanks to a turd he found himself home. His fingertips graced kitchen counter, bed sheet, Sweeney's hairbrush in the john. He had everything, didn't he? Work in the field he loved, a good wife, a decent house in a nice part of town, his tool kits for making stone tools and baskets and buckskin, a barbeque out back, yes? Even his health. He weighed too much but oddly he had low cholesterol and no sign of heart disease. He was forty-nine and with the same woman for almost twenty-five years. Half his life! But was every piece of his heart really "with" her? Janis Joplin, the sexiest female singer who ever lived, materialized there in his backyard that day, or at least the most crucial line she ever sang did: ...*little piece of my heart out, baby*...He fumbled for the shed, got out the lawn mower, and began his one act of suburban manhood, lost in a haze of questions.

The sound of a hawk keening pulls him to the present, and he walks out into the street. He sees Nina, at last, school over for the day. She must have lost her friends because it has been so quiet, so devoid of human activity, the town a still life of boats and small rain and window-eyed buildings, that he is relieved merely by her motion.

"Nina," he calls. She walks over, black hair in a loose braid, her shoes muddy.

She puppies up to him and he hands her the piece she left the other day. "You forgot this."

She looks at it and tucks it under her arm. "Thanks. Did you take my pieces to the museum?"

"I did."

"Well? What'd they say?"

It is all he can do to hide a smile. "They said they'd take them on consignment."

Her eyes go big. "They did? How much?"

He tells her. She lets out a whoop and pirouettes across a shallow puddle. "Wait till I tell my auntie and Dad!"

John releases his smile. "Hey, Nina."

She stops pirouetting. "What?"

"Where's your Uncle George?"

"Port Angeles." Her face goes more sober.

"Why?" he asks.

"Warrant out for him."

"What? Why?"

She shrugs the shrug of children who have been given only half the story but probably can guess the rest. "Drunk driving stuff." She lowers her eyes.

"When was this?" George hasn't drunk a thing in the month John has been here, and was on the wagon when he knew him five years ago.

"Accident was a year ago."

"Accident? What accident?"

"He killed someone," she blurts, and starts to back away down the street.

"What? Nina! Come back!"

But she's down the block, jogging, then around the corner. Fuck, John thinks. Fuck fuck fuck.

CHAPTER 5

I.

He wants George's salmon grease and wood smoke if he can't have George. He's almost aghast at his panic, at the thought of being alone on the extreme northwest tip of America. All his life, wanting aloneness, to hide – and now this? Wood smoke is a great comforter, and he sprints toward the trailer. The smell and campfire glow were what Steve at Tin Cup termed Wilderness TV. And it was true, you could stay for hours, hooked on that dance and odor of flames. The trailer is open, so he goes inside and starts up the fire. He won't cook any salmon; he just wants warmth after the chill of the ocean air, the trees backing it like dripping sentinels. They close in on him, the trees, whispering of timelessness and secrets. God knew what lay buried beneath their rotting leaves. He sits on George's little stool, brailling the wood, the cash register. He misses George, who always seems happy to see him, this missing more acute now that he finds George is at least as big a sinner as he is. To have killed someone! John curls his fingers into a ball, a kind of pained fist.

In honor of him, his one friend here, he has a sudden itch to attempt the *American Antiquity* article. For George, not for himself. For George and his crew and Meghan and Sweeney and everyone else he is sure he has let down. This makes him feel less alone. He dashes out of the trailer and extracts his laptop from the shack a block away. He grabs Mellars' lab reports, the first verifying the coprolite did, in fact, contain meat and almost nothing else, the second, six months later – the catalyst for his panicked fleeing to this tip of the continent – isolating antibodies to human myoglobin, a substance one can only procure in one's poop if one has eaten another human being.

Mellars' lab assistant, one Betty Jane Jaber, she of the quasi-beehive and Mardi Gras beads for a glasses chain, still thinks it is coyote scat. John will have to answer to that criticism. He will have to answer to the nay-sayers, to the incensed Hopi and the upset peaceniks who have cherished the Ancestral Puebloan – the Anasazi in old, un-P.C. lingo – for being Noble Savage Farmers, incapable of such brutality. He will have to fend off the witchcraft theorists. He has an email, three weeks old, from Mellars: *Call me. Where the hell are you? We have to announce this!*

Announce it! His breathing gets ragged again. The trailer feels dank and stuffy, no longer comforting with its residues of George's bulk and livelihood. Announce it! He'll feel like Bill Clinton in the aftermath of Monica Lewinsky. To read a press release out loud? About a kiva full of massacre and an act of defecation in its hearth that contains outright proof that at least in this one instance, cannibalism ruled the day? He never mastered reading Dick and Jane out loud! He starts reading out loud and the S's and J's and C's and P's get big and three-dimensional and start swinging their blunt black bodies into him from across the room. Sweeney will help later with the article if he asks, but he has been trying – trying for almost nine months now, really – not to go to her.

Nine months. He has not gone to Sweeney because every night at the site he would see Orion and think of that sentimental Dire Straits song about Romeo kissing the bars of Orion as a way to keep Juliet to him, and Meghan would be there. Meghan asks something different from him than Sweeney. He knew that the moment she said she hated lies in that lab full of stricken bones. Shit. He crashes open the front door to get some air. A woman is standing there.

"Oh!" he says.

"Where's George?" she asks. "I saw the smoke and thought –"

"He's in Port Angeles."

She looks disappointed. "I was hoping for some salmon."

"Sorry."

She's a thick-waisted native woman, probably his age or

older. She sticks out her hand. "Melinda Weeks. I run special programs for the elementary kids. You must be George's friend."

"Yes," John says, shaking her hand. *Special programs?* "I'm sorry I don't have any salmon."

"That's okay." She turns to go, then stops. "Do you know when George is coming back?"

"No." John takes a breath. "So, um, what do you do with special programs?"

She smiles. "You know. Kids with trouble reading, writing, math. Writing up Individual Learning Plans. Getting them through."

Tools. He stares at her. The only way he finally got a B.A. is because his comp teacher plopped him in front of a computer and said, You will do all your writing on this. You've dropped this course five times. It's time to finish. She didn't tell him she made different rules for him about the timing of his papers, but he knows other students did not get this treatment. He breaks his stare at Ms. Weeks, embarrassed. "Does the, um – does it work? The Learning Plans?"

"Sometimes. Sometimes not." She shrugs. "A lot of factors in a kid's life go into what happens when they sit down at a desk."

"Yes." Spokes of a wheel, drums, human lifelines. What's broken and what's not.

"I have to be getting back. I'm on recess," she chuckles.

"Nice to meet you," he says. But what he wants to do is to grab onto her and shout at her for help.

II.

He had a second Mrs. Carrington, he is ashamed to admit. The problem with the first Mrs. Carrington was that she lasted but a year. Her husband got a new job and they left the San Diego area. John timidly tried fifth grade without her, and found, if he worked at it, that he could use her techniques and keep up with the class most of the time. But he hid his ruler, his mock-up of a typewriter keyboard, from others as much as he could. To ask for more help? Mrs. Carrington had not come cheap, and his parents balked at first, but when Sister Theresa slapped them with that straight-lipped look only a nun can muster, they'd buckled. Nobody understood learning disabilities back then and he still thinks nobody understands them much now. Besides, as Sweeney likes to point out, back then there may not have been another Mrs. Carrington. She was cutting edge, pre-Disabilities Act, pre-anything.

So before Sweeney came along, John went to Lindsay, his older sister, to get him through junior high; then he went through two girlfriends. He wouldn't say they wrote his papers for him – he had more ethics than that – but he needed what Mrs. Carrington had started and not finished, and that was the right coaxing. The second Mrs. Carrington didn't come along for nearly forty years and when she did she appeared in the form of a woman named Colleen Jensen. He has called her, derisively, Diagnostics Lady most of the time. And actually, said Diagnostics Lady, what he needed was a sense of advocacy.

"Huh?" That sounded like one of those words people of her profession built whole conferences around.

"Advocacy," she said, standing up and pulling an article from a filing cabinet. She handed the article to him and he gazed at it, not even seeing the words. He was there because he flunked his PhD entrance exams at Mellars' esteemed university. Comprehensives that would simultaneously earn him a Master's and the entrance into the PhD program in archeology at the University of Utah. Comps that set up the worst possible environment for him – timed writing, pressurized writing, writing full of abstract thought with no room for oral discussion, for the drawing of schemes, for anything physical or auditory. It was also big picture stuff. No neat little packages of lithic analysis, no slices of place or time, but gigantic swaths of human history minds like Meghan's and Steve's thrived upon. (E.g.: "There is currently great debate regarding the entrance of peoples into the New World during the Pleistocene. Discuss at least two main theories and the data they are based upon..."; "Explicate Wittfogel's theory for the rise of state-level social organization and compare it to at least one other theory of your choosing regarding the same phenomenon. Based on your analysis, explain your own posture regarding this issue...") Ye Gods. The only thing auditory was the roar of panic fuzzing out his brain, like an F-16 going over, or the ocean crashing in but never receding. The roar was familiar, as old as school itself.

Diagnostics Lady was looking at him. He sat like a sack of potatoes, inert in the chair in her office. "You've been made to feel dumb all your life, right?"

He squirmed. "Yes," he said, dully. He pinched the bridge of his nose. He did not want to go back to his dreams, where his nakedness and fear of something so benign as the alphabet would render him paralyzed.

"Do you have brothers and sisters?" she asked.

"Yes."

"Older? Younger?"

"Older. Two sisters."

Diagnostics Lady grimaced.

"Why, is that bad?"

"Maybe," she said. "Our culture teaches boys they are supposed to be on top. But younger boys with strong sisters don't feel this way. So there's a conflict there. It can add to the sense of inadequacy." She said this as if she found it despicable that such a culture even existed, and then that young men should get upset at losing their sense of false entitlement. Then she added, "I bet your sisters had no problem with school."

"No," he mumbled, coloring.

"Look at me," she said.

He looked up.

"Now. Look me in the eye and tell me you've never been loved."

He was taken aback. "That's none of your business," he snapped. "What does that have to do with learning disabilities? With my 'kinesthetic learning strategies'?"

"Everything," she said.

"How so?"

"Because until I can get it through your thick heart – and notice I'm not talking about your brain here, but your heart – that you are a worthy person *as you are,* then you aren't going to solve anything."

They sat in stony silence for what seemed like decades. He remembers feeling ravenous. Finally, he said to her, "I just want to pass comps."

"All right, then," she said. "Take this to your professors and tell them to devise a test with these conditions met. If they have questions, they can call me." She handed him a sheet of official-looking paper. It said he must be given more time for tests. It said to consider oral testing. It said he should have access to a computer at all times. It said many things, all of which screamed at him that he was not normal and could not handle life as normal people do.

But he took it to his professors because it was his professors who told him to go talk to Diagnostics Lady – Jensen – in the first place. Eventually he passed his comps. But what did he lose?

He lost Meghan. The light's dimmer than ever now, the air pregnant with rain in the gloom of George's trailer with a blue screen of laptop and a small fire at the bottom of a barrel for company. He takes a napkin and blows his nose. Meghan, who refused to be Helper Girl #20. Or whatever she was. Diagnostics Lady continued to tell him how many football players and other boys had used their girlfriends to do their work for them. An "enabler," that's it. Is Sweeney an "enabler"? Hell, he doesn't know. But he does know since that disastrous day with comps, when he instant-messaged Meghan halfway through the Wittfogel question and she was not online (he told her to be ready; why was she not there?), and the phone calls that came later, it all tumbling out, how much he loved her, how much it frightened him, how he thought of living with her every day of his life, how they should have run away with each other years ago, how how how – but then, in the motes of dust stealing in on sunbeams in his comps cubicle, his computer screen totally blank, standing up and going to Professor Walker's office, saying, his face granite, "I can't do this," and turning on his heel to run as far away from the regal buildings and landscaped lawns of universities for good, Walker said, like some Mary-in-the-tortilla miracle they always used to laugh about in New Mexico, "Wait a minute, Thompson." He ripped off a piece of paper from a notepad, wrote a name on it like an Rx of some sort. "Go see this woman," was all he said. "Then we'll talk."

John just gaped at him. But I've *failed*, he wanted to shout at him. He wanted to take his fucking gun from sniper school in the Marine Corps and shove it in his face and say, *I was the best in my class at this, you moron. At shooting people with precision. But I don't give a fuck about that. Just give me the Master's. Give me a ticket to the one club I've only ever wanted to be in and never will.* But Walker merely looked at him, placid. He had round spectacles, a moustache, long tapered fingers with veins in them, dark hair with gray at the temples. He was one of the most brilliant men John knew. John looked at the paper. Walker was saying, he thought, that he still had a chance, that he wasn't, truly, as dumb as some of his Corps mates, whose IQs were seriously below grade. But he had to take charge of things. He had to go talk to the person on Walker's Rx, who of course was Colleen Jensen.

III.

By now it is nightfall and he has managed to write a page of description, then some thoughts on how Tip Cup does or does not fit in the spokes of the great prehistoric Southwestern wheel. He has eaten half a jar of salmon confit he found under the counter, and gone out for a Dr. Pepper at Neah Bay's one gas station about an hour ago. A question begins to form: What is the difference between *advocacy* and enabling? *Answer that, Ms. Jensen, will you?* Because he can't tell. He almost emails her. Almost. Then he dares to draft a message to Steve instead. He'll have to send it in the morning when he can hook up to the modem in the library, and that gives him time to balk, to not send it, to rescind himself.

He peers into the dank dark and wills George to appear. He does not. When John was sixteen and could drive, his father disappeared too. Not physically, but the brief years of occasional desert trips seem to have ended. Both sisters were in college and in their usual manner, his mother and father seemed to decide they had, really, no more children at home, and began venturing forth on weekends to auto shows (his father loved antique autos) and a cabin near Alpine that belonged to a friend of theirs. John did go to the desert, orienteering and flintknapping, experimenting with deadfall traps and atlatls, bows and arrows and fire made from a stick and a flat piece of wood with holes drilled in it from the stick. Then he would carry the ember around from campsite to campsite, just as he had read the Indians once did. He stayed away from Twentynine Palms, the enormous Marine base there; he stayed away from Edwards Air Force Base too, and its low-flying aircraft. He went south, between I-40 and I-10, and then south of even 1-10. He ran into the remains of what must have been an illegal Mexican, and flushed out a Viet Nam vet survivalist in desert camo who fingered an M-16 but never pointed it at him. His father had taught him enough about weapons for him to guess that, judging by the rest of him, enough sand had gotten in the rifle's mechanism that it wouldn't shoot anyway.

Maybe he was wrong, but maybe not. John called the INS, anonymously, about the dead Mexican, and on other weekends he went to the beach and played volleyball. He was big by then. Big and strong, athletic. A woman named Lanie Brooks caught him at the height of his physical belief in himself. He'd spend hours on the beach playing volleyball and body surfing. He'd take on sea caves at high tide and nearly lost his life several times during storm swells. Once he ended up on barnacled rocks at the back of a cave with about twenty seals; they could have cared less about him, but in that enclosed space their fish breath was enough to about put him under. He had to wait an hour or so until the tide began turning to go back out, and he was sure he smelled like a squid factory by the time he swam back to the beach. But he became good enough in volleyball that local coaches started to notice. Since he wasn't public school, he couldn't play on those teams, but their interest was enough to get him to stay around San Diego after graduating, with the SDSU coach bribing him with possible scholarships should he play well for them. He didn't have to have a great GPA to get in there at the time, though by senior year he was doing ok. He listened a lot in class, so that when Father Damien or whoever asked him a question, he could answer it back. They liked that. He'd get C's on papers and A's on participation, and stumble through with B-'s, C+'s for final grades.

John didn't know what else to do with himself anyway besides SDSU. He still wanted to do archeology, but it frightened him, as if it were something too far out of reach. Going to college for volleyball felt like a safe way in, as if as an athlete nobody would expect much out of him academically. So that summer he played beach ball, and Lanie Brooks, ten years older than he, married to an airline executive, a porn magazine's dream with the blonde hair, the big breasts, the eyes darkly mascara'd in a manner that was out of style by then but looked heavenly on her, paid attention.

Meghan, his sexual explorer, opening like petals after a storm, after incest and god knows what else in that family of hers – she was so jealous when, after she asked, he told her what sex felt like for him when he first had it. And even before Lanie it trampled him. Kinesthetic learner! He has to smile at that. The sheer physical overwhelm, the sensory range from prickles on the back of the neck to the flooding of warmth into his groin, his toes, his whole body. So he'd had sex before Lanie, but still nothing compared. He told Megan and Sweeney at different times that no nineteen-year-old was ready for Lanie.

They'd come seven times in one afternoon. He'd go over there when her husband was off on trips and after sex fall asleep in her arms, both of them naked, on the couch. They fucked in every room, outside, on the beach at night, everywhere. Johnny, she'd say, swirling his hair, you have such an intense physicality. Just intense. Years later, Meghan would say, "Don't you get it? The same grace by which your hands make spear points or cook me dinner or figure out lettering on keyboards is enough to do a woman in." Lanie taught him how to spread a woman's legs, touch her just so, put his mouth to that delicious triangle and tongue her till she writhed. Lanie'd buck and say, "Now! Now!" And he'd enter her, wet and plump as a plum, and she'd say, "Yes!" Just: "Yes!" She'd moan and fall back, blonde hair and big breasts spread everywhere. She looked hot in a bikini, hotter out of one, and he can still get fired up thinking about her.

She'd be sixty by now. He has no idea what happened to her. She kept promising him she'd leave her husband for him. Him, a freshman in college. The second summer when he got on a dig out in Arizona, he called her every night he could from a pay phone in Flagstaff. Come back now, she'd say. I need you now. But he couldn't. He couldn't. He had a job, a real archeology job. Somebody'd hired him as a grunt, a college crew grunt. He was thrilled. Come back now, she said. I'll fuck you till the cows come home, she breathed in his ear. He'd close his eyes into that and jack off in the phone booth. Lanie, I miss you so much. I miss you too, Johnny. Come back.

But he couldn't. Finally, he had a week left; they were hanging by a thread by then. Something had changed in her voice. Did she have a new boy? That thought made his stomach ball so tightly he thought he'd puke. That golden body, that laugh, that zest for running naked at midnight along deserted strands. She was desired by all the men on earth and she knew it. She was his first real love, and yet she had nothing to do with school, with archeology, with real life. He winces now at that. A "real love" when she had nothing to do with "real life"? *How many other loves have you kept in that place, that golden box?* He could love her because she was outside all that. She was above and outside all that. She lived in a plush, white-couched ranch-style house her husband bought for her. She fucked him, no doubt. But he was never John's competition, or so he thought. Now, he sees it differently. He sees a lot of things differently. But sometimes John still thinks if he'd just gone back early, or she'd waited three more days, it would have been okay.

On the last day of the dig he got in his pick-up and drove ferociously. He stopped in Seligman, Arizona, for gas. Seligman, a Route 66 town I-40 forgot. Transition place between Flagstaff's pine trees and the Mojave. Blonde grasses on round hills with yucca and juniper dotting them. Getting on toward night, The Brotherhood of the Third Wheel holding its rally here that Labor Day weekend. Men in black leather growled up to the gas pumps on Harleys with sidecars. It took John a minute to get that the third wheel was the sidecar. Across the street, a restaurant selling "road kill" entrees sat with a boardwalk and a false front and, on the top "floor," windows painted with women hanging out. Katie, one window said. Bessie, the other one said. The painted women wore mining-era corsets that revealed their cleavage, and ringlets for hair. Something in his mouth went dry. It wasn't till he got back on the highway and drove ten miles that it hit him that not only did the restaurant sell food off the backs of animals made into a joke by their roadside slaughter, but that the women, women painted above the restaurant, were meant to be whores.

* * * *

Lanie had left by the time he got home. He drove by the house, with its For Sale sign up and swinging in the breeze like a hinge in a ghost town. He played volleyball like an automaton that fall and the coach asked what the hell was wrong with him. He nearly joined the French Foreign Legion, in the same self-destructive spirit that he swam higher and higher tides into sea caves. Finally he parked his truck, an F-150 his father had had for years, in front of the Marine recruiting office and stared at it for about a week. Slowly, slowly, a path toward redemption filled his head. If he joined the Marines, he would have one more thread to connect to his father with. He could at least have that relationship solidify beyond a desert his father seemed to have lost all interest in sharing with John. He couldn't even take a shower and wash himself without missing Lanie so acutely it physically hurt, so he would give his body new memories. Boot camp memories. He was never going to be an archeologist anyway. So he joined up and when he told his father he didn't jump for joy or show John his medals or clap his shoulder like those ads tell you your father would do. His father, the history teacher wannabe, just looked at him and asked that Why question. *Why now? I thought school and everything was ok.*

What his dad really wanted to ask, John is fairly sure, is What The Fuck Are You Doing? Back in Neah Bay, he gives up on the computer. Out on the strand, the rain abated, the night dark, navigating by the white waves of the sea, he watches two fishing boats come in late, their lights on. Still no sign of George. Well? Dad voice morphing into Meghan: What The Fuck *Were* You Doing?

IV.

A car pulls up to the dock behind him, he hears a door open, then the thud of a heavy body on boards. "Thanks, cousin," says a sluggish voice. John turns around as the car peels away into the night. A pod of men are down the beach on the other side of the dock, surrounding a long object propped up on sawhorses. In the foreground, the heavy body picks itself up enough to brace itself against a piling.

"George?" John asks.

"John Wayne," he says feebly.

He hears the pop of a can and walks over to find him peeling back the lid of some sardines. He licks the oil off the lid. "Want some?"

"No. Do you eat nothing but fish?"

He chuckles. "Naw. Ate burgers for three days in Port Angeles. Ninety-nine cents at Burger King!" He finds this funny the way drunk and desperate people do.

"George…" John sits down next to him in the sand.

"Shit, John Wayne, did you know I went to Dartmouth?"

"What?"

He nods. "Dartmouth College. I quote, 'The Native American Program strives to provide spiritual, emotional, and personal support, oftentimes on an individual basis, to insure the success of all Native students.' I just looked that up again, on the internet in Angeles." He snorts and lets out a noise a hyena would be proud of.

"How'd you get in?"

He looks at John. "To Dartmouth? I was smart, bro."

"What happened in Port Angeles?"

He sobers a bit. "Had to go for a court thing."

"Nina says you got in an accident."

He merely nods and looks away, down the beach opposite the men with the long object. They can't see them from where they sit at the base of the first pilings.

"Nina says you killed someone." John pushes it, he can't help it. He has never pushed anything in his life and look where it has gotten him. Fuck it.

"Nina don't know when to keep her mouth shut."

John stares at him. "She's a kid! She's your niece!"

His face screws up and he puckers his lips in what John recognizes is an attempt not to cry. "I know," he mewls. "Sorry."

They are silent for a time. He finishes his sardines and pours out the leftover oil onto the beach.

"Know what I majored in?" he asks.

"What?" John asks.

"Economics!" He hyenas again.

"What's so funny about that?"

"I learned all about white man's money and I can't make a living worth shit! I tell you, bro, what it's like." He squats and faces John. "It's like someone telling you you didn't actually get beat up. That the people who made your reservation are 'nice.' It's a big mind fuck, is what. You know what the oil companies call all the pollution they leave behind?"

John swallows. "'Externalities.'"

"Yup! Externalities!" He owls in at him, mops his face with his paw of a hand, his breath fishy and close. "I ask you, John Wayne friend of mine, just what planet do they think they live on?" He flops back down in the sand. "Shit. We Injuns thought the earth was an externality we wouldn't be here." He cackles again as another thought swims in. "Sure is easy to do, though, when the top of the food chain is fucking ninety-nine cents and you get it in a nice little chemical patty with ketchup."

"True. Is that why you drink?"

"Naw, man. I drink 'cause I'm fucked up. Ok? Got to 'own my shit.' Make amends to all the people I hurt. People I killed. Step Four of white man's program."

John stands up. Offers him a hand. Across the way, a flame

spreads along the long axis of the long object.

"I'll be damned," George says, seeing it.

"What? What are they doing over there?"

"Makin' a canoe. They're burning out the middle to make the inside."

"Really? Let's go see."

But George shakes his head. Tears track down his round face, silently. "You got to be pure to go there. To be a part of that. Me, I'm hungover bad. Not pure." He shakes his head more violently. "They'd kick me out." He pushes John gently, though. "You go, bro. It's okay if you go."

"Are you sure?"

"Yup. I'm going home to clean up, dry out. Okay?"

"Sure."

"Fuckin' Dartmouth," he mutters under his breath as he shuffles off the strand. "Don't teach you nothing about your heart. What kind of education is that?"

PART THREE

CHAPTER 6

I.

His old UNM professor, Luke Sanborn, the one he deliberately wanted to study with, the one who drew Meghan and a host of other students to him, used to smoke a pack a day and laugh with a kind of southern "heh-heh-heh" that seemed both absurd and diabolical at the same time. His students called him an Alpha Male in the manner of great silverback gorillas, and Steve's book – the one on Orayvi with the bow laid across the kiva ladder – seemed, without meaning to be that at all, a surprising example of what Sanborn would call "middle range theory" – the practice of looking at the ethnographic present from an archeological perspective to tighten inferences about the past. Sanborn developed this theory by living with the Nunamuit around Anaktuvuk Pass in the Brooks Range of Alaska, and spent endless hours mapping bone debris around hearths, debris from eating the succulent morsels of caribou, debris representative of the remains of feasts, debris that fell out in rings around the hearth, a space between the fire pit and the bones that revealed where the humans had sat. His books were filled with his careful drawings of such hearths. Roast your leg of caribou, eat, throw the leftovers over your shoulder. Watch what the dogs do, how they drag things off, a confounding variable. Talk with the elders about when and where and how they move. How a man starts his life in one location, and does not come back to it for forty years. Why? Because that's how long it takes for the willow to rejuvenate, and willow is the sole source of firewood. How a woman might sleep with the man's hunting partner, a kind of polyandry never labeled as such in the literature. Why? Because hunting partners were crucial to each other's survival, to their families' survival. Few women would think twice about reinforcing that. John could only imagine Luke, heavy and smoking, breathing hard, in deep layers of down or skins or whatever it is that he wore, sitting with a clipboard around eternal campfires, asking questions, drawing hearths and bones, and flicking cigarette ash away until his hands grew too cold.

And, he would ask them, his focus off of hearths and willow for a while, knuckles on the oval seminar table, what of these "games" with the seal hunters to the north? What are those about? The inland caribou hunters did not have much use for the seal hunters, and vice versa. But they met now and then for feasting and games and what turned out to be statesmanship. For when the caribou crashed in the early 20th Century – the direct result of Euro-American mistreatment of the great woods to the south, where the caribou migrated to – on whom did the Nunamuit call? Why, the seal hunters of course, said Luke, guffawing slightly as he told them this. The Nunamuit went up there for a few years. Weren't treated with the greatest of respect, but they didn't starve either. And should the seal hunters face a similar misery? Why, south they would go, to the Brooks Range, to the hearths with their rings and rings of bone, and the dogs dragging the caribou hocks off into the dusk.

He'd hold their eyes at this point, John's or someone else's. And he'd say, "These meetings between the Nunamuit and the seal hunters are listed as 'games' in the ethnographic record. *Games*. We barely understand," he'd go on, appalled – "no, we understand not at all – how human systems work *on the ground*. We have almost no understanding of the adaptive purpose of social niceties such as games. Or, say, how a matrilineal group will distribute meat versus a patrilineal group. Once we figure these things out – once we make connections between what gets left behind in the archeological record and what we know of social organization – *then* we can start making some solid inferences about the past. Once we understand how things like willow and caribou and the distribution of impinging groups as well as available resources across a landscape affect human decision-making, *then* we will be getting somewhere." He'd kind of cough at a point such as this one, the heh-heh-heh of a laugh following.

The Ancestral Puebloan were probably matrilineal much like their descendants until the Spanish got a hold of them. Since the Spanish never got a hold of the Hopi, Steve's book nicely documented matrilineal clan structure at a point in time when Orayvi, a village occupied since 1300, split in two. What caused the split? The book asked, and for once, for once in the pages of mainstream, Margaret Mead cultural anthropology, John found teases of answers. Usually he relied on old explorer's accounts of tribal activity for middle range help with whatever he was seeing on the ground, since the explorers had had to live with the natives to survive at the level of whatever got left behind in the archeological record.

John looked at the graphs and charts about Hopi, his field groceries safely ensconced in a cooler in the pickup. He had since moved to the Laundromat, his weekend going by in dull and typical fashion, his wash spinning behind him. He had called Sweeney after starting the washing machine, encountering a sideswipe of surprising comfort in the small talk of married couples on weekends. He didn't understand his sudden confidence but he told her he loved her. He went back to the book. He loved graphs and charts. He read what Steve had underlined, Steve having unwittingly supplied a built-in ruler for his optically demented mind. Point One: The more important the ceremony that a clan controlled, the higher the quality of land that the clan also controlled. Steve had said that earlier to him in a campfire discussion, but it meant more. It meant control of ritual and control of economics had everything to do with one another. No need for the classic compartmentalization of ritual that archeologists and anthropologists were wont to do, thereby fomenting a potentially disastrous misread of another culture. The time-worn joke was that if an archeologist didn't know what an object was used for, she or he called it "ritual" and left at that. But that too was symptomatic of much, much more, of the deepest rent of all in the fabric of Western thinking. "Ceremony" was a product of the glorious human "mind." Economics at the level of horticultural land use was a product of "ecology," "nature," something "out there" that wasn't important to the human entity, the human "mind," to whatever Descartes had decided four hundred years earlier. Good God, he heard Meghan snorting in his head from a time long ago, and then Steve snorting too, from a more recent time, because Steve had more or less arrived at the same conclusion as Meghan after three beers around a late, loud campfire. "So 'ritual' could have *nothing* to do with the ecology of its location, and to find evidence that it might was somehow demeaning? All those post-modern guilt trippers pissing and moaning about how such thinking is 'environmental determinism' and the lowest blow possible. Give me," said Steve, spitting out a pistachio shell off to one side, "a fucking break. I'm proud to be environmentally determined." He blinked around at all of them. "I mean, really. Is there another planet you'd rather be from?"

John breathed, his clothes done washing. He started the dryer, went back to the book. Point Two: The split that happened at Orayvi did not necessarily go along clan lines. This was because, Point Three, as Steve had said, the split was "nothing if not a revolt of the landless" and, Point Four, there were two ways to be relatively landless, and that was either by virtue of being a part of a marginal clan who got to the mesas late by historical reckoning and had to make do with so-so agricultural land, or by being a marginal part of a leading clan – for instance, being born the fourth daughter of the fourth daughter of the fourth daughter. "Opportunity for participation in the ceremonial life was sufficient to prevent the alienation of the common people under the normal conditions of life." But when the going got tough…well, as he had said, the tough might slaughter the weak.

He heard the metallic slap of a zipper stop slapping through the open door of the Laundromat, and knew his wash was dry. He folded it, put it back in his laundry sack. Outside it was warm, mid-80s, the late August air crisper and yet somehow more forgiving. He got in his truck, still dreaming, marveling that his own head could hold all these thoughts. He hadn't known he could be capable. The August day seemed alacritous, clairvoyant, not of this world. What if we said, Luke Sanborn asked again and again in a million different ways, that the human mind is not an isolated thing, not the only thing that makes us human, not the only interesting thing? Gad – for a learning disabled kid that question was a lifeline, breathing space, sanctuary. What if we said, Lew went on, that like animals we are subject to evolutionary pressures, but unlike particular animal species, how we respond to those pressures will vary immensely? Later, when Jensen shoved Gardner's Multiple Intelligences at him and said: Here, you are gifted with your hands, a "kinesthetic learner," he remembered that question. He remembered thinking, astonished, *I am part of an immense variation; I am adaptive.* He remembered Jensen saying we needed the world full of people like him, not just those who could pass tests. There are two things that separate us from animals, said Luke: The fact that we know more than one way to skin a cat, and that we have a sense of the future and can plan for it. And even those two things are a matter of degree, not kind. *That's* the importance of our minds – how they function in evolutionary terms to facilitate our adaptation. These are the salient points about the human mind for archeological purposes. You want motives? He would ask, and stare at them in a vaguely crass, jaw-jutting way. Pot sherds that whisper in the dust? A wave of the hand, dismissal: "Then go write a novel."

II.

George's salmon shack is up and running again and John is

happy. It's Saturday and Nina pedaled by earlier with a friend. "Sold a piece!" She yelled at him.

"Really? Already? Which one?"

"The salmon. Terrence wants more so I'm gonna go look for wood!"

"Great," John said, happy at that, too. He is working, desperately now, to get the day at the Laundromat back. He dreamed that day the night before, after watching the canoe makers burn the log for a little while. In the flame the sorrow of George eventually slipped away, and by the time he turned to go back to his shack his mind was oddly stilled. Toward dawn, the dream came, and when he woke up he saw blue sky. The weather had cleared up, a preview of weather later in the summer, when for two whole months they tell him you might have nothing but morning fog for clouds. He takes his box of files outside, humming. He finds his notes on Steve's book, on the site. He can't believe this, but he feels for the first time in his life as if he really might be able to do what Sanborn would call "building an argument."

It's not that he hasn't, actually. He has built small ones around stone tool debitage, and with Sweeney he has built others. But it has been Sweeney's lead, her writing, his contributions in bed in the mornings, mulling it over, or on lazy afternoons with Coco perched in her lap. He misses this terribly now, a pang zinging through him as he leafs through Mark Varien's book on the social landscape of the Mesa Verde region, then looks up the kiva's tree ring dates from the U of Arizona lab reports. What was it that Megan asked him, so long ago? They were driving in his truck, having just looked at a road kill deer to see if it was salvageable for buckskin. Or rather, he looked at it. He got back in the truck and told her she didn't want to see it.

"Why?"

"She had a fawn."

"Oh."

Silence.

Then, "John, when did you ask Sweeney to marry you?"

"I didn't."

"What do you mean?"

"We'd been together five years, and she came home one day and said we were getting married."

"Just like that?"

"Just like that." He saw some edge in Meghan, as if that answer bothered her, but he didn't pursue it.

After a minute, she asked, "So why didn't *you* ask *her*?" *Like a normal red-blooded American male,* he could hear her thinking, though that discredited Meghan and it was his thought, not hers. But he had no answer for her. Just as he has no answer for the other tacit question, which is why he went along with it, "just like that." Well, he has some answer, staring now at the box of books, reports, papers, his own scrawled notes. First of all, he loved Sweeney. They got along well, shared a number of interests, most of all work. But that was it, wasn't it, he thinks, his mind and heart snagging the way kelp might on driftwood. The boy who never thought he'd be an archeologist had, for the five years he had been with her, found consistent archeological work. She'd "overwintered" him for that long. She also prodded him to finish his Bachelor's, that boy, because without that even she could only do so much. He remembers the day she came home and said they should get married; they'd been together long enough and it was time. He kind of froze. And then he thought: What if I said no? What if I need to think about it? He turned to look at her, face pale. He was lying on the couch in the livingroom.

"What?" she said. Her own face drained. "You don't want to?"

The many-headed hydra sprang forth at the look of her. A clutching guilt – *oh God, Sweeney, I don't want to hurt you* – that he took as a sign of love (was it? Is it?): the huge fear that without her he had no career, no archeological life; and most clearly – *don't you see, Meghan, don't you see?* – if he'd said no to Sweeney

88

when she said it was time to get married, if he said he needed to think about it, he felt she wouldn't wait. He felt he'd lose her altogether, just like he lost Lanie. And he couldn't stand that. He can't stand that now.

* * * *

He calls her at work from the pay phone in front of the gas station. He has deliberately left his cell phone at home in Salt Lake. He tries to tell her what he is doing, why he needs to be here to do it.

"You don't want me there?" She asks, accusatory. He can see her, hunching into her cubicle so others in the office won't hear.

"I don't even know where you are."

"I'm in Neah Bay."

"*What?*"

"Remember George Ward from the dig out here? He gave me a place to stay. It's just a shack –"

But she's crying. "This is just like when you went to school in Albuquerque."

"What?"

"I knew you'd find someone else. That you'd get through school without me."

"But I didn't, Sweeney! I ended up leaving. I didn't finish there, remember?" God that time was such a disaster, Meghan or no. Sanborn left UNM, Sweeney couldn't stand to stay anyway in the aftermath of Meghan, he flunked freshman comp for the third time. They went to Oregon then, worked up in Neah Bay and other places, came to Salt Lake where they retreated to the familiar rock of Great Basin archeology.

But she's silent here.

"Sweeney?"

"Ten to one Meghan's there, isn't she?"

"What? Honey, that was years ago. Meghan has a kid! She's

married!"

"Never stopped you before," she mutters, through her tears.

"Sweeney, I've been thinking a lot. Don't we have a lot more to us than just you helping me be an archeologist?"

Silence again.

"Sweeney?"

"Yeah, well," she says, "maybe we do, maybe we don't." And she slams down the phone.

* * * *

He goes out to the beach, where the long log lit by flame the night before rests on its sawhorses. It is the only place that does not seem a disaster. He approaches it, no one around though the fog has lifted and the sea is blue and he can't believe the sight of blue sky. He can see the length of it has been burned and gutted, the primitive start to forming the inner shape of the canoe. Leaning up against a sawhorse are long, shaped sticks of yew, and he hefts one up. One end is hafted to hold a barb, and John bets this is the beginnings of a traditional harpoon.

He glances around on the beach. Walks down it to a small set of tide pools, finds some mussel shell. He gathers the shell, gets a Dr. Pepper at the gas station, then his flintknapping kit. Because the sky is blue, and beautiful, and there is something nourishing about the canoe, he comes back out and sits on the sand. He takes his antler and gently hits at the mussel shell until it approaches the shape he wants, then pressure flakes the rest with a copper dowel. What else does it need? Another barb? He closes his eyes, trying to remember the harpoons on display in the museum two blocks away. Several of them had iron or steel tips, but the prehistoric ones use shell. He puts the mussel shell down. Goes to get some glass from old transformers that he keeps in his pile too. Works that. After about an hour he looks up and sees two men watching him.

He reddens. "I need pitch now," he says, for lack of anything better. "And sinew."

"What for, bro?" The two men have implacable Makah faces, brown and weathered. The both wear jean jackets.

The one who asked what for is elbowed by the other. "To tie the point onto the yew stick, dummy, that's what for."

"Oh yeah."

"You George's friend?" The elbower asks, the thinner and shorter of the two.

"Yes," John says. He stands up and offers his hand. They shake.

"I'm Peter McCartney, this here is Howard Ward. Howard's George's brother."

John looks at Howard curiously. "George never said he had a brother. Are you Nina's dad?"

"George and I have our, uh, problems," Howard says. He's built like George, stocky and prone to weight. "But yeah. Nina's my kid."

"Howard's not sure he likes you bailing out his family," Peter says, throwing Howard a half-teasing, half-lasered look.

Howard scowls. "Shut the fuck up, Pete."

"Huh?" John asks. "How am I –?"

"It's okay," Howard says. "I just didn't see Nina's wood stuff as anything but something she did when she didn't like being at home."

"Took a white man to see it," Peter ribs again.

"Shut *up*, Holmes," Howard says, this time punching him in the arm. "Pete says he's my friend but sometimes I wonder. He likes to think he's Russell Means. AIM. Celebrity Injun." Howard's eyes dagger at Pete, and Pete says nothing. "Anyway, I shoulda seen it. I'm a damn carpenter, you know. It's me who taught her to sand, use little saws and chisels to shape things."

"So she gets the wood thing from you," John says, trying to be helpful, skirting on what he feels is a potentially fatal conversation around Indian self-hatred, and white paternalism that just re-enforces it.

"And she did hide it from me. Never showed me the finished product."

"So you see? You didn't know." John's breathing harder now. He never meant to upstage her father.

"Teach us," says Peter, gesturing to the flintknapping mess and shifting the conversation. "Might as well use you now that you're here."

John is relieved to be off the subject of Nina's woodworking. "To make harpoon points, you mean?"

"Yeah," Howard says.

"We won't hunt till November, if then. But we need to do it the traditional way as much as possible," Peter says.

"Will they let you hunt?" John asks. He dimly recalls some hoopla over the whole idea of reinstating whaling among the Makah.

"Yeah, if we can get rid of that Sea Shepard idiot first."

"Who's that?"

"The most righteous of the 'environmentalists.' Look him up on the web. He *gloats* over my Uncle Tim drowning, thanks to them, when we built the first canoe and took it out for a voyage."

"You're kidding me."

Peter looks John square in the face. "No I do not, white man. They chased the canoe, overturned it. Now, teach us to knap and maybe if George can stay straight and not kill –" he stops, glancing at Howard – "anyone, you can help him get back on the crew."

"He was on the whaling crew?"

"Was till the accident."

Howard purses his lips and Peter falls silent. "Okay," John says, more to break the silence than anything, "in the museum it says you used to use mussel shell…"

The two watch intently. They ask questions, go collect more

mussels, take their first tentative stabs at shaping them. The morning ticks on, till it is time for lunch and John sees George watching off in the distance. If he's not mistaken he sees a small smile playing at his face. George moves off as he sees their party breaking up, not ready to talk. But the smile helps, and between that and Peter and Howard's interest, John feels more useful than he has in months.

* * * *

When he gets back from the beach, he finds a note tucked into the steel curlicues of his torn screen door. *Sweeney says to tell you to call Warren. She says he says you want to get fired?* It's signed *the gas station guy.* Shit. The phone must have rung off the hook till the attendant went out there and picked it up. And though John came here to do just that, he realizes with a terrible lurch that he does not want to get fired at all.

CHAPTER 7

I.

"Warren?"

"Son of a mother fucking cowboy. Neah *Bay*? Sweeney ought to ream your ass to Timbuktoo."

He has nothing to say to this.

"God, one minute Mellars is treating us all to beers because finally, *finally,* eight months after we found the thing, he has sorted out the real from the fake and gotten us proof of our cannibal. And what do you do? Next day you've disappeared. Je-*sus.* Now you are going to stand there and tell me just what the *fuck* you think you are doing."

A car swishes by him and someone rattles the bell over the door of the gas station.

"Where are you? Grand Central Station?"

"Sort of. For Neah Bay, that is. I'm sorry, Warren. I panicked."

"About *what?*"

"You haven't talked to Sweeney?"

"I've talked to Sweeney every day for the past two and a half weeks. I've cooked her dinner. Let her cry on my shoulder. All that."

John's stomach drops. He has really fucked up. He doesn't know what to say, and for a minute he freaks and thinks maybe Sweeney will leave him for Warren. He never once, in his marriage, even when talking about Meghan, feared she might leave him till now.

"Sorry," he says again. "I – uh –" and John Gregory Wayne Thompson, ex-Marine sniper, lover of sexy women, extraordinary body surfer and beach volleyball player, gulps into tears. "I can't write very well," he scratches out. "I hate public speaking."

"No *shit.* And this is the reason to abscond to outer Slobovia."

But John hears a softening in his voice that reminds him of the time Warren looked at him in the kiva and his eyes were far too kind. "John Wayne, we all have our Achilles' Heels," he says.

"Huh?"

John can practically hear him roll his eyes. "Oh for God's sake. You are dumber than hammered owl shit."

John starts to crack up. He feels the way he used to feel in church when he was too tired from surfing the day before or some other emotional delicacy gripped him and the words to the hymns pushed him to the brink of hysteria in all their dippy Christianity. "Hammered owl shit?"

"Yeah. I had a boss who used to say that. He had a really nasal voice you could hear for miles even with the wind going the other way. We'd do imitations. Ok, John Wayne," he says, getting back on track. "I talked to Dr. Walker. You hang up and wait for the phone to ring, okay?"

"What?"

"Just stay there. The phone will ring in a minute."

"Warren, what are you up –?" But the line breaks. He stands there like an idiot, the fog creeping back in for its afternoon nap.

The phone rings.

"John?"

He can't believe it.

"John, this is Colleen Jensen."

II.

That evening he makes a large fire in his stove. It may be clearer out but it has brought a colder night, and he's finding himself shivering here and there, mad for firewood, for tea, for his wool sweater and roar and pop of fire. He grabs at a memory of Sweeney and then his brain says No! and flips to Meghan, that useless ghost of a love; then No! again, back to Sweeney, and God but this probably has nothing at all to do with them. *What do you want them to rescue you from? What?*

Colleen Jensen, this afternoon: "John, you need admit you have a problem."

"That sounds like AA, Ms. Jensen."

"Well? It sort of is, isn't it? Alcoholics go for decades denying they have a problem. It becomes a burdensome secret."

"So, is there a DA, Dyslexics Anonymous? An LDA?"

She chuckles. Then, so softly, "who do you need to come clean with?"

"Warren. Dr. King, the boss. Mellars. Steve McLean."

"Who?"

"Steve McLean. He was on my crew. Smoked too much pot but he was sharp. I want him to help – "

"Ah. So maybe a collaborative effort. Is that possible?"

"Maybe."

John is weak by now. To tell his boss? Warren, who has known him but not really known him for twenty years? But John softens on him. He already knows.

"John?"

"Yes, Ms. Jensen?"

"Anybody else?"

Just every woman I have ever known, he thinks. "My father," he says instead.

And that's where he is now, his hands splayed before the flames, all lights out, the sea rising a bit on the shore a block away, hearing the swoosh of it and sensing its great dark power. He closes his eyes. *You have to be sleek to survive that water.* Sleek and blubbered and bullet-shaped.

But he is not. He is in dress blues, back from the Marines after boot camp. He is to be shipped out to Okinawa in three days. He knocks on the door of his parents' house. His cap is tipped forward just like in the advertisements, and this member of the few, the proud, the brave, stands with his round, bespectacled face waiting for his dad to open the door. His mother does instead. When she sees him, she puts her hand to her mouth and says, "Oh!" Then she blushes and tries for a smile. But it's too late. John senses the withered posture, the shrinking back, the pained swallow. "Mel," she says, hoarsely, turning her head behind her. She knows who he wants to see.

"What is it, Lou?"

His dad comes to the door. His mother disappears as if saturating the wallpaper in the hallway, some ancient shame bearing her off to invisibility.

They stare at each other. "Come in," his dad finally says.

They go to the livingroom. Pictures of John's sisters at college graduation adorn the mantel, as well as pictures of his oldest sister's wedding, of her with her ninth-grade class in Old Town. His youngest sister beams from a nursing school photo. His own photos consist of high school graduation and one of him playing volleyball on the beach.

The silence rings and rings. John sits as ramrod straight as he stood at the door.

His father finally clears his throat. "Where are they sending you?"

"Okinawa."

He nods. "Japan," is all he says, but old reels of World War II Pacific battles play before John and he's convinced his father is seeing exactly the same thing.

"Yes," John says, simply.

"And – and you're sure about this?"

He snaps a little. "Too late now, don't you think?"

His dad nods again, paying no attention to his tone but looking absently at the photos of Lindsay, Syd, and, John supposes, him. Then he says, "Why not have stayed in school?" His voice is paper-thin, a corn husk of a voice, wavery and sad.

John stares at his profile, unprepared for this. He thought the uniform, the boot camp posture, would recall his own military pride. "Are you all right, Dad? I thought you'd be proud of me!

Semper Fi!"

When his father turns his face to John, it's sunken, heavy.

"Dad!"

"The Marines were good to me, son. I went in at sixteen. Lied. Did you know that? I lied. I had an eighth grade education and my folks were starving on a farm in South Dakota that the Depression ripped to pieces, and I lied. I almost didn't get accepted."

"Why? Because they found out your age?"

He snorts. "Naw. They would look the other way a lot on that. But not on your health."

"What do you mean?"

"One in three recruits in those days was so malnourished even the military didn't want 'em."

John is silent.

"Too skinny," his dad goes on, "if you can believe that. Teeth looked bad, too." He smiles. "But they took me."

"And you stayed on through Korea. And you were a damn good fighter."

"Yes."

"So why aren't you proud of me now?"

He smiles feebly and says, "Of course I am, son. Of course."

But John knows it's another lie. They stand up, shake hands. He will return to base. He can't possibly stay there, at his parents' house. He can't possibly stay there and be swallowed up by Lindsay and Syd's college graduation photographs, most of all Lindsay's history degree, the one his father'd wanted and never got, the one John knows for sure now that his father hoped above hope his only son might get in his stead.

V.

You want history, I will give you history, Dad. Two a.m. now. He has drafted a joint email to King, McLean, Mellars, and Warren the leprechaun Heaney, well past all their bedtimes, erasing the first one he drafted to Steve and never sent. It gives him some comfort to write this message while they are not actually on the computer. He has resorted to stealing firewood from George's pile out back of his salmon trailer, and will pay him back with a wood expedition tomorrow. He'll go to Port Angeles to send the email, first thing, where the library has WiFi, unlike the Jurassic and glacially slow dial-up the little school library has here. Then he'll get wood and some fresh fruits and vegetables.

He tells his crew in the joint email (he couldn't bear to write more than one) that he is dyslexic, etc., and has a hell of a time structuring arguments on a page, but that he has a good one. He lays out Points One through Four of John Thompson's Hopi Village Split model for Turd Wash, or a variant thereof, where the folks in his kiva are decided losers. He tells them he knows it has problems. Then he says he knows they need to back up and simply do the science first. Present the evidence. Mellars will write back and ask to be the lead on another paper about the turd analysis, by itself, to appear in something totally intimidating like *Nature* or *Science,* and John will be more than happy to let him. But after that? The *American Antiquity* article is up to John to take the lead on. Not King, who would never write up a report for a project at which he was not physically present most of the time, not Warren, not anyone else. No, the Project Director heads that all up. Him.

History. All right, Dad, history. Once upon a time two people, a boy and a girl, drove west from Zuni Pueblo into the Arizona desert and out the other side to the great California Mojave. They both had fathers who had sought out the desert themselves, and so that vast expanse of sand and bony mountain ranges became associated with their fathers' hearts. The girl's father so hated his own heart that he married a woman he did not want to marry and took out his rage on his daughter by coming into her room at night and raping her. That girl now lay in the back of the boy's truck, sleeping a little and wearing, under her sweat pants, a loin cloth that she made, with his help, from animal skins pillaged for free from the alley of a game processing business on east Central Avenue in Albuquerque. They had kissed a lot for two hours once but had not made love yet and the boy's wife had no idea that such a thing was a possibility. There were going to the east side of the Sierra to lead a workshop for Forest Service personnel on how to determine different types of stone tool manufacturing and other scat left from prehistory.

At three a.m., under what she said a poet named Gary Snyder called "the tough old stars," she asked if Route 66 still existed anymore. They were out by Ludlow, before it somewhere, past the long incline up from Needles but not at that solo Texaco in the middle of the black desert night. Yeah, said the boy, there's stretches of it.

And so the boy, who was a man, thirty-six by that time to the girl's twenty-nine – the girl who was trying to become a woman – found that road. That road, Dad. The one you drove before they made I-40. The one her dad drove, too, the one he came in on as a little boy when the wind sheared Nebraska down to a skeleton and his parents realized no hope existed there anymore. Not dust bowl, but close, though her granddad had apprenticed as an architect and that was as far from farming as you could get. He groveled odd jobs in L.A. before landing a job with City Hall, where he stayed for the next thirty-five years.

People don't do that anymore, Dad. They don't stay with VA hospitals and military industrial firms and city halls and universities for all of their working lives. No. They skip from job to job, downsized or bored or hoping or whatever. So John took her to the strip of Route 66 he knew about, and stopped when the rip-rap of destroyed asphalt reared up in his headlights. They both got out. Went pee. Then she said, "I want to be in the buckskin. Nothing else."

"Go ahead," John said, because he'd said this before, shortly after she fell apart on the anthropology bench and they went for beers while listening to Patsy Cline. In the weeks that followed they'd gone up into the mountains east of Albuquerque and he'd given her an atlatl he had made and she said, "I want to be naked doing this," and he said, "Go ahead," and she said, "Really?" and he said "yes" and so she threw spears from that atlatl for an hour with nothing on but her tennis shoes. And he did not come on to her, did not make any sexual jokes, did nothing but witness a woman throwing a weapon each and every human had in their blood from six thousand years ago.

In the Mojave, she peeled down to the loin cloth and said, "I am so mad at my father."

"So be mad," he said. This too had precedent. She'd already beaten her fists against his chest, allowed herself to be held after waking up from a nightmare on the floor of his little apartment in Albuquerque. Once she threw glass out at a dump along I-40 west of town for over an hour.

She screamed for at least half an hour this time. Maybe more. In between her shouts the soft breeze fluttered on the two of them, stroking her bare skin like feathers, the smell of creosote almost reminiscent of rain, the stars looming close and brilliant. He'd kissed her several times by then, and he wanted her. He wanted her despite eleven decent years, by then, of sex with Sweeney. He wanted more than he'd ever wanted anyone save maybe for Lanie. But he sat, crouching on his haunches at the level of the creosote, waiting for her to be through.

She stood a good while after falling quiet for the last time, after screaming God Damn you Dad, you fucking asshole, how could you, I *Loved You.* The breeze played on her breasts, round and firm and high and small. Not Lanie's breasts, not Sweeney's heavy Renaissance femininity. Meghan had been a swimmer. She had broad shoulders and long legs. She looked down at the bushes as if searching for snakes or game. She looked back at the stars. Then she smiled.

"What're you thinking?" John asked.

"That I have a baby," she said. "Right here, right now. I am a mother. A Chemehuevi, a Mojave, a Yuma Indian mother. I see myself with a baby."

His heart went dead still. "Who is the father?" he asked, and he was shocked at how much he cared about her answer. He was as hard as a rock and kept his hands in his pockets to hide it, fearful that not even darkness was enough.

"I don't know," she said. "That's – that's not the point. The point is that I am alive and I can hunt and gather and be a mother, in the dark in the middle of the Mojave. I can picture setting deadfalls for rabbits, tracking roots and seeds."

"Good," he said, swallowing something huge and deep, knowing self-sufficiency and survival were everything to her. Good, the flames popping in his shack and his vision sheathed around a diver in high waves, a diver sleek and bullet-shaped, at home in the sea, sewing up the whale's mouth, all over again.

VI.

Port Angeles is bright and busy compared to the soggy shuffle of Neah Bay. It has a wider view of the Straits of Juan de Fuca, for one thing, and he watches the ferry leave for Canada while eating a mid-morning pastry from the dock. He has sent the email. Found dry wood, though he has yet to purchase it and load it in the truck. George has come with him, as he has a minor court requirement he was putting off till he could get a ride. The two hours to drive here were silent, George dozing on and off while John negotiated snake turns and watched the ocean eat in toward the road, then recede to more distant beaches through the trees. He finishes his pastry and stands up. Whale Watching! Shouts a sign next door to the ferry dock. Orcas! Gray whales! Harbor Seals! Eagles! Tours on the hour!

"Hey George," John says, when he sees him come back. "Let's

go whale watching."

George looks at him like he's crazy. "Get in a tourist boat with a bunch of people from Iowa?"

John laughs. "I know. Big come-down for a native. But why not? I'll pay. I have to go back to Salt Lake soon anyway."

George pales. "You do? You can't."

"What do you mean?"

"I said to Howard and Peter and the whaling crew that you could teach us for a while."

George looks straight ahead, his jaw clamped to keep any expression from creeping into it. John remembers something Howard said. That maybe he could help George get back on the crew. Good karmic padding for George, him of all people, this odd fat white guy who can make arrowheads and harpoons and leather bags and willow baskets. Who has learned to make cedar cord and the trademark conical hat from the elders in the museum in three short weeks. Who gets Indian girl nieces their first artistic commissions.

"I'm sorry, George. My wife and my, uh, job are, uh –" John takes in a big bite of air. "George. I may not have killed anyone but I fucked up pretty bad. I have to make it right. I could lose everything. I came here because I was running away."

George looks at him. "I figured that, John Wayne Greg."

"John Gregory Wayne."

"Huh?"

"That's my name. Not the other way around."

George squints at him. "Does it matter? I call you John Wayne Gregory-bro. That's guy-talk for saying I like you, you dumb-ass." He stalks off to the other side of the whale watch dock, his arms crossed and his hands tucked under his armpits in a huff. He's wearing an old hoodie sweatshirt, blue jeans, tennis shoes. His hair looks like Dennis the Menace's. Great impression for dealing with the law, John thinks, but maybe it was just a clerical issue.

"Sorry," John says. He sits heavily on a bench and runs his hands through his own messy hair. This being human business about does him in. He raises his head. "I can come back," he says.

"What?"

"I can come back. Give me a couple weeks. I can come back."

"For how long?"

"I dunno. A month? I could do longer maybe but I need a better internet connection to do the research than I have at Neah Bay. Besides, I, uh, need help from a, uh, disabilities specialist."

George turns to look at him. "A what? A disabilities specialist?"

"Yeah. I'm not the best reader and writer, unlike you."

He snorts. "I had other disabilities. Like being born Indian with a shitty school system."

"But you still got into Dartmouth."

"Yeah."

"Graduated, even."

"Yeah." He turns to look at John, his arms dropped, his posture more relaxed. "I was way behind at first. Caught up. But that wasn't it. It was just like what those Dakota and Apache felt like at Carlisle over a hundred years ago. I about died of loneliness out there."

John doesn't say anything to that. What can you say? You can kill someone in many ways and all of them were used on Native Americans. A whale boat returns, about twenty middle-class tourists disembarking.

George breaks the silence. "Could you come back in November too?" he asks.

"I can try. Why?"

"That's when the whales usually run back south. We hunt grays, not orcas. Right now, they're coming back up north. So May and November are good hunt times."

"Okay. I'll come back in November. You gonna stay dry?" John has to ask it. Otherwise, why come back? Why come back except to be what he has been all his life, an Indian wannabe, a seeker of tools and methods by which to live more tangibly on his planet?

George smiles wanly, reading John's mind. "Got to be a good reason, eh? You don't just want to watch the boats go out?"

"I'd love to watch the boats go out. Those are the most beautiful canoes I've ever seen. Like Viking ships, only sleeker, smaller. That, in a thirty-foot swell? Whew."

George has to grin. "Yeah. They're pretty in a simple way."

"The best." The next bunch of tourists gets on. "Hey, George. When you were training for the crew before your, your accident – what was your job?"

He pats his tummy. "See this blubber? Even when I run five miles a day and swim the ocean I still have more heft than the other guys. So rub me with bear grease and I can go in the water and not freeze."

John stares at him. "*You're* the diver?"

"Yeah. Sew that whale right up." He colors a little. "When I get a chance, that is. We haven't done it yet. Not for a few years, before my time."

"Wow."

The whale boat guy is looking at the two of them. George taps him lightly on the shoulder, jerks his head toward the boat. "Let's go."

"Look at stuff?"

"Sure." He giggles a little. "Be fun. I'll tell Nina all about it. You can watch for orcas and I'll watch for seasick Nebraskans."

* * * *

They see no grays, though George has his eyes peeled for them. He doesn't care about the orcas skimming right next to the boat, the feeding frenzy at the mouth of the Frazier River when the orcas hit upon a salmon run, the fact that those orcas, bless their hippie hearts, are run by elder females and mate freely. They might be vicious killers, but they live in the happiest of communes. The harbor seals lounging on a rock near an inlet don't seem to do much for George either, though they remind John of when they lived in Oregon and Meghan came to visit. There were harbor seals too, there, and he pulls out the one poem of hers he keeps in his wallet, worn to frayed cloth by now, when George steps inside the cabin to buy some potato chips.

> *...In the delta bob the heads of seals*
> *while out past the harbor, sea lions*
> *emerge from caves and troll the breakers*
> *for salmon meat and foam.*
>
> *Driftwood clings as I do to cliff's edge*
> *while you face a rabid surf and a multitude of rain.*
> *At low tide we have a shelf of runneled sand,*
> *the entire continent behind us,*
> *and I dream the mutual weight of our affection*
> *might tilt the whole damn plate up*
> *leaving New York and Jersey's happy gamblers*
> *dangling in the air...*

He puts it away before he starts sobbing right there in the noisy boat, with its outboard skimming them to a new spot for viewing. She wanted him to see her. To see what they were together. But he knows how the poem ends. He knows in the next stanza he sends some of her poems out to sea, and that they both shutter their hearts back up like a cabin in the face of winter, so that Sweeney will not see them herself. How little he understood that by doing that nobody got to see anything, much less themselves.

Back in Port Angeles, he runs to check email. To his surprise, all of them have answered. Must be a boring day back in Salt Lake or Albuquerque, where Steve is. He saves them to his computer to read later, goes back out from the library to find George, and load up groceries and wood. When they get back it's near dark, a drizzle hitting them about an hour from the bay. He piles up George's share of wood behind the trailer, and stands up to say good night.

"One thing, John-boy," George says.

"Yeah?"

"Neah Bay is full of disabilities specialists."

He blinks. "It is?"

"Well, three. But that's a lot for around here. Three ladies. Two native, the other not."

Melinda Weeks' round form comes back to him from her visit to George's salmon shack. "How come you have them?"

"We Injuns are just disabled, I guess."

"Come on, George. Get off the pity pot."

"Well, what do you think, John Wayne? We got seventy percent unemployment. White-ass teachers who hang out for a year to get their Indian fix and then leave. ADD, ADHD, fetal alcohol syndrome, diabetes. Do I have to go on?"

"No," John says.

"So I understand about needing the internet, and the wife. I do." He puts a big hand on John's shoulder. "But come back for me, okay?"

"Okay."

John rattles off in the truck with the rest of the wood, and dreams that night of orcas, the lone male dancing between two females, one with a baby, the other not, each adamantly self-sufficient and no longer putting up with him, for all his lover boy ways.

VII.

In the morning he opens his lap top, steaming cup of real joe in his hand for the first time in a week. The fire is crackling nicely, and outside is a shroud of the most intense fog he has ever seen. Perfect for a date with the blue screen.

Dear John:
Great on theory with Points One through Four. One problem I see: the Hopi village system comes about at least in part after local springs start drying up past 1300 A.D. and lack of arable land becomes an issue given the number of people. Can we really argue this is happening in 1150 in Tin Cup Wash and vicinity? Maybe...it'd be a good dissertation to run around assessing all the soil types and their carrying capacity relative to numbers of sites from various time periods in that neck of the woods...thanks! Think I'll take that one. Offhand look at settlement pattern data (and having spent 4 godforsaken months there in high summer) suggests it's a shitpile of a place to do agriculture. What does pollen say? Ratio of cultigens to wild foods? Are they making it? Hmmm...

But maybe we *could* make some just-so story about something like that Hopi system hammering itself into place, albeit not too kindly – *evolving* would be the right terminology – with incidences like our site's...you know, taboos on cannibalism evolving, clan-based hierarchies doing that too, as a best-fit-for-everyone type of compromise in the aftermath of events like what happened at Tin Cup...shit I don't know. I tend to blab. But yeah, a collaboration is a great idea. How 'bout Pecos for that gig! Nice and informal for a conference, no intimidating microphones, lotsa beer post-talks...Glad you are back among the living. Steve.

Steve, as John suspected, is still capable of making his head spin. Pecos. Huh. Early to mid-August conference given toward the end of the summer field season for southwestern archeologists to compare notes and get drunk and look at sites in whatever area they've chosen to pitch the Pecos tent that year. Hmmm...that could work. Next email is Warren: **Fuck, John. No worries. Collaboration's great. War-War.**

"War-War"? Ick. Sounds like something out of Star Wars and he wants to tell him that. Resigned, he stumbles in the fog to the library, hooks up to the modem, and eventually is able to tell him he is to sign his name "The Leprechaun" if anything, but Warren is online and shoots back, saying to remember the Achilles' Heel and that one of his is how short and Irish he is. Fine, John says. Fine. Gad, are they all confessing now?

John! I had no idea you too were a fellow dyslexic! I write science papers with heavy help from a computer. Oh, and Betty Jane Jaber as editor. But you are right about needing to write up the poo data first. Man, I had so much help from the colorectal department you would not believe! If it's all right with everyone else I will take the lead on that article, Jennie Schultz, my blind bone analyst, second. John, you third? You get to be lead on the archeology article, after all. I need your site descriptions at the very least. It's lovely in Salt Lake these days. Everything green and starting to grow. See you soon? Mellars.

"Mellars, if you are dyslexic then monkeys will fly out of my butt," he says out loud to the computer. But he says this because he is completely, infuriatingly jealous at the ease at which Mellars seems to accommodate this problem. He sighs. Next email.

John:
I sent in our Pecos Registration this morning after getting word from Warren as to your status. Took Steve's advice.

Smart cookie, that Steve. You have a week to get home to start organizing lines of evidence. King.

Smart cookie. Thanks a lot. King has a way of digging into people's wounds just so. He looks at the date on his watch. May 26th. He has a little over two months to prepare. Well, that's fair. In the meantime, maybe he can figure out how to write his article. Steve emails back with an addendum to the settlement pattern data that raises his eyebrows, but he is beginning to overload. He tries someone else.

Sweeney? (Instant message. He might as well, since he is hooked up and the modem is sailing relatively smoothly.)

Yeah?
You're there! I love you.
Please come home, John.
I am. Monday night.
I have to go back to work.
All right.

But dammit. Dammit dammit damn her independence, her shroud of competence, her focused career life, her solitary nature, her stony demeanor in the face of pain, her her her – Sweeney had her tubes tied at thirty-two. They'd been together two years. They both said they didn't want kids. One day she just went and did it. Told him about it after he got back from a week in the field. He gazed directly into his bowl of pasta, Coco's predecessor mewling at his feet.

"John?" Sweeney asked. "That's okay, isn't it?"

"Sure, sure," he said, all of twenty-seven and not once thinking, until that very moment, that fatherhood was something he could dream about but now would never know.

PART FOUR

CHAPTER 8

I.

He debates, on his route home, whether to side track down to central Oregon and pick up some more Glass Buttes obsidian. This is the most beautiful obsidian in the world, with its variations of color ranging from mahogany to pumpkin to black to red to snowflake patterns to rainbows. Working with it is like working to modify a piece of art already made, and adds a whole new dimension to flintknapping. People knap not only to replicate perfect arrowheads, or make spear designs of their own, but to integrate whatever shape they are aiming for with the patterns in the rock. Hold up an exquisitely flaked Desert Side-Notched arrowhead of "midnight lace" Glass Buttes obsidian to light and note the translucence, the play of black stripes against the nearly clear silver those stripes are embedded in. Knap a Clovis point so all the stripes are running diagonally from the top left to the bottom right of the tool. Turn it over and notice the stripes running the opposite direction. Take a red mahogany with black swirls and knap a sturdy Archaic point, the red somehow looking more solid than anything in sheer jet black. A well-knapped Clovis of "silver sheen" looks like water captured in stone, rippling in whatever light is offered its way. Someone in Ashland actually ran an art exhibit of modern, flintknapped Glass Buttes in their gallery, and sold several pieces.

But this time John sticks to the straight and true, Eisenhower's interstate system, sixteen hours of shotgun drive, jacked up on Dr. Pepper and Slim Jims. He does eat a salad in Pendleton for good measure, and falls, with periodic help from country radio, into remembrances of other road trips, trips with Sweeney where they pulled over and made love in nearby forests, trips to Malheur Field Station in the Oregon desert to learn basketry, knapping, survival skills, the journey with Meghan through the

Mojave and up to the east side of the Sierra. The back spine of the Cascades and Sierra Nevada is the most compelling country to him in a vast territory of compelling country. He makes a living these days by virtue of the Ancestral Puebloan of the Colorado Plateau and the Fremont of Utah and northwestern Colorado, because they leave behind the most sites and this is what you find when you run surveys for pipelines, or gas well pads, or access roads. He understands Meghan's love affair with red rock and twisted juniper; he has seen Warren, too, wistful in the face of impossible ruins tucked up five-hundred foot cliffs in southeastern Utah. But when Sweeney and he were first together, when he was learning archeology above and beyond his summer college stint near Flagstaff, he learned it in the eastern deserts of California and Oregon; he learned it in Nevada, with its ragged and steep ranges of rock jutting up out of pancaked desert basins dotted with waterholes that have no outlet.

When he feels it – that line of volcanic, plate tectonic rupture, the abrupt end of moisture from the west as you drive down, down, down, into the east, the seeps and hot springs and pounding geothermals rising up through creeks, the spill and tumble of cold streams into more sluggish desert rivers, the oddity of Mono Lake with its salt and birds, the raped and pillaged Owens River, along whose banks the Paiute once manipulated native grasses for better harvests, the sheer granite – one monstrous batholith – of the Sierra – he stops breathing. He stops breathing the way he stopped breathing as a child when he brushed the outstretched hand of Jesus on a statue and it fell off. Six years old, he thought he was going to hell for sure. Only here he stops breathing because he thinks he is in heaven, rapture hitting him as the sun goes down behind him and as, of all twists of fate, the Stones' "Wild Horses" twangs on the radio about how you can't keep him away and the truck cab smells of smoked meat and mildew. And when Meghan stepped into Hot Creek with him near Mammoth and they sank low and stripped and he entered her and she closed her eyes, he doesn't think it was just him she was with then. He thinks she was with him and the earth, the earth thumping up through the sand beneath their feet, the drumbeat of its core breaking out to the surface in that creek, urgent, like spring, like the new leaves and mating rabbits and newborn calves and erupting flowers, who seem to be saying, *I want everything*, palms open or touching, the blind courage of it all, to reach up, to pound up to the surface from a million miles below, for Meghan to wrap her legs around him after being torn apart as a child, for her to be doing that with her other lover, with Jason, the one she would marry, for John to be there with her in that watery heat, to be to be to *be*.

The Stones stop singing. He turns off the radio. An image lasers in and he needs dead calm to possess it, even as he knows how futile such an attempt is. He pulls over into a deserted rest stop in the oncoming dark. He has four hours to go and he is by now in the Great Snake Plain of Idaho. It is desolate country even by his standards, but the dark drops a curtain over it and he is not there anyway. He is in the silence, he is back with Meghan, in an ancient grove of juniper growing out of pumice. The great Sierra lies behind them and they are in foothills of the next mountain range to the east. The junipers are over eight hundred years old and have healed strips of their wood cut out of them. This for making bow staves, vertical lines five or six feet long, the edges of them grown over with bark. The sun is long, delicate and bright in the late afternoon. She touches a tree, then another.

"What'd they cut them with?" she asks, and he points to the ground – his grand surprise, because there, like ancient tears, like drops of some jeweled piece of the past modern America has utterly forsaken, lie dozens of stone axes.

They are not in the late 20th Century anymore. They are in some other time and space, not separate from the ancient wisdom of the gnarled juniper, who are the tree version of Yoda, not separate from the pumice or the axes or their shadows extending out in front of them as they walk downslope, hands held. There is no need to speak. Just a need to kiss hard and deep, hard and deep, as if the world had ended, to not be anything but one and all, atomic particles colliding and emerging whole in the aftermath, nothing Newtonian or gravity-born or on the scale of daily life, but quantum, sliding to the ground, him, her, Sweeney, Jason, every love they have ever felt, every love the trees have ever felt, every passion from every volcanic outbreak, right there, right then, right now, in a pickup stopped by the side of the road in southwest Idaho, its engine ticking, the dry plain a dusty breath through the open crack of one lone car window.

II.

"Sweeney? I'm here."

It is about 10:30. The light is still on in the bedroom.

He goes in. She looks up at him from where she sits in bed, reading. Her blonde hair's tussled, her old nightgown hanging in furrows from her shoulders.

"Nice of you to come home," she says, but her tone isn't awful. Just quiet, unsure.

He sits down on his side of the bed, buzzing from being in a car so long, the hum of tires on asphalt running through his veins. He wants to cry. He wants to collapse onto her lap and sob. But what will she do? She is not a woman inured to crying. She cried when her last cat died; she cried stoically, several tears, when her father was ill and it looked like he might die; she cried and screamed and threatened to slit her wrists when he told her about Meghan. He has cried exactly four times in front of her. He cried more in front of Meghan than in the twenty-five years he has been with Sweeney.

He tries resting his head on her lap. He closes his eyes and breathes in the smell of her, of their bed, of their house. He is not sure he has ever done this with her. A small whimper escapes him. She puts her hand on his head oh so very tentatively, as if it were going to bite her, as if it were some rare artifact she found in a cave that might fall apart if she touched it. He wants her to touch his head more, he wants her to cradle it the way Meghan cradled her son's head the very last time he saw her, the way he cradled Meghan's head when she woke up screaming. But Sweeney just rests her hand there. He knows for her to have him fall on her lap like this, needy in some other way than the academic, is terrifying. He knows she is doing the best she can, that she is not kicking him out, not snarling, not shrinking away. He could cry even more for how hard this is, for how much work he now glimmers is ahead of them.

They stay that way for several minutes. Then he lifts his head, and kisses her, and retreats to the bathroom, where he runs a hot, hot bath, the road and the terrible, beautiful visions it wrought, draining away from him into the water.

* * * *

His plan to be so tired from the long drive that he sleeps well in spite of all his anxiety works for about six hours, which is better than he had hoped for. He gets out of bed at five, makes tea, and stares into the black well of the living room going gray with dawn. Coco sits with him, purrs. It is Tuesday. He realizes he has spent all of Memorial Day driving.

Sweeney and he talk little once she is up and fixing breakfast. She gazes at him, then opens her mouth, then closes it. They sit across from each other at the table, and he gazes back at her, blinking through his fogged brain. Her blonde hair is leaching into gray, her eyes sad. She opens her mouth again.

"Big day?" she finally says.

"Yeah. I have to see everyone, but especially King."

"Warren told me. He was here yesterday." She says it with a faint underbarb and John wonders if she wants to make him jealous. He tries to ignore it.

"Yes, he told me over the phone he'd been – " He'd been what? Helping her? She hated any sign of needing help. And helping her with what? With his stupidity, of course.

"He's been here a lot," she cuts in.

Fine, he thinks, a slow fume building. The old John would have simply clamped his mouth shut, let it pass the way you let your boot camp sergeant's remarks pass in the Corps. But the old John is slipping and he worries, briefly, that he'll erupt into an abusive cad. "You sound like you're trying to make me jealous," he says, trying for steadiness. "Because if you are, you're just making me mad."

She colors, surprised at him. "Shouldn't *I* be the mad one? You come back last fall from that dig, you hardly say a word to me about it, you meet with that doctor at the U and talk to Warren on the phone and then you sit through the winter doing some lithic work for me but really just waiting to hear results. It's just like with Meghan."

"Meghan?"

"When she was in your life you'd do the same. You'd be online at strange times. You'd call her once a week when I was at the grocery store, only I'd come home and you'd still be on the phone and your face would just be *glowing*." Her eyes are hot. "Like you have some secret that doesn't include me, some life. Was there someone in Neah Bay? Why there? How come," she says, her voice etching like a knife on glass, "how come you don't want my help on this?"

All her sense of worth is wrapped up in that question. Patricia Sweeney, PhD. Patricia Sweeney, project director. Patricia Sweeney, helper of pathetic husbands. Is he nothing, then, in her eyes? Because he had to fight so hard for every grain of education he got? Did she support him because she wanted him to have what counted for *her* – an advanced degree? More prestigious work? What was *her* motive for "overwintering" him for so long? That she could mold him into the being his father wanted him to be? She wanted him to be? He feels like a terrible cynic. Surely she did it because she loved him. Surely.

The world is too bungled for speech. And even if he could talk, what can he say that she will understand? How does he tell her that George is in Neah Bay, and that a whale is waiting to die at the hands of men in a cedar canoe made out of a single tree? And what does that have to do with anything? The lone bead of blood she drew when keening about Meghan nine years ago, the scarlet drop so efficiently brought to the outer world by an obsidian blade she made, scares him death. It has been waiting in the wings of their marriage ever since. So he bites back, now, his impulse to further anger. What if he starts shaking with rage? What if he says the wrong thing and she runs to the closet and finds the .22? All the detritus of them balls up in his stomach. He reaches sideways for an old envelope sitting with a heap of mail at the end of the table, his movements as stealthy as Coco's. He finds a pen. "Here," he says. "Call her. You might be able to listen to her better." And he leaves Colleen Jensen's number on the table while he gets up, suppressing again any signs of rage or sudden anger, finds his keys, and drives away from what he thought was his house.

III.

He pounds on Warren's door. Warren lives in a quaint little Craftsman kind of thing in the old part of Salt Lake next to the largest Mormon cemetery in the world. The U is blocks away. "What?" He blinks, as he opens the door in his bathrobe, cup of coffee in hand. He's five feet six with a big red nose that makes him look like a drunk in bad moments. It gives John a pang to think of Warren cooking dinner for Sweeney, because she lets almost no one in her life but him and her sister and the cat.

"Sorry. I know it's early."

"Sweeney kick you out?" His jaw juts a bit and John can see he's mad at him too.

John looks hard at him, his own jaw twitching under his skin. "Don't joke. I left. She doesn't want to listen to me. She doesn't trust me."

"Well, gollee, dude, you leave over a month ago with just a note and an apology. And you did have an affair."

"Can I come in?"

"Certainly."

He plops into an old stuffed chair while Warren sits on a futon that doubles as a couch. Old hardwood floors, scratched and venerable, glow faintly in the morning light.

"So she told you about Meghan."

Warren leans forward and puts his cup carefully on a beat-up coffee table in front of the futon. The décor on the walls is a mix of ski bum and archeology, old telemarks crossed over the futon, a National Historic Preservation Week poster with a Grand Gulch ruin on it on the wall facing John. The careful placement of the cup and Warren's heartbeat of silence soften the room. Warren can never stay too long in an angry place. What happens instead is that bloody compassion, as if Buddha himself woke up in Utah and found Alta powder, fantastic archeology, and a lovely little hobbit home on the hill near the U. John squirms. He feels he has been angry all his life without knowing it till now, and that compassion is not something he deserves.

"You know, I knew Meghan too." Warren's voice is soft.

John's eyebrows rise. "You did?"

He nods. "A long time ago. She worked with me at Bandelier. Near Los Alamos. She was maybe twenty-five."

Well, Meghan did work at Bandelier then. John knew that. The summer after he worked Wupatki and met Warren. "Did you – did you like her?" Now his voice is soft. Why does this matter so much? But the relief at finally, finally being able to reveal Meghan is too lovely. He wants to keep talking.

"Of course I liked her. She was a lot of fun." Warren kind of smiles. "But we were friends. Nothing more. Although..."

"Although what?"

"I always got the feeling she had a lot of backbone underneath her. I liked that. I had a cat once, when I lived in Flag. I named her Simone after Simone de Beauvoir, and she loved that."

John nods. A man who names his cat after a feminist would make Meghan gleeful. *I hate lies, John* comes back too, the stalwart adamancy of a three-year-old who knows what's up and won't stand for it so close to the fury of a woman opening up secret doors to find out why she was shattered into a million pieces in the first place, why there was such punishment for being feminine and receptive and intuitive and alive.

He looks around the neat little house. "What about you, Warren? Are you ever going to get married?"

Warren shrugs. "If I find the right gal. I dunno, John Wayne. I'm forty-five and been skiing every winter and doing archeology when the sun shines and in two weeks I shall have a PhD." He snorts. "Dr. Walker wants me to apply for jobs."

"That would be grown up. I thought you wanted a 'real job.'"

"Do not lecture me on growing up, O Peter Pan of Neah Bay." He looks down his bulbous nose at John as if he were a high British lord, but the Irish stevedores that were both his male grandparents win out and John ends up laughing.

"Shit, Warren, you couldn't pull off the high and mighty if you tried."

"No. Probably not." He fingers what John now sees is Mellars' report on the table. "None of us can." He stands up. "Breakfast, dude? Eggs and bacon!"

John follows him to the kitchen. "What do you mean, none of us can?"

"If you hadn't left your wife and holed up in that godforsaken rain-infested dump at the end of the American continent, I would think this is funny. But look at us! Steve is a gangly thirty-year-old pot head with red hair and a secretive Baptist past. Mellars looks like –" He bangs a frying pan down on the stove and John finishes the description for him.

"Santa's elf."

Warren starts laughing and can't stop. "Exactly! And me! 'The Leprechaun,' you say. Fuck you, you big ex-Marine cocksucker who reads and writes with a fucking ruler."

The heat on his face is so instantaneous that he looks to Warren's stove for flames. But there are none. Just the shame, and after a startled millisecond of shock (This! Out of the great Buddha Warren!), he runs out of the room, slapping the screen door behind him. He flops on the stoop, arms crossed, face more flushed than when he has the flu, eyebrows pinched into a strong scowl to prevent schoolboy tears from falling out of the eyes below.

But Warren is a brave man. "Sorry!" he squawks, coming out to join him almost immediately. "I'm sorry, John-bo. That was beneath me."

He swallows and the two of them say nothing. Women would be working toward language, no doubt, by now, but that has always been a secret cove for John, a sanctuary he could use on his own terms, without ridicule. And, well, even Warren is a product of what he knows Colleen Jensen would be calling an autistic male culture, where more gets said in the flick of a fly-fishing wrist over a good trout stream, or in the gathering of wood for fire, or in sick jokes in sad kivas, than anywhere else. Is this wrong? John puzzles. In a twinge of the gut he realizes what he feels is something akin to love. A word not meant for male friends before. And a word he has associated either with sex, or with the sterile Jesus-love of Sunday school.

So he says nothing, and Warren says nothing. They sit on the stoop until the smell of hot grease gets to them. The air is cool and the trees stir and the gravestones of polygamous pioneers perk up at them from behind shrubbery at the end of the block.

John sniffs back tear-induced mucous as innocuously as he can.

Finally, Warren finesses a voice. He talks softly. "We're all mighty social fuck-ups, is all I was trying to say, Johnny-boy. And this site, with its death and turds and all that, is taking us for one hell of a test drive." He sits upright then, his palms on his knees. "I smell a grease fire if I don't go tend to breakfast."

John nods, and Warren goes inside.

* * * *

After Warren, he goes to the U to find the bones. He finds some of them in shoe boxes, others on table tops, clustered by long bone fragments or smashed vertebrae or crania. Jennie Schultz, the blind osteology person, is not around and he is alone with them in a lab filled with comparative skeletal collections of animals. They lie in boxes, rows and rows of them, floor to ceiling on industrial metal shelves, organized by species. He is surrounded by the sleeping power of bones.

Like Meghan's collection, the bigger fragments and long bones lie on black lab countertops, but with an old section of sheet over them. He is surprised Jennie hadn't put them away, but it would be quite a task and maybe she is around, coming back to them soon. He lifts the sheet, rolls it back. Some of them are burned, some the pale color of bone defleshed and rapidly deposited. The day they found them he remembers other reactions – worries about NAGPRA, thoughts of Meghan, most of all the beginnings of having to organize and write a major research finding. But today his hands find the burned cranial vault of an adolescent and he is back in that kiva, picking the vault up from an ash dump between the deflector and the ventilator shaft. He holds it up and sees that the inside of the vault is not blackened like the outside, and in a flash he knows that the whole head, brain intact, was laid on the fire to be roasted. They screen the ash dump, and shattered fragments emerge – vertebrae, long bone slivers and knocked-loose teeth. Next, Warren dismantles the ventilator, mapping each fragment found there in place, and then handing them off to John for bagging. One by one a parade of cracked humerus bones, broken ribs, mandible fragments, clavicles with cut marks on them, scapulas, temporals, orbitals, heads-bashed-in parietals, a femur and tibia, completely whole and probably once articulated, pass through his hands. Metacarpals, phalanges, tail bones, patellas, tarsals – Jesus.

Warren stops. "Fuck," he whispers.

"What?"

He gently extracts a gracile-looking skull, nearly intact save for a good cave-in on the right temporal bone. Hands it to John. "Now watch what's next," he says. And out comes a complete atlas bone, that first vertebrate of the neck, and then his left hand, clasped as if with treasure.

"Hold your hand out," he says. Into John's palm slides twenty or so turquoise beads. A necklace.

"Fuck," John says. He stares at the beads for a very long time, Warren breathing next to him, watching them too, as if they might come alive and start writhing in agony.

"I'll bet she was decapitated," Warren whispers.

"Don't say that."

But it's too late. The sun is an oblong box hitting the east wall of the kiva, the afternoon air still and filled with the small noises of archeologists working above them, troweling or scraping or taking notes on clipboards with their papers held down with rubber bands. The smell of dirt is pervasive.

"What happened here?" Warren asks, fingering the beads.

They both have noted the presence of roof beams when usually these are burned or scavenged for use elsewhere; they've both noted metates and whole pots and beautiful ornaments left as if their owners were coming back the next day.

He puts the beads in a plastic Ziploc. Labels it. Puts it in the box with all the other bones that are wrapped and bagged and labeled too. "I don't know, man," he says. "I don't know what happened."

But they both get out then, crawling up the ladder and out of the kiva for more air, for the assurance of sunshine and the sound of birds. John doesn't know about Warren that day, but he remembers feeling utterly blanched inside. Back in the lab, his hands on the child's head, the blanched feeling comes back. He swallows and puts the skull down. His fingers graze against another skull, then a femur. And he thinks: for scientific purposes, all these bones are "circumstantial" evidence of cannibalism. It looks bad, but you can't "prove" that they were eaten. It is Mellars' turd that will provide the "direct" evidence. What speaks more volumes to his lame and shaky heart, however, is exactly the opposite. The turd is almost funny in a sick way. The bones, though – the bones are devastating.

IV.

King is conciliatory, throwing John the puzzled look of an alpha male who cannot understand why anybody would run off to the Pacific Northwest in the face of such spectacular evidence. For him, this is a career milestone, a one-up on his competition, his firm's name to be known in far broader circles, the findings meticulously rendered and presented. He is tall with a paunch and used car salesman hair. But every archeology firm boss has either an MA or a PhD, usually the latter, and the give-away to that much education on King is a pair of John Lennon glasses. "So," he says, looking at him from across his desk, an owl out for prey, "what have you put together?"

John's not sure what he means by this, but he starts with the turd. "The turd decidedly has trace quantities of human myoglobin."

"Yes. So does the inside of one pot and two of your flakes, the ones with sharp edges." He's at least read some of the reports that have come his way, John thinks.

Nodding, John adds, "The pollen analysis is interesting, too."

King sits up. That report he clearly hasn't absorbed. "More, please."

John fishes through his files and finds it. He adjusts his glasses, and then, with a glance at King, takes out a ruler and concentrates on the scientific prose in front of him. "'Flotation samples collected from 5MT15403," he begins, "had very low ubiquity of cultigens and high diversity of wild plant foods...the only cultigens were an unburned squash seed and a single, charred maize cupule.'"

He looks up. King is gazing wide-eyed at the report. "God. Almost no corn. Them dudes ain't makin' it. Surviving on rice grass and pigweed is not my idea of a good time."

"Nope, it's not mine either." John thinks on that desolate site, the battered bodies, the feeling of everything left in its place for the wind to howl into. "Steve wants to go back and look at soil types," he adds to King, "but he did tell me something about settlement data for that piedmont area past the toe of Sleeping Ute, where we were."

"And – ?"

"It's abandoned more often than it's occupied. Seven hundred years or so of potential human horticultural history, and only about three hundred of it with any sign of human life to it."

"So what are his conclusions about that?"

"That maybe it is kind of a marginal area to do agriculture in to begin with."

King's nodding vigorously and rolling his lips. "That's my guess. It's below the p-j, for god's sake."

P-j is pinon-juniper woodland, the usual habitat of Ancestral Puebloans. "Yes. Barely, but it's still pretty hot and dry." John sees Steve's coveted lone juniper-and-chaise-lounge reading spot and misses it, suddenly. "Five thousand foot elevation in a shallow wash that cuts through a slope facing south to the San

Juan."

"Especially dry then," muses King. "Big drought time if we believe our tree rings, which we do. Anything else?"

He nods. "Steve, when he was doing settlement data research, ran up against a host of other sites from that time period that had bodies like ours."

"Really?"

"Really."

King sits back. "What do other time periods look like?"

"They look like purity itself compared to 1150."

"Well, well. What the hell is going on at 1150 in the Four Corners?"

John fingers Steve's book on Orayvi, lying next to the other reports in his book bag. Steve also told him about other studies that suggested that factionalism was a constant problem for the Pueblo. How to translate that information into what might be at their site? "My guess is they are already shoved out of somewhere else, somewhere more productive. A loser clan among loser clans in a loser location."

King pouts, weighing that idea. "Good just-so story. Any evidence for that?"

"Maybe with some of the pottery. A lot of stuff from the south, in the Chuskas."

"Huh." They're silent for a minute. Then he says, "Now John," in an alarmingly fatherly voice, and John's blood freezes. "Do you know how you are going to go about putting this all together?"

The question and tone betray the fact that he doesn't trust him and John buries his face to hide a deep blush. "Scale," he mutters.

"What?"

"Three scales. Site level, nearby settlement data, then regional scales."

King is quiet for a minute, tenting his fingers in front of his perpetually pursed lips. John wants to knock his hands apart and tell him to go drink a beer. Christ.

"Good," he finally says, though John feels he has been pretty vague. "Start with that. I'll want a draft of the article in two weeks."

A weight falls off John's chest at King's return to trust, and then back on in what John knows all too well is a precursor to panic. *Two weeks!* He stands up to hasten his leave. They shake hands and King looks him in the eye. He has never been so grateful for his tinted lenses in his life.

Still, King has to say something. Fuck. *Men are no good at this.* King's trying to be jocular and concerned and he comes across instead like a pompous patronizing pig. John holds his breath.

"Warren said you were a damn good dirt archeologist. I trust Warren, and I believe him."

"Yessir," John says, slipping back into Marine Corps grunt mode disturbingly fast.

King chuckles. "I'm not your drill sergeant, John. But you'll be all right with the write-up now?"

"Yes," he says. He shifts on his feet like the same errant six-year-old he was at Warren's. He says he has to go. King nods and John beetles out of his office, masking his discomfort as much as he can. Food his great solace in times of stress, he eats a Super Combo from Del Taco next door. He pulls out his cell phone, only to stare at it during his entire bean burrito. Finally, he dials and leaves a message for Colleen Jensen. Step One: Admit that you are powerless over your learning disability.

* * * *

When he gets home the answering machine is blinking. He presses the button and his mother's voice comes on. She doesn't sound like her usual overly chipper self. "John, your dad's in the hospital. Please call me on Lindsay's cell phone –" then an aside, "Lindsay, what's your cell? – 619-555-3050. Okay, honey?"

His heart slides to his feet, even though he has been half-expecting just such a call ever since Sweeney's father had a heart attack five years ago. John's fifty, his father is eighty-three. When he saw him last Christmas, he seemed healthy, still beachcombing on weekends or hiking a bit around Alpine. Not fat. Some arthritis, but overall health good. John calls Lindsay's number.

"He's had a stroke," she says, picking up the phone before John even hears it ring on his end.

"How'd you know it was me?"

She sighs, forever the exasperated older sister. "Ever hear of caller ID, John?"

"Do I need to come home?"

"He's dying, John."

"All right." And even though he knows he will have to fly to San Diego this time and not drive, he's already on a stick-straight road in the middle of the Mojave, veeing into a mountain range that forever recedes, and never reveals its heart.

CHAPTER 9

I.

With stitches in his throat, his sternum, his chest, he lies back on the bed he shares with Sweeney in the same way he lay back on a nursery log in the forest back in Neah Bay when the ocean held no answers and he was trying to make sense of Tin Cup. He spokes his hands up into overlapping wheels again, too. Boolean logic. Venn diagrams. Who overlaps with whom? If the Southwest is myriad fluctuating circles and the Northwest a string of Christmas lights along a rich and dangerous coastline, then what is he? How do his patterns fit together? He sits up. *You aren't supposed to have a pattern, son.* The rifle loose and loaded in the hand, lowered but ready, the belt of bullets hung low around the hips below another belt, a leather thing with oval buckle with brand on it, the kerchief tied at the neck, the flinty squint out from underneath the brim of a curling hat. This from a movie poster of his namesake. Then: His father in dress blues, 1945. Then: His father on Iwo Jima, with two other buddies in black and white, leaning against a coconut palm, exhausted, smeared with dirt or blood or something, cigarettes dangling from two of their mouths. They are all smiling, ghost smiles, smiles too old for teenagers, for twenty-year-olds. But they are doing what they should be doing. The smiles also say that, because in spite of the exhaustion they exude a certain pride, the pride of pleasing others, of reaching the pinnacle of what their society has told them to reach. Three GIs on a remote Pacific island full of dead and rotting bodies. The pinnacle. The photo is framed in his study.

Then: this just a simple one. The lone man, silhouette, walking off into the sunset. Alone alone alone. *There is no pattern. No web. Your life is linear, save for the occasional woman who likes you too much, wants too much, demands you pay attention. Forget that.*

Meghan, in the hotel room in Monticello, the last time he saw her. "If you could, John, would you marry me?" Her son was four months old and lay sleeping in her arms.

"You mean if Sweeney were not in my life? If Jason were not in yours?"

"Yes."

"No, probably not."

"What would you do?" Her voice was still, as neutral as she could make it.

He couldn't look at her. He looked off to the wall of the motel. "Probably drive. I like it best when I'm alone, driving in the desert. I think best out there."

"Oh," was all she said.

He still couldn't bear to look at her. She was nursing her baby on the other bed. But after he went to the bathroom and came out she was still there and the baby was there and he had never seen anything more beautiful in his life.

Later they made love again and she nursed again and then he gazed at her. A huge swell rose up in him, a rolling wave, and "I love you" ripped out of his mouth like a flood, like whatever forces swirl after twenty-four hours of rain and then slot down the steep canyons for which Utah was famous. He had never meant anything more seriously in his life.

She closed her eyes as if in pain. "I love you too," she whispered, but he was saturated with unease, the flood sloshing into a queasy sea. He knew he had hurt her, that the old days where they both could float along in a dream world outside of every other world were over, because she was too strong now.

Six months later, after he couldn't find her during comps, she asked him, phone line a taut wire of silence and implication stretching between Santa Fe and Salt Lake, "Why don't you like being with me?"

He was stunned. "Huh? I love being with you."

"Then why aren't you?"

Silent wires. Ravens perching. *Don't get too close to the trans-former. Caw! Nevermore....* His reply came with a voice that was a scratch in the desert, rice grass breezing on red dirt. "Sometimes my feelings for you are so intense that it scares me to death." He could barely breathe.

"So what do you want to do when you have those feelings?"

He remembers snorting. Tough-guy snort, the blown-out air of the man with the lowered rifle, the knotted kerchief, the exhausted smile. "What do people usually want to do when they're scared like that? I want to run five hundred miles in the other direction."

The line was cold, deadly silent, crackling with freeze. He just said what he said to a woman with more emotional courage than anyone he had ever met.

"I just love it," she said dryly, "when people choose their fears over love."

Click.

And then the final nail, when she phoned to tell him that she told Jason everything, when she said that at first John had helped (*so much*) to heal her wounds, but that now it was creating a new split and she refused to live a split life. The wires crackling again, heavy and swaying in the winds between them: "You've never once really said you'd go be with me, even though I know how much you love me. I can't do that anymore, John. I want home. I want my family. You always said we were friends."

He hung up. She wrote him a long, long email nailing him on all his stashing of her, all his closeting of her in a jeweled box to be taken out at his convenience, and of all her need, the revelation that from the get-go something in her knew whatever baby she had would not be his. That he would never go there with her even though without him she would have struggled so much more when things so completely fell apart and she left a first marriage, left a career, left everything. *And why, John? When I saw your stricken face as I boarded an airplane in Salt Lake? Why,*

*John? When you see me nurse my child and die with love? Why, when
after eight years you still call me every week? Why Why Why? John, at
some level I have simply loved two men. And for* me! *A marvel, to learn
that I can love like that! But who is really there for me? Who loves me
on a daily basis? Who? Go to Sweeney and heal whatever there is to heal
between the two of you...but I cannot be your secret lover anymore; I
cannot replay what I was asked to play with my own father...*

He did not respond. He banished her, red with anger that she
wanted out of the special place, that she compared him to her evil
father, that in some way she had flown past him in her growth,
become someone who didn't need his help the way she used to,
become the other train shooting past his through the desert in
opposite directions at midnight.

Two days later, at work, the phone rang for the last time.
"John. I would be with you." As if to say, *even though this is
hopeless, even though you have thoroughly rejected me, I want you to
know I loved you enough to make you a full partner.*

And what did he say? No pattern, linear life, no strings
attached, off into the sunset. He was a specialist. Lithics. He
didn't 'do' relationships, interconnections, bigger pictures. He
said: "Leave me alone."

II.

He looks Sweeney in the eye when she comes home an hour later
and tries to reassure her that everything will be all right. Not
about his dad – his dad is dying and there is not much to do there
– but about the two of them. He tells her he will call from his
sister's house as soon as he gets there. He asks if she wants to go
with him, but he knows the answer. She has a report due in two
days. Someone has to hold down the fort. She'll go to the funeral,
when it's certain. Then he leaves a voice message for King and
Warren to tell them he has to go to San Diego. He clears the decks
as best he can, but he can't help feeling, once Sweeney drops him

off at the airport, that he is leaving behind a posse of people looking at him with the disappointed eyes of so many elementary school nuns.

On the plane he drinks a beer and sweats through fears that his father will suffer the fate of Terry Shiavo. His mother can have a fundamentalist Catholic streak to her, and he wonders if she will go there at a time like this. But mostly what he fears, the beer not doing much to nullify his guilt around it, is what he really wants to say to him. He really wants to say God damn you, Dad. Where the *fuck* were you? Day in and day out, working his way up the V.A. food chain until he pulled a good wage. But the more money he made the less anybody saw of him, and when they did he seemed gaunt in spite of his jowls, hollowed out. If anyone asked them if he was unhappy they'd all no doubt look completely startled and say, "No, of course not!" John can see the obituary now, written by his mother, full of his achievements in Knights of Columbus and the VFW; his list of war medals; his three children; five grandchildren; thirty years of service to the V.A.; the final sentence saying it all, and trivializing everything: "He enjoyed hiking and was a history buff."

A history "buff"! He finishes his beer and slaps the can a little too hard on his flimsy airline table. The woman next to him stirs in her sleep. Is that what such an interest was worth? "Buff-ness"? What the hell is a "buff" anyway? Christ. He hasn't been this angry since the Marines, when his sergeant screwed with his head in sniper school. "Shoot at anything that moves," he said, while he guarded an embassy perimeter. So he did. Dead shot, ground zero, middle of the target. The gun turned out to be blank save for a red paintball. He looked at it in amazement. A red-splattered figure moved toward him, up the stairs of the tower. His sergeant popped his head up, grinning. "Good work," he said. John wanted to fucking wring his neck.

He's in a mood when he lands. Lindsay picks him up from the airport sporting extensive gray roots and bags under her eyes.

She takes one look at his face and says, in that way only siblings can, "Oh, boy."

"The sins of the fathers," he responds, not knowing why, his voice like that of an automaton. He feels like a fish swimming in a murky tank.

But she nods. She, after all, lived out the "buff" and became the history teacher. "Yes," she says. "We'll talk after we see him."

* * * *

His mother is tittery because she is unsure how to behave. The nurse in her would take over from the hospice workers, her body language oozing contempt for every other kind of care besides her own. She checks his oxygen, which is the only thing he is hooked up to, and strains her neck to see how much morphine they are giving him when it is time for his next dose. "Aneurysm," she says, before she even hugs him. "Right to the brain stem. There's no communication between the brain stem and the brain."

Then she does hug him, her hair gray in tight curls, her body a dumpling in old age, her face his face. But John has his dad's build, and for one brief uncomfortable moment he feels her feeling him as her husband, and she holds him to her longer than she has ever done. It transforms her and the nurse visage drops as she lets go of him, her chin trembling.

"Sit down, Mom," Lindsay says, gently, and leads her to a chair up against the window in his room. His father has utter privacy here; he's in a hospice wing, and John's Terry Shiavo fears fade.

"Where's Syd?" he asks.

"She'll be down with Rob and the kids tomorrow."

He nods. Their middle sibling lives in the Bay Area and it occurs to him that she keeps as much distance as he does, if not more. Huh, he thinks. The monolith of the two perfect sisters

Chapter 9

forms a crack in him. Why has Syd kept so far away? And why hasn't he traced out the possible implications of this before?

"You want some time alone with him?" his mother asks into their small silence.

"Uh, sure," he says, startled. He hasn't given it any thought until then, what he wants, but an alm offered is an alm offered. She and Lindsay leave the room.

Alone, he finds he has almost nothing to say to him. He is surprised. At other times he has felt like Meghan, who shouted reams and reams to her father out in the desert, or outside Albuquerque while throwing glass, or wept quietly about him in the back of the pickup under an obsidian cliff face near Mammoth that was less than a thousand years old. But now in the stark quiet of a room filled with nothing but sunlight and his ragged breathing, John has nothing. He would like to shout at him but he is no longer the looming silhouette on the beach when John was ten, the silhouette who finally noticed him after a decade of John's existence in his life. He's a dying old man, shriveled, utterly mute, worthy of pity.

"Did you expect this, Dad?" he asks, with faint Marine Corps jocularity. His voice sounds both echoey and feeble, all at once. "I bet not. I think you expected it at Iwo Jima and Chosin Reservoir, but not now."

He rubs his fingers together and looks at his father's hand. Does he dare take it? Isn't that what you do with dying loved ones? Hold their hand? Stroke their forehead? The thought makes him squeamish and his breathing picks up. He has never taken his father's hand before. He has no memory of doing this, even when he was little and doing everything else with his hands. Building Legos. Feeling the grain of wood on his little boy workbench. Holding a square of American cheese in his fat kid fingers. He looks at both sets of their hands in astonishment. How, then, did that little kinesthetic learner know his father loved him?

135

He pulls up a chair next to him. Now he is at eye level to his torso, the gut rising and falling, the arms palsied from stroke. Jesus. His childhood attention consisted of being Syd and Lindsay's kid brother. They didn't need toy dolls. They had him. They dressed him up, propped him up, made him pet the cat, laughed when he tried to run away from them. He finally punched Lindsay when he was five, if he remembers right, and thought for sure he was done for. But maybe Lindsay never told on him, or maybe his mother decided she'd had what was coming to her, but he was never picked on quite so much again. So began, he thinks, wondering if he could at least reach up and touch his father's head, the Long Years of Neglect. A boy who spent many days looking at more of his father's Marine Corps photos than he did at his actual father. This Is My Dad, said the photos. World War II, Korea, medals and plaques, a wedding picture, a pair of pictures with all of them as a family. When John was in junior high, about the time he watched National Geographic and found out about Louis Leakey and PhDs in archeology, he extended his knowledge of his dad to his bookshelf. Rome, Greece, Great Battles of the Civil War, Strategies and Tactics, The Great War, The Rise and Fall of…endless history. Most of it military, but still.

He takes a deep breath and puts his fingers lightly on his father's forehead. His hand does not burn off; smoke does not curl out of his father's skin. But the dam holding back tears he didn't know he had completely fails, as if his touch were a magic red button to open floodgates. He feels like George on the beach, listening to the sea and weeping with rage. "You stupid shit," he sobs, as he slumps in the chair, his arm collapsing onto his father's own useless limb. "You stupid, stupid shit."

It is the most loving thing he knows how to say to him. It is this because he says it tenderly, and most of all because it is the truth.

III.

Lindsay and John drive in silence to an Applebee's five blocks from the hospital. It's past dinner time, though because it's high June the light is still strong and if it weren't for the sea breeze it would be hot. A year ago, he remembers, Warren and he were just beginning to get into the kiva.

"So, brother o'mine," she says, sitting down as the waitress brings ice water and silverware, "how are you?" Lindsay has that efficient confidence of oldest siblings, her fingers taking strands of errant hair and pushing them back into a loose bun, her other hand taking off her glasses and plopping them unceremoniously on the table.

"Other than Dad dying, you mean?" He tries to smirk, to keep up the kid-brother banter, but with Lindsay that has never really worked. She could surf all day in twelve-foot waves in her prime, and even now she runs 10Ks on a regular basis. She has a thicker waist thanks to being over fifty, but John wouldn't call her fat. Syd, he realizes, he never knew how to talk to. It was Lindsay, with her help on Shakespeare and geography papers, with her Mother Bear protective streak (was that an oldest sibling thing too? Paternalistic in men, motherly in women? Was King an oldest sibling?), who got to know him a bit.

They order food and Lindsay starts to talk. "You looked like hell coming off the plane."

"Thanks."

"What'd you say to Dad in there?"

He looks at her. "Isn't that supposed to be private?"

She blushes. "Sorry. Sometimes I fall back into Bossy Sister mode, still."

John laughs a little, thinking how often these days he has felt like a child, too. "You know one of the things I thought about in there? With Dad? How you and Syd dressed me up and pushed me around and made me a doll." He can't say it without an edge of poor-me bitterness, and he's immediately horrified at himself.

But Lindsay is already on it. "Cut the crap, John Wayne. You stood up for yourself in the end, left me with a nice bruise."

He's silent. She's right. The waitress refills their water and takes their order. Lindsay sits up. "Look, let's do a little exercise. Close your eyes and imagine feeling superior to us. To me and Syd."

He's surprised. "What?"

"Just humor me. Close your eyes and imagine feeling superior."

"How old do I have to be?"

"It doesn't matter, but since we're talking the doll phase, be five."

"Ok." He takes a minute, settling into the booth, closing his eyes. A whiff of resistance rises up but he realizes Dad is dying and he could barely touch him and this bothers him. He also realizes he is in a booth with his older sister whose dad is also dying, which turns out to be as effective at holding him to the spot, somehow, as an interrogation cell. "Ok," he says after a moment. "I feel superior." Hah hah hah, he thinks. Take that, sis, as he punches her in his mind's eye. But he is not feeling exactly himself either. As if punching and being haughty requires an out-of-body experience. "Now what?"

She gives an annoying small smile. "Shift it. Imagine feeling inferior."

He sighs. Who else would get him to do this? Lindsay the lapsed Catholic, Lindsay of the semi-annual Buddhist retreat. Fine, he thinks. He feels inferior. Yuck. Picked-on boy.

"Now imagine feeling equal."

He blows out air. When would this end? He works his way into the idea of equality. He doesn't know what he expects, but as soon as he makes the adjustment the shift in the atomic substrate is phenomenal. It's as if a storm has ended, the tide gone out, the sand remaining smooth and wet and full of little plovers, running on little stilt feet. He is not an out-of-body asshole, nor is he shriveled into a victim's ball, nor is he an out-of-body asshole because he is covering for being shriveled into a victim's ball. His eyes fly open. "Shit."

She nods. "It's all in your head, bro. All in your head."

He's chastened, almost appalled. Superior-inferior, the rage of a five-year-old boy who *already knew* he was supposed to be superior but felt inferior. *But I'm better than you! I'm supposed to be stronger! The MAN!* And there you are, making me pet the cat.

"What happened when I asked you to feel equal?" she asks.

He feels immensely sad. He looks honestly at her. "Equal, and I punch you and we're all fair and square. We're friends, actually. The world is at peace. But instead, Lin, instead…" He drifts off. The idea that he could have had friends for sisters all these years makes him feel lonelier than ever.

Lindsay smiles a wan and knowing smile. "Instead you pay for your high and mighty status. You pay with I'll-Do-It-Myself Shit. You pay. It's lonely at the top."

"But I've never ever felt 'on top,'" he protests. Their food comes and they pause.

"Of course not," she says, sprinkling her fries with ketchup. "That's the other lie. Because no guy is ever, ever, ever, allowed to feel less than in front of a woman – and we won't even go into race and class – because when he inevitably does he feels like a total weenie. Emasculation 101. So you go around fucking the world to feel better." She takes a bite of an enormous Rueben sandwich. "Okay," she says, to her non-rapist brother, to the one who saved an incest survivor's life, "maybe that was a little harsh in your case." She smiles, though, as she chews.

"How do you know all this?" he asks, chewing his burger.

She looks at him. "You think I ever got Dad's approval? I know you never did." She puts her hand on his, something that seems far easier for her to do than it is for him. Could she do that with their father, too? "All this gender stuff between us still doesn't negate that you really didn't have a dad. I know that." She shakes her head and tears come up. "I wish he had ever figured out that all we wanted to do was *know* him."

"Yeah," he says, the feel of his forehead coming back. But he is bothered, now, about Lindsay. "What do you mean you never got his attention either? You were everything he wanted. The history teacher."

She laughs. "Yeah, right. Somebody once said oldest kids tend to track Dad, middles the mother, you both. I don't know, but that works in our family. So I got to live out the dream he never did for himself, huh? But don't you see, John-bo? That meant I had to come at history for myself, not him. So I subscribed to the Howard Zinn school of underdog history, not the Stephen Ambrose-cum-John Wayne history of great battles. But I sometimes still think I did it all for him and who the hell am I, really? Sometimes I think I should shove it all and go to massage school. It's funny," she says, drinking water, "how the greater a man's absence, the more he looms like a dragon you have to fight."

Now she is the one looking haggard. Wow. He'd always assumed the calm, competent sister, who never failed his father in the ways he did, had it made.

"It must have been easy to do the history thing, though," he says uneasily. For some reason he remembers a drive across the Mojave with Sweeney once, in which it had rained voraciously. Huge puddles sat in the median of the freeway. It smelled of wet creosote when they got out of the car to go pee. It wasn't the desert he knew, and it unsettled him. "He must have loved that," he says.

She shakes her head. "It brought up uncomfortable things between him and Mom."

"What do you mean?"

"I mean they raised holy hell when I told them I'd applied for a teaching license. I had to," she grins. "I had a job offer."

"You didn't tell them beforehand? That you were a history major? What about student teaching?"

She's still shaking her head the whole time John is asking these questions. "Nope, nope, and nope."

He is incredulous. "Why the hell not?"

She eats her Rueben, wipes her mouth again, and takes a swig of water. "Because, John-bo, I knew it'd bring all sorts of crap up. I overheard them fight about it when I was fifteen. He wanted to do a degree, even by night, and teach history. She said the salary cut was too much and besides, he'd have to teach in public schools and they were Catholic." Lindsay laughs a little. "Dad would have to become a monk to teach in Catholic schools. Can you see that? Or at least work truly for squat."

John has stopped eating. For the first time in his life he has zero interest in food. "So he squashed that dream. For those reasons." He states this as if it is the saddest fact he has ever heard.

"Yes."

His parents' marriage unfolds before him, another childhood illusion shot down. Did every family go through this when a parent lay dying? All this unraveling? How simple! To talk to your sister. To really talk. It has grown dark outside and Applebee's glows like a strange island, the low murmur of other diners fading to nothing.

"So what happened when you did tell them?" he asked.

"Mom turned a little green and muttered something about how I was going to teach in public school, then? So I said Duh, Mom. What do you want? That I become a nun? She had no answer to that. She'd just told me earlier she hoped I'd marry Kyle and have kids." Kyle was Lindsay's ex-husband.

He is so floored at all this that he just sits there.

Lindsay eats a French fry. "I shouldn't have these. At my age, you get fat instantly. Meno-calories."

"Meno-calories?"

"You know, menopause." She rolls her eyes. "Doesn't Sweeney tell you anything?"

John colors. No, Sweeney does not. Lindsay catches it and scoots in over the table. "Are you and Sweeney okay?"

He holds her gaze and then lets it drop. "I don't know," he says, and tries to explain, in as few words as possible, the last year's trials. He tries to tell her about the disabilities, how jealous he was of her and Syd, especially of her history teacher career, how he has this terrible, terrible site full of butchered human beings and a turd, and he has to write it all up. He's a lithics man, he says. Rocks don't require weaving a story about human relationships. Besides, his entire career as it is has been is thanks to Sweeney. How she is pissed and hurt that he won't ask for her help on this. That he loves her and they have a good many shared experiences but like Dad with Mom – he stops. The parallels hold him rigid. *She said the salary cut was too much, and besides, he'd have to teach in public schools and they were Catholic.* Sweeney, announcing marriage. Announcing her tubes tied. Announcing the trajectory of the rest of his life, just as his mother announced his father's trajectory. And his father – that tough Marine, the man who rarely let his emotions crack the surface – why, he buckled. He did not stand up for his life. He did not.

Appleby's reels in muted light and voices ring suddenly sharp from far corners. Lindsay is staring at him. But it's all right. It's all right because Lindsay, in her Obi-Wan clairvoyance, her older sister intensity, in her fight, he sees now, to insist on life on her terms, seems to get it. They just sit there and stare at each other, each in their imperfect lives. He has never loved her more.

* * * *

The waitress comes and Lindsay asks for a box for the other half of her sandwich. He says no when she asks if he wants one for his half-eaten hamburger, too.

"I wish I knew then what I know now about LD kids," Lindsay says at the end of his saga. Tears rise up in her for the second time that night. "I've taught high school for nearly thirty years, John. I know a great deal about what you have to go through." She looks away from him and puts her hand to her mouth. "None of us saw it, did we?"

"Lin, I was in fourth grade before someone noticed I couldn't read, and it wasn't Mom or Dad."

She sighs very, very heavily. "If I'd known, I could have truly helped you instead of set up a pattern."

Now it's his turn to want to hold her hand, but all the old fears rear up again. So he just says, "Give yourself a break. Nobody knew anything about disabilities back then. You know that. No legislation, nothing. And it's bigger than you, Lin, anyway," he says, thinking about what Colleen Jensen said about women enabling their silly football players. "It's all that cultural garbage you just called me on." Christ, he sounds like Gloria Steinem. "It's a boy not being able to ask for help because he isn't supposed to ask for help and because he doesn't know what's wrong anyway."

"So women become the place to hide your weaknesses." She snorts. "And I was the first."

"Maybe," he admits. *And Sweeney may be the biggest hide-out of them all.*

She looks sideways at him. "Did any woman ever call you on that?"

He blushes so deeply she smiles.

"You had an affair, didn't you?"

"Yes."

"How long ago?"

"Years," he says.

"She was brilliant, yes?"

He nods. Lindsay goes on. "But she called you on it so you broke it off."

"Sort of." He shifts uncomfortably. Trust a sister to read right through your seven layers of skin and Saran-wrapped heart. He closes his eyes. "I wish I hadn't. Broken it off, that is." This is the first time he has ever admitted this, even to himself. Guilt over Sweeney, over his whole life, fills him up, a great bilge from some sewer he has never wanted to visit. His world becomes a fragile bubble that would pop if he were to leave it for Meghan, or anyone. He thinks about her and her baby boy, nursing at her breast. He remembers pulling up to the base of an obsidian cliff on their trip to the Sierra, and making love in the back of the truck. He remembers, three years later, going back there to collect obsidian with two Forest Service archeologists, and telling them to pull up a little further, off the spot where he'd parked the truck before. It was too sacred, that spot. It burned with something he wanted no stranger to see or feel or understand.

IV.

In the bluish dawn he wakes up to that same image of Meghan. Did he really want her? Or just her adoration? Or her baby? *The baby.* His heart accordions and he folds into himself, fetal. *Sweeney, why couldn't we –? And Meghan – did I use you? Did you use me? Why have I never stopped missing you?* Then the reality of being in San Diego slips in with the growing light, and the reason why he is here returns. His heaviness grows deeper. He gets up slowly, takes a shower. It is early and Lindsay is not up yet. Summer vacation is barely two weeks old for her, he realizes, whereas his field season should be just starting. He should be working somewhere. But he's not. Not in that sense, anyway. He eats eggs, and slides out into the sunrise air.

His father just has to slip away. His systems will slowly shut down, one by one, as the brain no longer sends signals. This could take three days or three weeks. John pays him a visit, again fidgeting over this notion of touch, his jaw working to say how he'd wish he'd understood anything about him. A notepad with the name of some drug across the top lies on a nightstand next to the bed, a cryptic nurse-note scribbled on it with the remaining pen. He tears the note off, putting it back on the nightstand, and stares at the subsequent blank page. The pen's an odd heft in his hand. Meghan was picky about her pens. No fine point, she said, as it made writing akin to chicken scratch, or fingernails on a chalkboard. Something smooth, flowing. Blue over black. This is just a fat ballpoint, also swag from a drug company, but it is medium point and its fatness fits his big hand. It doesn't occur to him until he starts writing that he *is* in fact writing, that he is doing the one task for which he carries more shame than any other. Dear Dad, he writes, then stops. It hits him, what he's doing. *Don't you care about your spelling? Your backward b's and occasional d's that still want to about-face?* A wave of humiliation surges through him, catching in his lungs. He lets out a noise, the pen clutched in his hand. But his father simply lies there, breathing raggedly, a hundred cells dying with every release of air. *Well it sure as shit doesn't matter anymore, does it, Pops?* Dear Dad. I wish I knew... *I wish I knew what? That you loved me? That you had far less courage than I thought you did? That all your Purple Hearts don't make up for an unlived life?* He writes that, then scribbles over it angrily. What a bunch of self-pity and too-late recriminations. Surely he's a better specimen of humanity than to leave his dad with that. He tosses the pad down on the night stand, sick of this no man's land halfway between speech and silence, this struggle to communicate with a man who never knew how to communicate himself. He wipes his face and pulls at his collar. The room seems hot, his father's breathing unbearable, and he catches sunlight slanting in through the window. It's as if he can hear the sea in the light, and he bolts then, makes a beeline for the beach as if the hospital room were filled with wasps, mosquitoes, invisible gnats. His rental car directs itself to La Jolla and Seal Rocks. If he hangs out with the seals maybe he'll be clean of something too human, too close.

He may be forty pounds too heavy but ocean swimming is bliss, is pure body memory, and he knows just what to do. The waves are decent – five feet or so – and he rides wave after wave after wave, salt water sluicing up his nose, sand in his swim trunks, kelp sticking to his fingers as he coasts into the strand. He gets out to put on sunscreen and lets all his pores shrink into a laminate of salt. When it gets too hot, he goes back in. Four, five, six bouts. Bout seven, tired and inured, he slowly realizes that two shapes are swimming next to him, belly to his belly save for three feet or so between them. One behind him, the other in front, a threesome of swimmers. The miracle of this contact brokers no argument. His astonished flesh fills with a satisfaction he has never known before, a kind of enormous yes vote spinning as the seals spin, happy in their dance with him and the sea. He follows their lead and rotates, pirouetting horizontally through the water. They take him right along, to the backside of their rock, where the pull can be dangerous at certain points of the tide. But they're not at that point. In home waters, more seals slide in to greet the two who have reeled in this strange wreck of a man. He finds himself surrounded with smooth and shiny bodies, and as he bobs for air, they swirl around him, caressing him with sleek bellies and flippers. One of them pops up right next to him and barks what John, in some animal way, knows is a welcome. *This!* All those nights spent shivering in the Great Basin, digesting mice and stalking deer and searching for good rocks to make arrowheads with. All of them were about this! He saw a picture once of an Apache man wearing a buckskin deer hood and crouching in a stalking position in a sage-filled field in Arizona. The Apache had ceased to be just a man, but was half-deer, half-man, a shamanic crossover of species. John has ached for that world, for that place where you were not judged by your ability to form complete sentences, but by your ability to intuit the living universe. He'd always been able to intuit it. Always. Women knew it, those that cooed over his loving. His hands on obsidian knew it and still know it.

He stays in the reverie of seal-life for a long time. A young seal nudges him to swim, and John begins to laugh. Since he's underwater, he laughs silently, with all his body, until he senses a shift in tides. He bobs up and waves goodbye to the writhe of seals on the rocks. They too have pulled up out of the sea as the waves move in. Some stare back at him, others seem not to notice. He frog-kicks around the treachery of rocks and oncoming surf, the sea now a creature in its own right, directing him in. He could tell time by that tide, but he has no desire to. How many minutes or hours or days he has disappeared into another world, he does not know or care.

On the sand he is hypoglycemic with hunger and crisp with sunburn. He puts on a shirt and flip-flops, walks to a hot dog cart, eats, gazes at a pay phone across the street at a 7-11. His cell is back at Lindsay's, a deliberate move on his part. He doesn't want Mom, Lindsay, Syd calling. In a haze, munching his dog, he walks to the phone. Some unbelievable grace has just happened to him and he rests in its stupor. He puts in change, ask for information. Information comes back with the number and puts him through. The phone rings and rings, but he lets it. Someone will pick up eventually.

"Hello?"

"Hi. I'm looking for George Ward."

"He's down smoking salmon. Can I take a message?"

"Uh, I'm on a pay phone myself."

"Ok."

The station attendant leaves and John hears the sound of tires on what sounds, actually, like dry pavement, the bell tinkling over the door of the gas station. He finishes his dog and downs his entire Dr. Pepper before "'Lo?"

"George?"

"John Wayne Gregory-bro! How the hell are you?" He sounds

genuinely glad to hear from him.

"Good. You?"

"I'm getting in shape. Running five miles a day. Beach running, bare feet if I go where there aren't too many rocks. Great for your calf muscles."

"I know. I used to do that for volleyball."

"I'm staying clean, John-bo, so you better come back."

"I will."

"When?"

John sighs. "My dad's dying, George. I'm down the ocean from you in San Diego. I surfed all morning."

"Is it hot?"

"Yup."

"It's beautiful here, John. Sunny, warm for here. Which is to say, about seventy degrees."

John's silent a minute. It occurs to him how much they both love this ocean, this sea. Miles and miles of coastline, reefs, earthquake faults, bays, coves, sandy beaches, timber, Japanese-looking trees shaped by wind and foam, lie between them. But it is the same sea.

"I swam out by the gray seals today. Thought of you," he says. He waits a beat, then says, "George, they swam with me. They came and got me and took me to their rocks for a while."

George laughs. "It's a good ocean, enit?" As if that were nothing unusual. Then, "How's your marriage? Your job?"

"What, do seals do that for you? Do they come and get Makah boys and girls and take them for a joy ride every once and a while? Jesus, George, that was *sacred*."

"I know, bro. But I also know it happens. So yeah, they come and get you. A lot of things do."

Silence floats in a peaceable way up and down the coast between them. "That's the pain of being Indian, isn't George? Knowing those things can happen in a world that doesn't – doesn't – "

"Doesn't want it to happen anymore. Yeah, bro. It's like taking the whole cathedral and smashing it to death."

He could cry if he doesn't watch it. Dammit. This awful grace. This awful beauty. He squeezes his eyes free of tears and inhales and answers George's other questions. "I don't know, George, about things," he says. "The job, okay. I'll get through it. Sweeney I don't know. She's mad at me. I told her to talk to the disabilities specialist because she was too mad to listen to me. But she hadn't done it when I called her last night."

George is quiet, then says, "Sorry about your dad, bro."

"Did you have a dad, George?"

"Not really. Why?"

"I guess I'm assessing how much I had one, either."

"Maybe they got their own secrets, you know?"

"Maybe."

They're quiet another minute. Then George says, "I've gotta go. Just put a batch of fish in the smoker. Nina's watching it but you never know. We got tourists now the weather's nice."

Nina. Nine-year-old Nina. Same age as Meghan's boy. A surge of affection wells out of him, like surf spilling into a tide pool. "Say hi to her, will you? Has she sold more art?"

"Yeah, she has. You're coming back, eh?"

"Yes, George. I'll email you through the museum and let you know, okay? I'll keep you posted."

"'Cause I ain't doing no November ocean swimming just for me and my damn brothers and cousins."

"You aren't?"

John can almost hear him shake his head. "Sad to say, they never got me to stay sober. But the whale might. Like those seals of yours. And you. You and I have a bet going, eh?"

"We do?"

"We do, bro. Nose to the grindstone. You keep yours, I keep mine there. Ok?"

"Is this a race?"

He laughs. "No, bro. You white men are such idiots. It's a love affair, you dick."

John hangs up and he stares at the phone for a few minutes before a smile breaks over his face, and then a laugh escapes his throat, and then another one, till he goes back to his car, feeling wrung out and better than he has in a long time.

V.

He leaves a day later. Mom and Syd are an odd unified front of nursing mania even though there is nothing to do, and Lindsay and John start to feel useless. "Go home, John," she says twenty-four hours after he has called George. He is staying at her place, where she lives with her youngest son, who is in college, and two dogs. Kyle she left years ago, and another husband has not materialized. She pats his back. "He'll die, they'll have a memorial service, you'll fly back. But it could take a bit and it sounds as if you have things on your plate."

John feels her hands on his shoulders. His sister, whom in one sense he barely knows but in another knows him better than anyone. He does nothing to remove her hands. She can be pushy and pugnacious but in his current state he is not sure anything less would work with him. He'll beat her up later, he thinks, smirking. Equality.

"You know," he says, "I think the funeral will be an after-thought."

She nods. "I think so too."

"All those movies have you think differently, though. Like that's where you realize all your grief and stupidity and such."

She raps his head affectionately. "If you've let Hollywood dictate your emotional life, no wonder you're a wreck."

He chuckles. She puts on some tea, and they pass the afternoon in relative silence. He finds a stand-by night flight out of San Diego, kisses her cheek goodbye, and boards the plane.

Aloft, over the mountains and into the Mojave, he tracks mountain ranges, alluvial fans, dry stream beds that he can't even see because it is dark. It is all in his fingertips, that territory, that map of his dad's heart. All in his mind, just as Lindsay said. With a jolt he realizes that the Mojave was the first thing he brailled, the first landscape he learned to feel with his hands, since he could not feel his father.

Something detonates. Boom. Him. A giant coyote lopes all over the entire Mojave Desert. John stares down out the plane window. *Trickster, trickster.* Coyotes are clever but not wise. *A lot for you to learn out there, Dad.* He thinks back on dead Mexicans and prehistoric tracks at springs. *A lot to learn.* Then the desert leaves and as the pilot guns the engines for reasons John will never know, the ocean swims up in his ears. He can feel George's feet pounding the beaches of the Pacific Northwest, like the earth pounding up through Hot Creek. And then a whale, a whale, cruising deep water off the coast of the one ocean that has ever been his home, lets loose its low and haunting moan, demanding that he listen.

PART FIVE

CHAPTER 10

I.

It is late when he gets home, but Sweeney rolls over and says, "Let's go camping tomorrow. It's Friday and I'll call in sick. Nobody else knows you're home yet."

His heart beats in the dark. "You talked to Jensen, didn't you?"

"Yes."

* * * *

In the morning they do what they have always done best as a couple. They stash sleeping bags, camp stove, five-gallon water jugs, into the back of the truck. Foam pads, pillows, dry goods, cooler. A duffel bag of fleece and clean underwear. Flintknapping kits, a basket Sweeney is working on. They leave a mound of food for Coco and head for the mountains, for the uplift around Flaming Gorge in the northeastern part of the state, nearly in Wyoming, for a vast forest with plenty of campsites away from other people. They don't say much on the way up, slipping pleasantly into the working silence of two people who have been with one another a very long time. They get gas in Logan, eat lunch, continue on. They find a spot near a small lake, set up camp, take a walk around the lake before cooking dinner, noting frogs and herons and the swoop of an osprey, whose nest resides on a pole stuck high in the water. The light lingers late, summer solstice just past. John waits for Sweeney to start talking this whole time. Finally, a fire started, the fleece brought out against the oncoming chill, she says, "She says I have to let you do this by yourself."

"Who?"

"Jensen. She says you have to 'own' it. Not let other people take over where you should be struggling on your own."

"What did you say back?"

"I told her you always knew you had them. The disabilities, I mean. You never denied it. To me, anyway."

John walks over to their little camp table where the stove sits, and primes it again. "Want some tea?"

"Sure."

She adds another small stick to the fire. "But we denied it to everyone else, didn't we?"

"Yes," he says.

"Till you managed to get a job that landed you in this current mess."

"I didn't plan on cannibalism and the smoking gun of a turd," he says, trying to keep an unbecoming whine out of his voice. "I thought I was doing a simple project for Ute Irrigation. Rote write-up. Plug in the standard descriptors about environment, local prehistory, history. Do a little analysis. Done. I can do that."

"I know."

He pours water into the kettle, tipping the five-gallon container, and puts it on the stove. The gravel crunches under his feet in the dark.

"It's just – it's just – " she starts. "I don't know if you love me except for that. For helping you." Her voice sounds like she's pinched her vocal cords off. John knows then she is fighting rare tears. He comes over and squats next to her in her camp chair. The fire reflects in her face and he sees streaks of wet down it.

"Of course I love you." He puts his arm around her and looks into the dark at the shadow of their truck, the flickering fire, the hiss of the propane heating water. "I love this. It was smart to say let's go camping."

"It was?"

"We do this well. We've always done this well. Sweeney, I've eaten mice with you in the middle of the Oregon desert, for God's sake."

She guffaws a little. "That *would* make for a solid marriage, now, wouldn't it?" But she knows what he means.

"And coming up here. We know each other so well. Pack, get gas, eat things the other knows the other's going to eat. I guess, well, all that matters. It matters more than I realized," he says, thinking back to his dad, who for all his war medals, is dying curiously alone. The countless ghost towns, the kill zones of myriad tiny mines pawed out of the earth by loner men at 12,000 feet, the fact that in spite of their beauty western states have the highest suicide rates in the nation – all this worms in and out of his gut. How was such lunatic loneliness even possible?

Sweeney is grimacing at him, her face lit by campfire. Then she starts bawling for good. She heaves and hiccoughs and puts her face into his chest. "Why did you marry me? Why did you say yes?"

"Because I loved you."

She pulls back. "But that's not all, is it?"

So many things hang between them, laundry wrung out but never drying on thick string in the backyard. John is on one side, she's on the other, and they are batting against it to try and find the other. "What do you mean?" he asks, but his mouth is dry.

"I mean you hesitated when I came home and said we should do it. I mean, you never asked *me*." This last comes out hysterically, the same voice she used when she grabbed the obsidian blade. John winces.

"You were waiting for me to ask you?"

She snorts. "God. Men are so dense."

"Sweeney. You never mentioned marriage till then!"

"What did you think? We'd float along forever, through all the field seasons and endless winters? It'd been five years by then."

John is stumped. He sinks, cross-legged, in front of the fire. "I don't know, Sweeney. That was a long time ago."

"Oh come on. Talking to Ms. Jensen, I thought – I thought: this has been with you all the way along. Like you knew me 'overwintering' you wasn't quite right. But you wanted it so bad, John! You wanted to be an archeologist so badly!" The tears are flowing again.

He has quite forgotten the tea until the kettle goes. He stands up and pours two mugs. "Here you go," he says. "Mint. Your favorite."

She tries for a smile but fails. "I did all that for you because *you* wanted it! And I saw how hard it was for you! What was I supposed to do? Look you in the eye and say, figure it out yourself? I knew you needed *help!*"

So she did love him. Does. He is not just her coattail. He says, "I think, uh, that that's what Jensen would say now, huh? That I have to figure it out for myself. Get the right kind of help from someone who is not my love –" he almost says lover but somehow this would trigger Meghan, or even Lanie Brooks, into the conversation.

"Am I your love?" she asks. "Why did you marry me if not to have this career? This chance?"

"A lot of it was right!" he says. "We'd been together five years and split willow with our teeth and made wikiups and searched for obsidian and worked side by side in nasty conditions in the middle of the Nevada desert and wrote reports. We work really well together!" John looks at her. "We sleep well together too."

"Well, if that's all true, why'd you run away? Why Meghan? Why hiding so much shit from me?"

"I thought – I thought – " He wants to stitch up, to remain silent, to not reveal. He has slipped through a thousand ecosystems that way – elementary school, high school, college, field seasons, graduate school discussions, campfire talks. But that won't work anymore. "I was young, okay? Stupid. I am just now seeing some things, Sweeney. Just now. But then I thought it was good. I could have a career and a wife. Both! A good deal."

That sounds a little callous, so he says, "I mean, what other married team works as well as we do?"

They could probably name a couple, but that's not the point and she knows it. "But that work isn't entirely clean," she says.

"In one sense I get to be hand-holder. Enabler, says Ms. Jensen. So you are beneath me but then I'm beneath you because I am propping you up. Ick."

John thinks back on Lindsay's little exercise about being equal. "I agree," he says. "Ick."

"But I don't know how else we are to be!" The hysteria's back again. "If we don't have work, what do we have?"

"Please," he begs. "Can you not sound like that?" His voice is now the one pinched beyond repair. "It reminds me of, of when you threatened to kill yourself."

One more piece of laundry falls down in the dark. She stares at him, wild and disoriented, the doe in headlights.

"That scared the shit out of me," he says, in the tiniest voice he has ever possessed, and then they are hugging each other, and crying, and he does not know how they will get through the night, or the next day, or the next year, with such wet failure between them.

II.

July 1. He has five weeks until their presentation at Pecos. Mellars has already written a tidy, strictly biochem-oriented article for *Nature,* about the turd. The draft of it sits in front of him, a lovely shorthand of data for him to plug in to the larger site report – *his* site report, *his* baby – for *American Antiquity,* the official journal of the Society for American Archeology. Colleen gives him voice-activated software to try, but he is not sure it is any better than simply typing things out, the way he has always done, letter by painstaking letter, each letter known only by its placement on the keyboard, not by visions of a's and b's and c's dancing in perfectly spelled order in his head. Lithic reports he could often cut and paste the bare bones of, especially if the site was in an area he and Sweeney had already done work in. Then, because he had done the analysis himself, spent hours with a magnifying glass or microscope, peering at flake after flake, what he had to say on the keyboard seemed less abstract, as if the distance between the lithics themselves, the statistics on their attributes, then the meaning wrung from those statistics and typed onto a screen, was shorter. For the Tin Cup report Colleen says to allow himself to roam, to stand up and take a walk, to eat. To take the big picture requirements of it all in short chunks, just as he has done for lithics in the past. In turn he allows her, once, to watch him try to work through a one-way window, and she wonders if he is not a little ADD on top of everything else. Great, he thinks. Just fucking great.

Don't fight it, John Gregory. Don't fight who you are. Well, home now, the house echoey because Sweeney is out by Wendover monitoring a gas pipeline survey and Coco is asleep and it is afternoon, who he is seems to be merely a puddle of memory, is simply the strings of roads he grew up on, the arc of thousand-mile mountain ranges and boiling deserts and the lonely lovely reality of coming of age in the American West. He is not the child of fifth-generation ranchers, he has no miners buried in histori-cally recognized ghost town graveyards, his parents did not ride wagon trains out from Missouri. Whatever confidence he has lies in growing up in Southern California in the 60s and 70s, when that state was still truly Golden, when people like his father remembered its pre-smog palm trees, swaying in the ocean breeze, or the smell of orange blossoms permeating the air from orchard upon orchard of citrus. Now? Even when he was in high school he and his classmates fantasized, Ed Abbey-style, about burning down the stick-built condos and faux-Italian villa houses that were replacing the groves. He first made love in an orange grove. Tried a clove cigarette there with Syd and Lindsay; he nearly barfed but he still remembers the grove. Hunted rats that hung out in the smudge pots in one of the rare times he ran with a pack of boys. But mostly he body-surfed and played beach volleyball. So after trying five different first sentences to his article, he Googles "San Diego beaches" and feasts, for a good ten minutes, on postcard shots of places he knows well. Then he screen-saves one, and bookmarks the website for future reference. He tries writing a first sentence of the article again. *Around 1150 A.D., a violent sequence of events took place at a small Puebloan habitation site (5MT15403) in southwestern Colorado...*Ok. Is that okay? He has no reference point, no trust. He tries a second sentence but by then it is like trying to stand on a surfboard in turbulent water. He wants to call George, yet he knows he is the wrong person for this.

So he calls Steve's cell phone. His heart is beating loudly, but when Steve answers, it sounds like he's driving a semi.

"Where are you?" John asks.

"I drive a backhoe a couple of times a week," he says. "Pays my tuition when I'm not out on a project. Or sometimes I dig the trenches for a project."

"Oh. Can I read you something?"

"Sure."

So he reads him the sentences. "Good," Steve says, a beep-beep-beep sound emanating now. "Keep going. Call me tonight. I gotta go."

No doubt, John thinks. He was probably backing up into a ditch.

But it worked. The phone call worked. Steve the Brilliant said the sentences were good. John lets out a lot of held air. He switches out his screen saver to a new one, to a photo of Seal Rocks, heavy with seals. *Hello my friends.* A weight drops on his sternum. What he would give to be with them right now. He writes the whole first paragraph on that memory, his fingers now registering more quickly the position of letters on the keyboard, his brain warmed up. *Seven individuals* – S fourth finger of left hand, e third finger of left, v second on left – so much of this is left! He even smiles a little. He is wildly ambidextrous, always has been. Maybe the act of typing is not so bad. The phone rings.

Jensen.

"How is it going?"

"Colleen!" he says. He is appalled at his own elation. "I *like* typing!"

"You do? Why?"

"It uses both hands. I use both hands a lot."

He can practically hear her smile. "Rock on, John, as my freshmen would say."

"Why haven't I noticed this before?"

"Fear, John, makes people unbelievably stupid." And she chuckles good-bye.

Men, women, and children – were systematically dismembered and defleshed... Ick. New screen saver. This time he Googles Mammoth Lakes. Inyo Forest. Tioga Pass. Another ten minutes staring at all that, the habitat of his deepest hour with Meghan. The scene of many a trip with Sweeney. Considerable archeology. Two more paragraphs, very slow because now he is doing the literature review and he has to reference every sentence. Sweeney used to do this, not him. The flipping back and forth between text and reference could send the gigantic p's and q's flying again. But Jensen has suggested colors, and so, when he has to stop, he highlights the last word in bright purple. Then finds the reference. Comes back. Thanks to purple, he can find it again easily. He also puts it in caps. Then changes it out when he is done inserting the information.

He stands up and gets iced tea. Returns, spends ten minutes Googling on the Puebloan southwest. Taos. Zuni. Old Shalako dance pictures, the looming Katchinas in the dark December night. Hopi. Then prehistoric ruins. Mesa Verde, Betatakin, Hovenweep. A glance at the rocks of Monument Valley, one final Google to Goosenecks State Park, where the San Juan nearly doubles back on itself through deep layers of rock. Not too far from their site. Not too far.

Out of the literature review. It's dark by now. He is not even hungry. He hears, dimly, Coco go to his food and crunch with sharp little cat teeth. Then the delicate slap of water on his tongue as he drinks, the swish of the cat door. Coco is out for his nightly prowl. John looks up. His reflection comes back to him in the dark pane of glass on the other side of his computer. He almost smiles at it. Two more sentences. Then, as his stomach makes its first growl and he realizes his rear end is nearly asleep, he Googles the Mojave. Joshua Tree, Death Valley, Kelso Dunes. He is on the fifth photo, of Death Valley in rare spring bloom, when the phone rings again.

"John." It's Lindsay.

He has been waiting.

"He died, didn't he?"

"Yes," she says, simply, and it is all she needs to say.

III.

The funeral is a full Mass, a hundred or so people, sprays of white lilies around his father's coffin. Old men with their World War II hats, a cadre of nurses and administrators from the hospital, his mother and father's friends from over the years, his sisters and their families, John, Sweeney, cousins, aunts, uncles. The church is spacious and light without being too modern, stone and stained glass still the predominant architectural materials, the incense floating in curlicues up to the ceiling, altar boys in white robes, the hymns and smell of the incense and the light through the glass working on him in a way it has always worked on him, as if he were wrapped in a strange, heavenly woman's body. He can stand Mass because he finds himself in a lush riot of sound and smell and light; when he was little sometimes he would just close his eyes and breathe in the incense, or the clean soap of the man behind him, or his mother's perfume. The maroon cushions on the fold-down prayer benches, the dark gloss of the pews themselves, the formality of their layout in rows, the pulpit higher than the rest of the altar and jutting, the organ with its pipes off to one side. He loved all that ethereal beauty, that paean to heaven, that creation of sacred space. The Catholics are good at this; as Meghan once put it, at least they never forsook art and beauty the way her Puritan ancestors did. The unmarried priests telling married people what to do, the strictures against abortion and birth control on a planet with too many people, the primacy of the Pope, the guilt trip laid on him every week in Confession – he can do without these. But can he do without his history with it? Can he do without his Catholic genes, some French Canadian, some English in spite of Henry the Eighth? And can he do without a Jesus who, as one of his padres taught in high school, was a champion of subverting the social order, of upending power structures? ("Turn to Mark, Chapter 2, verses 1-12. Look at 7. 'Why does this *man* speak blasphemies like this? Who can forgive sins but God alone?' My, my, how upset the powers-that-be were!") This was the 70s, and liberation theology in Latin America was this padre's passion, but John knew he was lucky to be taught by a bunch of socially conscious Jesuits in general. He absently picks up the Bible while one of his father's VFW buddies drones on, and flips to The Gospel of Mark. Sweeney throws him a curious look. John smiles slightly at her. The sad reality of Christ being co-opted by new power structures will hit as soon as he runs into language that makes his toes curl, so he flips to Matthew, the Beatitudes, then accidentally ends up at John: "Whoever eats My flesh and drinks My blood has eternal life, and I will raise him up at the last day. For My flesh is food indeed, and My blood is drink indeed. He who eats My flesh and drinks My blood abides in Me and Me in him."

In light of the kiva at Tin Cup Wash, whose details he has been immersed in, this makes him bilious, as if he is reading a vampire book, not the Bible. He puts it back, his stomach balled and his mouth wanting to spit. But the butchered bones do abide in him, and he in them. He remembers jerking awake, once, several days after Warren and he had finished wrapping the bones for transport and analysis. The night was dead still, no moon, the oppressive cloud cover of late August monsoons waiting ominously to build into some kind of storm. Lightning flickered in the far distance and flashed on the walls of his tent, soundless. He was covered in sweat, and even though he opened his eyes he could not erase the image of a human skull laughing raucously at him. *No one's a Noble Savage, John-Boy. Not a one of us. Hah hah hah.* The skull was cracked on one side, carmel-colored from fire-roasting, but its awful teeth were intact in its mandible and bony gums.

He swallows, closing the Bible just as the priest recites the words he has just read, more or less, in preparation for Communion. Why this emphasis on the actual body – communion *the* central rite – when the rest of the time Christianity denounced the body as separate from the spirit, splitting heads from hearts, telling him that his tactile sensibil-ities and kinesthetic wiring and need for human touch were sinful? And why, when the body does show up in the Bible, it is so grisly, so devoid of joy? As if its sole purpose on earth was to illicit suffering and not pleasure? What, then, did this mean for his swim with the seals? His times of great sex? His love of the smooth feel of obisidian and the satisfaction of hitting a rock just so to form a tool? Was all that profane? Was *that* why he kept Meghan at arm's length? Or went for the married Lanie? He rolls his eyes. Was he infested, as Meghan would say, with a run-of-the-mill virgin-whore complex? God almighty.

He watches as people begin to form lines to take bread and wine at the altar. The appeal of history fades away, as does his Catholic ancestry. In the end it always comes to this – that he, the kinesthetic body boy, feels like a charlatan in this church, not human, not real, not legitimate. No respite from the shame of school ever awaited him in the hallowed halls of his church. No doubt some kind padre would re-interpret the whole thing for him, but the damage had been done. It whittles down to that for John – that for most of it to make sense he has to apply pretzel logic, a kind of psychotherapy, to the text itself. And he is struck too, his chaise lounge conversations with Steve in his sights even as they stand for a hymn and his father's coffin shines under the chandelier, how egotistical Jesus sounds, how much the "I" voice predominates, how much they are supposed to believe him and only him, as if that alone will make the rains come and benevolently shelter the corn at Chaco Canyon. Why didn't Europe do what the Pueblos did, when faced with the failure of a system grown too large for itself? Why didn't they retrench and start preaching sustainability to their kids instead of expansionism, colonialism, nightmare?

He smirks, the archeologist that in the last analysis he will always be back in charge in his pew. *Ship technology, Dude,* says Steve in his ear drum, a disembodied voice. *Imagine if Europe had not had ship technology. And horses. And gunpowder. And a ton of malnourished landless young men for whom the promise of land could never be fulfilled in the home country.*

He rises to begin his own march to the altar, his mother and sisters in front of him. *I am not heaven-bound by these reckonings,* John thinks, looking at the coffin. And his father, the Coyote loping in the desert, in spite of all this Mass and lifelong service to the church, is not either.

* * * *

His parents' home becomes the scene of a potluck after the service. Sweeney finds herself in conversation with Lindsay, and John can tell his sister is probing gently into the folds of their marriage, ever curious about her baby brother's life. They eat fruit salad on the patio. Syd asks how he is doing, tells him about his niece and nephew, who are in late adolescence and standing by a deli platter with fruit punch in their hands. They look tall, big, athletic. Indeed they are, she says, droning on about volleyball scholarships and all-state this and that. John says hello to them and then slips into the cool dimness of the house. His father's den retains the wood paneling so popular in his childhood, and is therefore a dark room. He turns on a light. His mother has begun cleaning out his drawers, and on his desk John sees a baby book. His baby book.

He had no idea his parents kept this, much less that it existed. He opens it. Faded Kodachrome photos with pretty serrated edges greet him. Black-and-white, too. His father holding him, grinning, his mother's caption reading: "Mel gets a son!" As if to say, "Finally!" The Legacy.

John swallows. Some son. He dares to glance only at a few more pictures before it becomes too hard. John, in kindergarten. Already, a hollow look to the eyes, swimming upstream in school, not understanding why he feels so different. He moves away abruptly from the album with its hollow-eyed child, and is looking again at his father's Iwo Jima buddy picture when his mother quietly enters the room.

"You can have that," she says, standing next to him. "You always seemed to like that picture."

"Thanks," he says.

"Oh, and your baby book. Did you see I found that?"

"Yes."

"Take that too." She smiles at him. "He loved you, you know."

He looks at her funny. She flushes. "I found the note you wrote him in the hospital. The one you crossed out."

He doesn't know what to say. The room ticks. His mother swallows. "He wasn't perfect, John. I hope you can forgive him."

She touches his arm lightly. This is too easy and too hard, all at once. He wants to run screaming from this forced religious sentiment, from the urge all too-nice women have to gloss over the pain and preach forgiveness when it seems to him that forgiveness has to come from some long process of rinsing and cleansing. A fierce anger at her for holding his father back biles up in him. Then anger at Sweeney for doing the same to himself. He knows it's not right, that anger, and he shifts it once more to his father, to himself, for capitulating so easily. To forgive all that? Here? Now?

His mother looks at him curiously but when he says nothing she turns to the baby book, still wistful. "Do you see how cute you were? Lindsay was frankly chubby. Syd, colicky. You were my favorite baby. Did you know that?"

"Mom…" he says, because he is about to cry. She's already crying, quietly.

"Did you ever think you wanted children, John?" she asks. After a lifetime of chit-chat, she seems to need genuine talk now that her husband is gone.

He feels desperately sorry for her even as her question feels invasive. So "Yes," John says, barely able to stand this confession still. But he has already confessed to Lindsay and so he has less hesitation this time. "Yes, I think – now – it's taken a while – but now I know I would have liked that very much."

A sound makes them turn. Sweeney's in the doorway, her throat clearing. John knows immediately that she has heard every word of his confession. The air goes unbearably thick. They stare at each other, wary in the forest. His mother freezes, as if she can sense she is too close to some animal misfire. And then Sweeney's wheels on her haunches and forfeits, leaving the doorway an empty rectangle of light and accusation.

IV.

"You *bastard*," she screams at him in the rental car. They're parked outside Lindsay's, post-potluck. Lindsay and her son James are inside and so the car is the only place of privacy.

"Sweeney – "

"No, you listen. You *never once* told me you wanted to have kids."

"What good would it have done? You tied your tubes two years into our relationship."

"You could have said something then."

"You never talked about it with me before you went and did it."

"I did *too*. In a tent in the Oregon desert. Or don't you remember? It was cold and the wind was howling but we were happy. And we talked about archeology and how hard it was to even be married in that life, much less have a family. And I asked you if you could see yourself being a father and you said no."

John stares straight ahead at the dark street. "I was twenty-seven. We didn't even get married for three years. I had no sense I'd be capable of being a father," he says. His failure sits on him like a wet blanket.

"So why do you know now that you'd be capable? When did you get this realization?"

"I don't know I'd be capable. I just – know – I just know –" John can't say more without Meghan coming up. Without her barely pregnant form getting on an airplane in an airport swarming with families. Without sensing her nursing her four-month-old son on a bed, the last time he ever saw her.

"Do you know," she asks, turning to him, her face bloated and red with tears, her fingers removing a strand of blonde-gray hair from her face, "how fucking *hard* it is for a woman to have kids and be a professional, *still*? Did any one of your women profs in school have kids? Or if they did, what kind of family life they had? I knew *one* woman, John. One. And she wasn't my idea of a good role model. I went to a conference just two years ago, John. For women archeologists. Remember that? You were out at Fish Lakes doing survey, but I went. And someone from the corporate world was there to tell us how to negotiate jobs as women, and she asked how many of us had kids. The room was half academics, half contract people. Most of us had advanced degrees. Do you know how many people raised their hands, John? Do you *know?*"

"No I don't know." He can't keep the irritation out of his voice. Of course he doesn't know.

"There must have been a hundred people in that room. About five – *five*, John – raised their hands. Even the corporate lady was stunned. She had two. Motorola took better care of her kids than academia or the archeology world ever did."

"But you made your decision about no kids long before that conference."

"True. But I knew I was up against all that, and it was way worse twenty years ago, believe me. All that *bullshit* where work and motherhood can't mix. Sometimes I envy the African women who run marketplace stalls and keep the whole nine yards together while five children go with them, crawling underfoot, watching each other, having other mothers around to watch too. But that doesn't really matter. I - I –" she chokes up, the fury sliding to grief – "I knew since I was ten I didn't want kids anyway."

"You did?"

"Yes. I had a horse. I loved that horse. It was enough. I loved being outside. I loved Laura Ingalls Wilder until she had a family. Then I lost all interest. I'm just –" she sobs – "That's just not *me*."

So I have, really, told her essentially that I wanted another woman, another life.

"Sweeney, I'm sorry," he says, his tongue so thick he can barely speak.

"I am too, John," she says. "I am too."

CHAPTER 11

I.

The next two weeks he moves through the world as if wading through molasses. Sweeney has to leave for the field and uses that as an excuse to pack quickly and get out of the house. He tries to ask if they still have a marriage but she has clammed up, and shakes her head vehemently, her lips sealed, when he tries to address this. Finally she barks, "I don't *know*, John! Why don't you figure that out for yourself?" and so he backs off, waving feebly as she disappears down the driveway and out to the western Utah desert. He has seen more emotion out of her in the past two weeks than he has for most of twenty-five years.

Mellars, on the other hand, is gleeful when King suggests they carpool down to Pecos together and stop by the site on the way down. His wood sprite happiness almost lifts John's spirits, and then he collapses back into the molasses as soon as he is out of Mellars' presence. Their site will already be backfilled, of course – standard operating procedure once excavations are completed and all parties satisfied. But the aura of the place, its situation in a dry and desolate land on an upslope toward Sleeping Ute Mountain, will still be worth revisiting. He wonders what he'll think, seeing the saltbush and sandy wash, the site covered over with innocuous dirt. Had he known what it would bring upon him he might never have ventured there, though King, unbelievably, has approved John's rough draft, albeit with extensive commentary. Something in King seems to care about his success; John has never seen a contract boss vet a report as heavily but without apparent exasperation. He called Steve at least a dozen times after his first day writing the introduction – Steve who told him to read Mark Varien over again ("people respond to social landscapes as well as environmental") and an historian named Gutierrez John had never heard of. ("Man, that dude taught me more about Pueblo social organization than all the ethnographies combined. Anyway, he says Pueblo culture is one constant mitigation against factionalization." "But what," John asked, "can I really say about that anyway in the article?" Steve was silent for a minute. "Maybe not much. That's the great thing about this damn field, huh? Answer one question and five equally fascinating ones rise up. And then your colleagues tell you you can't talk about half of them. Makes you want to piss in all their faces, I swear.") He hung up smiling at Steve's vinegar, elated in a way he could not explain. He was openly looking for help and therefore not slyly asking for a crutch from anyone. Colleen cheered him on in the background.

Mellars is building a toy barn with toothpicks when John walks into King's conference room for a meeting. Warren and John watch him idly until King comes into the room. Steve will join them at the site, hitch-hiking up from Albuquerque, and they will hash out, pow-wow style, their composite presentation at Pecos. The Utes have okayed their camping for a night on their land, though King thinks they will be rained out. It always rains in *torrents*, he says, in early August. Monsoons, you know, he harrumphs. John sneaks Warren a look that asks, seriously, how he has ever spent time with this man in the field. Warren hisses back, under his voice, "Ah, Grasshoppa. You must be patient," which brings on a fit of the giggles on both their parts that they have a hard time suppressing. It is the first time John has laughed since the funeral.

"Something bothering you boys?" King asks, his conference room empty but for them and Mellars.

"Uh, no," they say, but Mellars has taken the stage anyway.

"What will I need? Sleeping bag? Tent? What else?" He is hopping off his chair like a kid. His toothpick barn falls down.

"When's the last time you went camping, Mellars?" Warren asks.

"Ten years. I know, it's bad. I am like a mole who lives underground for most of my time, then pops up to find the real world exists after all."

"Only your mole den has fluorescent lights, multiple stories, a lot of sick people, and microscopes."

"Don't forget other moles."

"Gad, what are your parties like?"

"What parties?" And they all laugh.

II.

From: George Ward
To: John Thompson
Sent: Monday July 20, 2007
Subject: Life
Dear John Wayne Gregory-bro:
How are you? How's life?

Dear George:
I think my wife is leaving me. Life is terrible.

Dear John Wayne Gregory-bro:
I'm sorry. When you get here I'll tell you another story, just as bad. About a guy who rolled a car when he was drunk and killed someone. Killed two someones, really. Can you – I am hoping – you will fill the shoes, maybe, of one of them. Stupid, eh? Like that will rectify the whole thing.

Dear George:
Fill their shoes? Damn. That's pressure, George. I am a fuck-up. I repeat that: I am a fuck-up.

sent: July 21
subject: re: Life
Dear JWG-b:

I lost my best friend, among others. (::::::. Not that I could tell you this face to face. Too HEAVY all this. So let's switch the subject (Fake Guy Cheer, here. We are a beer commercial.) Why did you like Indian stuff so much?

Dear George:
Beer commercial relief coming back at you. I wanted to know how to live off the land.

Dear JWG-B:
Why?

sent: July 23
Dear George:
Because everything else is bullshit. Money is an abstraction. Shrink-wrapped steroid-infested beef at the market is an abstraction. How do you eat an abstraction? Why do you want to go whale hunting?

Dear JWG-B:
Because it's initiation, eh? We all lack initiation. We used to have it until you guys came along. And you white guys seem to have no clue about that. You do it all wrong.

Dear George:
What do you mean?

JWG-B:
For example, Everest. Everest???!! What the FUCK is THAT??? Guys in Spandex overachieving their way up a peak. Spare me.

Dear G:
Guys in bear grease grunting after a whale in a canoe for god's sake.

173

sent: July 26
Dear JWG-B:
With our elders. Our brothers. With boats we made ourselves.
Harpoons, seal skin floats, cedar line. All that we did ourselves. Our
teachers were right there. Older men. Fathers. Present. And the whale
– this is key, John Wayne – the whale was something brought back for
all the others. Testosterone's just an energy. Not good, not bad. It's what
you do with it that counts. Ever read Black Elk Speaks?

Dear George:
Ye-es. Long time ago. But isn't Black Elk Speaks written down by a
White Guy?

Dear JWG-B:
Of course. Typical. But no biggie in this case. There's a good little
lesson in there. Go to the part about the buffalo hunt. About what the
hunt advisors tell the young men. Go do it. Go. Now.

sent: July 29
Dear George:
Okay. I found Sweeney's tattered copy from 8 thousand years ago,
when she went to college. I found the hunt. I found the passage. It says:
You can be as macho as you like, but if you bring back meat and do not
share it with the widows and orphans and families without hunters, you
are less than scum.

Dear JWG-B:
Precisely. Now tell me Everest is anywhere near that.

Dear George:
I see your point. I humbly kneel at your Makah knee.

sent: Aug 2

Dear JWG-B:
Fuck off.

Dear George:
I am on the road for the next week. Big presentation. I will email you when I'm done and tell you when I'm coming.

Dear JWG-B:
Kiss my ass. Have a good time. I just got back from 6 miles on the beach. You better come. I don't like running.

I love you, too, John thinks, but George's confession about the best friend could make him sob if he doesn't watch it. He is stunned at all the pain in the world. His mother gave him a small box of his father's as he was leaving their house, and he hasn't dared open it. She said there were photos, maybe a letter or two, she wasn't sure. But it was from his Marine days and since he had been a Marine, too...John swallows. Was this his father's initiation, stuck in a box? He has his bag packed for Pecos, and tucks the box inside of it. Something buckles inside, sea swell, ripple in the firmament, seismic shift. He doesn't know if he will not explode into tiny fragments in the next five seconds. He wishes Sweeney were following him out the front door. He wishes she still had faith enough to be there to kiss him good-bye. He wishes her feminine form would remain in his rear-view mirror as he drives away. But she's not there, her faith is gone, and he has the neighbor kid keeping an eye on Coco.

III.

The company Suburban has the air of a vehicle inured to dirt but vacuumed for purposes of starting a trip clean. The cracks are permanently infiltrated with sand, telltale bits of red dust, small dried pellets of mud. These you find when you drop something between the seat and the door and go fishing for it, only to discover that your piece of paper or sunglasses or what-have-you has to be blown free of dirt, and that your fingernails need cleaning. Open the back doors and inspect the corners; scrape your duffels and tents and coolers against ridged metallic floors venerably scratched. From the rear-view mirror hangs a dream catcher, and a bundle of sage tied with red yarn rolls around, falling apart, on the dashboard. Small totems occupy cup holders, other parts of the dashboard, insets where CD players have not been installed: skunk skulls, locust husks, seed pods, chert flakes. It is, in short, like most vehicles whose lifespan has been spent out in the more remote corners of the West, driven by archeologists and other people who have their noses constantly to the ground.

They roll out of town, south toward Provo. The Great Salt Lake valley begins to diminish behind them, Mormon billboards prevailing in the near view along the highway. None of them are very talkative yet, as if the morning were a time of private contemplation. Southeast into Price Canyon the relief of pinon-juniper, then pine, then near-tundra passes by them, and as ever John is not thinking about modern things, not really noticing fences and corrals and then the mine on their left as they cut through the heart of it. He is wondering which pinon groves have produced nuts this year, whether the deer population is fat, where the springs are in the side canyons of this crack in the mountains. He mentally reels past known lithic scatters, places he has surveyed, sources for stone tools and clay. He can see Warren scanning the same landscape, too, eyes glued to the scene out the window. Mellars, by comparison, is asleep, and King is unreadable behind the wheel in the driver's seat.

They push on to Moab for lunch. The red cliffs it is famous for begin to appear on either side of the highway, farther away at first, then closer. King starts shaking his head even before they get to town. "This place sure has changed."

Warren agrees. "Used to be a sleepy uranium town. I remember driving through here as a kid. We'd get milkshakes and sit in the park. Only big trees for miles around."

· King turns his gaze to him. "Try growing up here."

Warren colors slightly, as if one-upped in the Know-Moab department. "You grew up here?" He looks out the window as they cross the Colorado River, then the entrance to Arches National Park.

He nods. "My dad mined uranium."

"No kidding."

Moab is now a mountain bike mecca, as well as ground zero for off-road jeep trails, hiking, and other forms of recreation. It sports a bookstore, several hip cafes, a microbrew, and a big supermarket. They pull into the microbrew next to a rental RV (Cruise America!) full of Germans extracting themselves to go eat lunch in the same place they are. The car on the other side has Iowa plates. It is early August and hot, though the thunderheads are building off on a couple of horizons and John thinks King is right that it will rain later. Their arrival thankfully ends King's and Warren's exchange, and they enter an air-conditioned restaurant done up in quasi-hip pizza tavern style, with old signs scavenged from god knows where and posters of top mountain bikers and rock climbers (Fisher Towers: The Ascent of Jared Ogden) strewn about the higher places of its echoey innards.

"Modern Moab always makes me feel as if I am the sloth of the universe," Warren says, gazing at the poster of a burly woman splattered in mud tearing down a trail on a bike.

Mellars blinks in awe elsewhere. "People actually climb rocks like that?" he asks, looking at the poster of the thin red spires that comprise Fisher Towers.

"Yes," King says, "all the time."

"Why?"

They look at him. "We have no idea," they all say more or less together.

They order two pizzas and a pitcher of amber microbrew. After chewing in silence, their pizzas demolished and the pitcher largely consumed by Warren and John, Warren turns to King.

"Your dad still alive?" he asks.

"Nope." King's gone a wee bit rigid and John debates kicking Warren under the table so he won't pursue things. But Warren is Warren, the kindly leprechaun, too interested in any human story for his own good.

"What'd he die of?"

King turns his face full-on to Warren, who is seated next to him in the pizza booth. "Warren, I've known you a long time, so all right. But, man, you know how to push a guy."

"Sorry," he says. The waiter comes and they pay the bill. Outside the pavement is too bright and Mellars agrees to take the wheel.

King and Warren are ahead of John. They each get in the back, and leave John to the passenger seat up front.

"Lung cancer," he says to Warren, as they settle in, his voice low so at least Mellars and John will know to pretend not to hear. "What do you think you die of when you mine uranium for a good chunk of your life?"

* * * *

To have an archeological sensibility in this country is to occupy a landscape, John realizes now, of grief. If he sees a film with a Huron Avenue in it, he doesn't think about Boston or whatever city the street is in. He thinks about something much older, the trampled remains after which the street is named; he thinks of the Huron on the Canadian border of New York. He thinks how they were the northernmost of the corn-growers before the season got too short and they moved into the boreal forest of the caribou-hunting Cree. He thinks then of the Iroquois and their League of Nations, how the Declaration of Independence was borrowed heavily from their form of governance, a fact his rebel priests from high school loved to point out. Moving west, he remembers, once, being on survey in the Badlands of South Dakota, and stopping at Wounded Knee on some weekend when camp seemed too windy and lonely to stay in. He knew then, Selma long past, the slave quarters of plantations dug up and exposed for their throw-away cuts of meat and ugly crockery, that somehow this, Wounded Knee, was now the epicenter of unresolved sorrow in this country.

Meghan said once that she was able to fall apart in Europe not only because it was far from lethal home, but because there was no break in historical continuity. A bench made in 1300 A.D. was still in use by the same relative peoples who made it in the first place. A bench made in 1300 A.D. in the Southwestern United States would likely be in a kiva, a ruined kiva, made by a people nearly destroyed by the invaders from Europe. "It's that rupture I can't stand, John," she'd say. "That total break. I can hold Holocausts and wars and famine and bizarre religions if it all makes sense. If you can connect the dots. But in America I am always feeling that to connect the dots is un-patriotic. I'm supposed to shut up and go to Wal-Mart. I'm not supposed to have a past."

John will see the name Winnemucca while driving I-80 in Nevada and think: Shoshone. He sees Minnesota on a map and thinks: the Sioux before they got kicked westward thanks to fur trapping pressure, before they figured out horses and roamed the Plains. Mississippi: The Natchez, Cahokia mounds, Arikara mass graves full of Indians diseased from DeSoto's men. Utah: old name for Ute. And by the time they roll toward Cortez (named by settlers who thought the ruins around there were from the Aztecs; hence, also, Montezuma County and Aztec, New Mexico) he is hung up on Narrangineap Irrigation Canal, Weeminuche Wilderness, Ute Pass, Moenkopi, Awatovi, Teec Nos Pos, Chinle, Tsaile.

What is left of that world? What is left of this one?

They arrive at their campsite. The air is cool, clouds covering everything. The breeze holds tinges of autumn, and John knows they are at the turning point of the summer. Turning points are thin places between worlds, like Hallowe'en. He has always felt them, even in relatively seasonless San Diego. He squats heavily and pulls up a twig of ephedra. Mormon Tea. Bright green plant that looks as if a bundle of praying mantises got together and formed a bush. The twig is bitter. But he knew it would be. Called ephedra, but really pseudoephedrine, not the stuff that kills athletes. Out here, out in the Mojave even, it was used as a way to keep going when the hunger pangs got to be too much. So it conjures up feeble hunting parties full of Indians with sinew-backed bows. Mormon hand cart crazies, their supplies low, their ruts still visible in red slickrock over by Bluff. All that in one, simple twig. It is odd to be back at the site after a year.

Warren squats beside him. "Do you think our kiva people were brewing Mormon Tea so as to get up enough energy to grind up rice grass?"

John chews. "Or to kill their own?"

They look out on this sere habitat, this dream of dust and backfill and Steve's lone juniper, occupied, lo and behold, by Steve.

"Christ," Warren says, heaving up to go meet their companion. "Je-sus Christ."

* * * *

Mellars gleefully tends the fire, telling them he first got interested in chemistry thanks to pyromania as a teenager. "I loved blowing things up."

"Great," Steve says. "How come you didn't go work for some bomb factory?"

Mellars pokes the fire with a stick. "My tastes matured,

obviously." But he smiles an impish smile as sparks fly from a knot undone by heat.

They extract the jerry-rigged grill from the back of the Suburban, an iron thing with legs and a piece of grate material more often seen on storm drains than barbeques. It spits a little at them from the sky as they put the steaks on, but holds out through dinner, dessert, a second round of beer as they begin hashing out their talk.

King, his used car salesman hair uncharacteristically flattened under a Burton snowboarding hat ("You snowboard, bro?" asks Steve. "Yes, actually..."), looks much more like an aging hippie than a business owner. His John Lennon glasses reflect the fire in their lenses, his five o'clock shadow a considerable beast John has never seen before. This is a man who must shave daily or achieve a beard in short order.

"John needs to introduce the site. And the participants," he says.

"I was thinking a panel. Four of us lined up in chairs behind one of those fold-out banquet tables," John says. "What time are we presenting?"

"It's a 3:15 session," King replies, scratching at his scalp from over the hat. "I tried to argue for a campfire discussion, to make it more informal, but they don't do that anymore."

"They don't?" Warren asks. "Damn, those used to be great."

"When's the last time you went to a Pecos Conference?" Steve asks.

"Uh, ten years? Embarrassingly long. I was always in the field, thanks to this putz." He lightly taps King's arm.

King scowls. "You could have just said the word, my friend."

"I know. I have no excuse. But they used to do these campfire things. Everybody'd be on their fifth beer by then and it could get lively."

"Probably why they canned that idea," Mellars says.

"Naw," Warren snorts. "It's because the folks running it now are uncool old farts. Old farts back then were trying to be hippie cool. Breaking up marriages, doing dope, brewing things in their basements, holding campfire talks. Nowdays it's all about being respectable."

"Too bad," Steve says, swilling the last of his beer.

"It's okay," Mellars says. "Biochem and doctors have nothing like even the modern Pecos. We think if it isn't taking place in a Hilton it can't be serious."

"That's because your research happens in civilized laboratories, not in the great outdoors," Warren says, breathing deeply and expanding his arms into the damp air.

"Maybe. But we're still looking at creepy little diseases you really don't want to know about."

They chuckle and agree that John will introduce everyone and set the stage for the site. They have forsworn high technology ("It's a Pecos Conference, not the goddamn SAAs!" Warren proclaims, referring to the Society for American Archeology meetings, which do tend to take place in Hiltons), and have a map of the site location on a big board, then an easel for a couple of other graphics. Mellars will then do the bone and turd talk.

"Too bad Jennie Schultz couldn't come," Steve says. Flickers of lightning line the dying sunset sky to the west, the thunder audible by now.

"Yeah. She did a great job. She gave me an easy report to read," Mellars adds.

"But a blind woman would have made us look a little more P.C., you gotta admit," Warren says. "Round out the panel."

"Of course," Mellars says. "But I am an elfin white guy with dyslexia, three advanced degrees, and a Pekinese. Isn't that okay?"

"You own a Pekinese?"

"Damn straight."

"Too bad you didn't bring it along," King says.

John stuffs a laugh. "That's the first scale, then. Site scale. I want Warren to continue that with the pollen analysis and descriptions of the site itself. You know, how everything was left intact, no wood burned or scavenged. Then Steve can take it out locally to the other sites in the area, to the soil types, then regionally."

"What do you get to do?" Warren asks. "Sit back and say nothing?"

"I'd, uh, like that."

"Forget it. You do the site descriptors."

John sighs. "Okay, okay. But I have to wrap everything up, too. And take questions."

"We'll all take questions, sweetheart," says Steve. And as he finishes, what was a growl of thunder rattles closer and then the next flash is blinding.

"Shit," John says. Mellars looks white as a sheet.

Warren licks his finger and holds it up. "Coming right this way."

"Fuck," King says. Flash boom again, and the wind begins sweeping through. The temperature drops ten degrees in seconds.

Warren beelines for the back of the Suburban and starts throwing duffels and sleeping bags inside.

"What're you doing?" Mellars asks.

"It's gonna douche!" Warren yells above the thunder and wind. They all pile in the truck. The lightning outlines them and the truck like ghosts. Mellars is still white.

"Holy cow," he says.

And the rain begins.

* * * *

After an hour, their tents soaked and sagging outside, King resigns himself. The thunder has gone, but the rain is quite steady. "Let's go to the Holiday Inn. I'll put it on the company card. We can pick up the tents in the morning."

"Aw…" Mellars says.

"You want to camp in this?" Warren asks.

"I would," Steve says.

Warren sighs. "That's because you are thirty years old and a mere babe. By the time you're my age you start thinking differently."

John has to say he is with Warren. It is discomfiting, this increasing reliance on fossil fuels and mattresses, but the Holiday Inn beckons, so why not?

"Mellars and I could stay out here," Steve volunteers.

"It's okay," Mellars grouses. "We're going to be camping at Pecos, right?"

"Yessirree Bob. It's all set up in Greer Garson's field."

"Greer Garson? The actress?"

King nods. "She owns a ranch out by Pecos near Santa Fe. The Forked Lightning Ranch."

Mellars pales again. "I admit I don't like lightning."

Warren claps his shoulder from the rear seat. "Don't worry, my friend. New Mexico has the highest strikes per capita outside of Florida."

"Sweet," Steve says.

"Pooey," Mellars says, and they all begin a desultory, slithery, slog to Cortez.

* * * *

King magnanimously insists that as Project Director, John should have a room to himself. Warren mutters that this probably has more to do with making Mellars feeling included – by bunking with the head cheese – than anything else, but John nonetheless feels a little special, as if the Great Father himself has deemed him important enough for his own motel room. Warren and Steve pair up and move in next door.

The silence, though, post-campfire camaraderie and the expectation of sleeping in a tent, seems odd. He cracks a window to let in the cool, rainy air and unpacks a toothbrush and a pair of sweatpants. His father's box spills out of his duffel and John goes still. The box is maybe six-by-eight, an old stationary box. It has old-fashioned embossing on the front, as if wedding invitations once nestled inside, or elegant thank-you notes. A funny box for a man, but then if his father needed a box he would have asked his wife or mother for one, in all likelihood. His life was not like Sweeney's, or Warren's, or even John's own; Amazon.com with its swooping insignia and two-day shipping did not clutter up his father's house with cardboard.

He puts his sweatpants on and sits heavily on the bed. He tenders the box in his hands. The lid comes off reluctantly, as if it has not been opened in a long time. His mother said something about the Marines, as if whatever contents lay within had to do with warfare, or at least armed service. The first photo confirms this – it is another, slightly less well posed, shot of his father with his two Iwo Jima buddies. Black-and-white, crinkled edges. He flips it over. In faded ink, he finds "Me. John Tate. Hank Latham. 1944." The second picture is of a Higgins boat. Huh. John associates those with D-Day, but when he flips it over he sees it isn't a Higgins boat at all. "Jap prototype for later Higgins," his father wrote. Gad. Even then he was interested in the minutiae of history. Underneath that is a small notebook, black with grid paper, like a portable accounting book, with photos tucked inside. In dark pencil, often smeared, John makes out dates, small notices. "Rough seas." "John T. owes me for poker." "Yelled at for not cleaning my gun but I did clean it." Then: "I am not good at writing but I started keeping this because I needed some place to put it all. We've been fighting for a month on this island. I have seen things I never thought I would. Goddamn bodies rotting in the sun. Tried to turn over a soldier today and his head didn't go with his body. I bolted off into the bushes after that." Photos, stashed in the pages. Dead bodies, boots in the Pacific. A dark object falling out of a cocoanut palm: "Jap shot and killed out of tree."

John squints closer at it, now that he knows it's a human body. It is mostly a blur, but he can see a hand, the shape of a leg. He puts it back and turns the page. "John T. saved my ass. I end up with just a little shrapnel in my shoulder, not dead, as he has a sixth sense and told me to duck even though I could see nothing coming." Photo: John Tate. 1945, March. "Shithead grin. Great." A few blank pages follow, then two months later. "It just gets worse now that it's summer. Rumors that the Japs don't have resupply, are scraping by on their own dead. I don't want to hear it."

The long-ago day when John hunted urchins in tide pools returns to him, his father an interested silhouette all of a sudden. What did he say? *Ate that way in the Pacific sometimes. Japs had us pinned...*

John hesitates. Reads on, more slowly than ever, his stomach doing slow figure eights. What did his father do with his own rations in short supply? But new angle of war greets him instead: "I had to kill one up close yesterday" his dad wrote next. "He was wounded, howling like a wolf. What bothers me is I killed him less 'cause he was beyond help but because I just wanted him to shut up. I even said SHUT UP before I shot him. Went away shaking. John and Hank and Scottie P. made me drink half a flask to put it out of my mind. John says we're all not right out here." Three days later: "John T. RIP. Fuck. John T. I will name any son I get lucky enough to have after you." A picture follows this, not too close, the generic shot of the dead soldier, lying face down. All his father could stand, no doubt, but wanting the memento, the final thing.

John puts the diary and photos aside, his finger marking his place. With his other hand he wipes his forehead. All these years and he thought John Wayne was the reason for his name. His father never once mentioned a John Tate. Nor Hank Latham nor Scottie for that matter. He talked about his superiors, his mess cook, the names of the ships he traveled on. But not those men, even though they grinned out of a picture frame in his study. *Did they all die?* John looks back to the book. This segment of his father's life even his mother knew nothing about. "Your dad never talked about the war," she said. "They were all like that. Only time they talked was in the hospital, moaning when the morphine wore off." His mother, the nurse. The good Catholic. The one who never questioned what price she paid, they all paid, for that colossal silence.

There are only two more photos in the book. John turns to them and stares. They are the grisliest he has ever seen. A man with his thighs completely gone, just the bones left. All the muscle stripped, the intact shins picking up, puttees and boots on, where the thighs leave off. He knows what he's looking at even though he has never seen such a thing before. It makes the butchery at Tin Cup look definitively more orchestrated, sacrificial, ceremonial. There the parts were disarticulated from the rest of the body, hacked up, the skulls roasted, everything finally and righteously stuffed into a ventilator shaft. In the photo the soldier with his thigh meat gone is simply the victim of defleshing for the sake of a long-needed meal, the butchery of desperation. The next photo has a man with arms and legs done in the same way, nothing left but a torso with bones sticking out.

He turns the photos over. They say the same thing. "Jap dead cannibalized." That's all. Then one last entry in the book: "Rumor has it they done this to a couple of our scouts. Hank L. is out on patrol to make sure. Jesus. We're pretty hungry too sometimes but Jesus. What do we tell those scouts' families if so? Jesus. Now I *have* to study history when I get done here. Have to. Because I need to damn well know why."

PART SIX

CHAPTER 12

I.

The Pecos Conference is at Pecos National Monument this year because it is its 50th anniversary, and Pecos was the first place it was ever held. Alfred Kidder "discovered" stratigraphy at that long hump of buried humanity southeast of Santa Fe, where tribes from the Plains traded with tribes from the mountains and mesas to the west for hundreds of years. The car ride down has been moderately quiet until Pagosa Springs, when, after good coffee and pastries at a trendy little bakery there, all tongues but John's loosen up a bit. His mind is stuck on what he heard, in the motel room after seeing the pictures. It was a small, soft cry, like that of a wounded animal. He must have made that cry, but he doesn't remember feeling it; it seems to have come from somewhere so deeply inside of himself that it remained foreign, a sound he had no idea he was capable of until he produced it. Sleep had been a business of sticky heaviness, then wide awake pacing at 3 a.m., and finally, in frustration more than anything, a few tears shed around five that roiled up all that he had been holding back. Wrung out, face puffy, he greeted the crew in the morning with motel coffee and an unreadable face. The shrapnel from his father's life floats and sticks inside of him, an impenetrable sorrow he dares not linger on.

Meandering talk about the possibilities of grizzlies still lurking in the south San Juan, King's story of hunting with his dad near here, the more open sheepherding land unfolding around Chama, the battered and now illegible sign appearing on the road near Tierra Amarilla, the only remnant of the politics behind a famous courthouse raid on the part of Hispanic land grant protestors who fought Anglo developers in the 1970s – all this rolls by John as they skate down the Chama river valley. They stop at the amphitheatre to pee and test their echoes against the vaulted dome of Jurassic sandstone that forms it; they talk O'Keefe and Ghost Ranch as they pass it; in Abiquiu Warren shows them how the gas station, convenience store, and land behind it is all one big site – "Hell," he says, "all of Abiquiu is just a tell. Like what they have in the Middle East."

"So is Zuni," John adds, speaking for the first time in hours. And what he has been increasingly staving off, his father's journal being replaced by another heartache, arrives full force. His time in New Mexico, the fear and hope of catching a glimpse of Meghan in Santa Fe, the memories of life out at Zuni and in town in Albuquerque – all of it comes crashing back in. He tries to ignore it, but the scenery is increasingly familiar, increasingly reminiscent.

Warren looks at him. "You all right?"

John stares back from behind his tinted glasses, a stone wall. "Yeah. Why?"

"Nothing," Warren shrugs, his kind eagerness dying back in the face of John's stare. "Seems like you woke up on the wrong side of the bed, is all."

That would about sum it up, thinks John. The Chama river dead-ends into the Rio Grande at Espanola ("heroin capital of the Southwest," Warren adds, for their edification), and they swing right toward Santa Fe. John closes his eyes, willing himself not to search for women on the street of a certain age, with long brown hair and the build of a swimmer. Comments ricochet around the truck about turquoise coyotes and street urchins with dreadlocks ("Trustafarians." Warren again. "Dude," Steve says, "is there nothing you won't comment on?" "No," Warren says). A sleek black Jaguar pulls up next to them at a stoplight and they all stare at the woman driving it.

"God, we're bad," Mellars says. "It's not as if there are no rich people in Salt Lake."

"Yeah, but they're an entirely different sort," John says. "Mormon."

"Nowhere near the hedonism you can sense here. Though Park City might compete."

"This is more like an artistic Vegas."

"Oh get out. It's not that bad."

"A hippie-shit Vegas?"

"No, that's Taos."

"How about a living adobe museum?"

"That's better."

Forty minutes later they've gone out the other side, threading through Canoncito and turning off at Glorieta onto State Road 50, where the p-j is thick and beginning to blend with ponderosa. John has always loved this little road, sniffing as it does of the only Civil War battle ever fought in New Mexico, an old Spanish adobe running at one point right up against its side as if it had never left Spain, the trees making for a narrow country lane feel. It dead-ends at a choice between Pecos National Monument to the south and right, and the higher mountains to the north and left. They turn left and eventually left again into Greer Garson's field, butting up into the Pecos Wilderness foothills. It's late afternoon by now and save for a microwave burrito at Abiquiu John hasn't eaten very much. Warren and King procure the improvised grill again, and this time the clouds hold off. It thunders up-canyon, deep into the mountains, but they've settled into a modicum of happiness with grilled rib eye steaks, a fantastic gourmet salad courtesy of Mellars ("I like to cook"), and a choice of red wine or beer. Other archeology crews mill in their sights, campfires flickering, low talk spattered with sudden laughter, the movement of one or two now and then toward the port-a-potties lined up at the edge of the field.

Visiting other fires is part of the Pecos protocol. People not seen for many field seasons show up from your past. Daryl Chapman says hi. Roger Gastineau stops to chat. ("Where you working these days, man?" Warren asks. "Mogollon, as usual. Silver City." "Oh yeah.") Then Shayla Greer, an old timer, limps their way and stops in recognition.

"Well, well, well, if it isn't Mark King." She peers at him and then the rest of them in the firelight.

"Would you like a beer, Shayla?" King asks. He seems slightly embarrassed.

She pulls up a stump and takes him up on his offer. "Thank you." Then she turns to all of them, gray braid long down her back, frizzy ringlets setting off a round and deeply creased face. Her fingernails are cracked, her hands permanently dry. But she has the tough beauty of western women who've lived outside all their lives, and if she weren't an archeologist John would say she owned a ranch, was a crack shot, and could break horses in no time flat. In either case, he'd say she had lived well and was, somewhere, profoundly content with herself.

"Mark here was my student back in the Pleistocene," she beams.

Warren sputters in mid-swig. "He's that old, huh? What kind of student was he?"

"Well, I'll tell you. A complete goof-off as an undergraduate. But then he did a transformation act five years later. Came back with some serious recommendations from folks in the field and we let him in to grad school."

"Where was this?"

"New Mexico State, back in the day," she slaps her knee. "As the kids say now. 'Back in the day!' And they mean, you know, 2001."

"It's fun getting old, isn't it, Shayla?" King says.

"You bet." She pulls in a little closer and waves her beer hand over toward them. "Now, I hear you've got a pesky little site to tell us about tomorrow."

They glance at each other nervously. They've tried to be very, very good about not saying much in public yet, but since the pollen had to be sent out, and the bones farmed to Jennie, and the tree rings went to Arizona, and archeologists of all stripes love to give each other the context for all their little laboratory pieces, and they are an incestuous bunch anyway, they're not totally surprised. They're just curious about the rumors. "What are you hearing?" Warren asks.

"The C-word, boys. The C-word." She looks at them expectantly, like a reporter awaiting verification.

"Come to our panel tomorrow, Shayla," King says. "You'll hear it all there."

"No preview of coming attractions for your old teacher?"

King smiles. "Sorry, Shayla."

She sighs and stands up. "I should have flunked you, Mark." But then she cackles. "All right. But I'm warning you –" and she again points with her beer hand, which reminds John vaguely of a gun – "expect a full house. You've got juju swirling around you like autumn leaves."

"Shit," John says, as her stout figure retreats into the fire-spotted dark.

Warren reaches up and massages John's neck, giving it two or three hard kneads. "No worries, Bro. Hakuna Matata."

"Huh?"

"*The Lion King*. Hakuna Matata. It means, in Disney's version of some African language, No Worries."

"Jesus Christ," Steve says. "What will they bastardize next?"

"Who knows? But we're all gonna be just fine, you hear?"

They clank beer bottles together, drink up, and go to bed, though John drinks – downs, actually, rather quickly – another dark microbrew ale, a poor substitute for a sleeping pill but between the histamines and the alcohol, one that works for a few hours. Then he is up again, with the moon poking out between shredding monsoon clouds, and the soft hacks and coughs of a camp asleep, popping in the dark all around him.

II.

In the morning, the Sangres in blue shadow while eastern light stripes long rays through Glorieta Pass to the south, John begins walking. He heads out to the road, catches a ride up toward Cowles with an old Hispanic man towing a trailer with a saddled horse in it so he can check some sheep he has at high pasture. He and the man start up the same trail, and he says goodbye as the man's horse takes him up faster. John hikes into the ponderosa, the smell of wet pine clearing space inside of his sinuses, his lungs, his heart. It is always uphill climbing out of canyons, but this suits him. He wants to be tired; he wants not to think; he wants to come back to the conference wrung out and in need of one sixteen-ounce Dr. Pepper to keep him adequately awake but not rankled during the panel.

He slips, once or twice, on steeper inclines that are muddy with rain, but he never falls, and eventually clears the pine into rolling meadows. To the west he sees the backside of the mountains above Santa Fe, storm clouds already forming by ten o'clock. At Wupatki he remembers the merest of clouds over the San Francisco Peaks billowing to full-fledged thunderstorms by one or two in the afternoon. He could watch another great metastasis form here, but he doesn't want to be caught in it and he wants to be sure he gives himself time to catch a ride back down the road. So after a half an hour in the meadow, where he finds a rock under a lone ponderosa to sit on and alternates between fear and hope, he slides back down his wet, tree-shaded trail. He is offered a ride back with a Benedictine monk, of all people, and it dawns on him that the upper Pecos valley, like so many in New Mexico, harbors a religious retreat and sanctuary. The monk wears ordinary clothes and tells him it is his "day off." He has been fishing the upper Pecos and is now going to Santa Fe for better groceries, and when John tells him he went to Catholic school under the Jesuits, the monk beams and tells John his own stories. He says for John to call him Peter. He uses the word "sin" once and John blanches. Peter sees it and laughs. "Sin is just not living up to your best self. It's not looking in the mirror and taking full account."

"It's not devils and hellfire?" John jokes, afraid to get into deeper religious conversation.

"Ever looked at yourself, full of accounting, in the mirror?" Peter laughs back. "Here's something," he says, turning off a very low radio. "I have spent most of my days pissed off at the Book of John. All that egotistical 'I' this, 'I' that, especially since the early Christian cults of Mary Magdalene and Thomas didn't like that gospel. It served the power interests, you know? 'I am the bread of life!' 'He who does not believe is condemned!'" He looks quizzically at John, an eyebrow raised. "BUT – I'm getting it now. I'm fifty years old and I am finally growing up."

John nods, oddly willing him to continue. "I didn't know about the early fights."

Peter the monk laughs again. He is the most joyous monk John has ever met. He stinks mildly of wet, trout-filled river and has a cooler in the back of his pick-up full of fish. "Who would? You think all those early church fathers wanted you to know about Mary and Thomas and all the other possibilities?" He snorts. "Not hardly. But anyway. Back to looking at yourself in the mirror. Open the glove box, will you?"

John does, and finds a frayed Bible, New King James version. The monk smiles wanly. "Some Bible Thumper gave me that a long time ago. 'Christ's words in red!'" He snickers.

"Is that bad?"

"No, not really." He throws John a grin, as if to say he is a hopeless man. "I just love language. I read the thing in Latin. But I'm odd, I realize. Flip to John, Chapter 3, verses 20 and 21."

"Okay."

"Now read it," he says.

John clears his throat and nervously uses his fingers to follow the lines as they bump along. "'For everyone practicing evil hates the light and does not come to the light, lest his deeds should be exposed. But he who does the truth comes to the light, that his deeds may be clearly seen, that they have been done in God.'" John looks up.

Peter beams. "Perfect. Now, what's that cringing part of yourself when you look in the mirror, but all the little demons that don't want to be seen and are therefore 'practicing evil'?"

The act of reading in a jostling pick-up while a monk watches him is about as "seen" as John would want his failures to be, and he smiles bitterly at himself. The lesson is all too clear.

Peter the monk slows down for a flatbed truck loaded with wood that is meandering in front of him. "Do you see?" He asks. "I don't know about you, but that's enough hellfire to last me the rest of my days, facing that."

They approach the Forked Lightning turn-off and John tells him to drop him there. "Thanks," he says, though he is not sure for what.

"Any time. Come do a retreat with us."

That is a notion John would never have entertained until that moment, and the strand of it that he seriously considers, fleeting as it turns out to be, startles him. He lets out air he didn't know he was holding till then, and watches the pick-up disappear down the road. He stands in silence for a minute or two before he finds legs to walk to the campsite and its cooler. He extracts the long-awaited Dr. Pepper and sandwich fixings, and eats a late lunch in relative peace. He assumes his colleagues are off listening to papers in the big circus tent northwest of the camping area, as he can hear the drone of someone's amplified presentation from his camp chair. Pieces of himself stab at him, the Catholic school boy a knife in the right ribs, somewhere near the heart; his left temporal pounding a rhythm of the twenty-year-old who, after Lanie dumped him, wanted to go with the Hispanic sheepherder into the hills or join the French Foreign

Legion or anything to leave his life behind. If his bones could pulse, what colors would they be? What sounds? But he clinches at that since immediately his left head begins a wail worthy of Muslim women at a funeral. The moment makes him physically cringe but he forces it back because if he doesn't he won't be able to eat or drink or talk. He breathes out heavily, struggling, and gazes at the southern hills where Pecos Pueblo guards the Pass. He wonders that by age fifty humans should not all be mostly dead or dying, as the human heart can only hold so many memories. He would be an elder in Ancestral Puebloan culture, lucky to be alive, but he does not feel like an elder. He feels very, very, very young.

* * * *

At three, they set up the map and line up the other posters behind it. They test the mics. A good crowd has formed; the rows of folding chairs are full. Low thunder echoes from what was his ten o'clock cloud, and the sun goes in and out of presence.

"Let's hope it doesn't do a light show," Warren says, eyeing things to the north even though he can't see the sky from under the tent.

"No shit," Steve says.

"Ready, boys?" King says.

"Sure," everyone but John says, and then a mic is in his hands and he is clearing his throat in public.

He has one brief second of seizure, of *I-can't-do-this*, but then he breaches into open air, and it is past. He knows in that moment that the gray whales have made it safely to their southern grounds off of Mexico, that George is pounding the beach in anticipation of their return, that all is about as felicitous as it can possibly be. *Now or never, John-boy,* he thinks, and something about that imprisonment frees up speech.

"Thank you all for coming. I realize, uh, we have a

provocative title to our talk, something about 'social terrorism,' I believe, and Shayla Greer informed us last night that we have 'a lot of juju' swirling around us." People actually laugh, Shayla's reputation intact and serving John well at this point.

"So, uh, yeah, Tin Cup Wash was a site with more juju than we wanted or expected. It lies here –" and he takes a pointer to their map, a blow-up of the Four Corners, and touches the location of the site. He relates the official site designation, what it was composed of, why it was excavated, etcetera and so forth. He then lists off, in a preview of coming attractions, the various analyses the site demanded of them – bone, stone, ceramic, settlement pattern, soil, turds. He introduces Mellars more thoroughly than he will the others, as he is unknown in archeological circles, and then sits down. Somewhere in his mind he is moderately astonished that he has done what he has just done, but he can't stay there or he will lose track of what's happening in front of him and that thought causes him to panic.

Mellars, though, is good. The bone descriptions are not so bad, Jennie Schultz' report practiced at bone-speak for archeologists in general. But the turd is new territory for most. Mellars teaches first-year med students and fills in for the occasional undergraduate anatomy class, though, and it shows. He dumbs it down just enough so that people get what he's talking about without being made to feel as if they are, in fact, being dumbed down to. Words fly by John: *biochemical analysis, an immunological detection assay method (ELISA), immunoelectrophoresis for blood residues, human myoglobin-specific purified antibody.* Mellars never once uses the word turd, though at a Pecos Conference, with its beer and dirty jeans culture, it would be awfully tempting.

When he's through he beams expectantly, as if Santa's elf has just laid the perfect golden goose egg at everyone's feet, and John is about to turn it over to Warren when a hand shoots up amid low murmurs.

"I knew we wouldn't get to finish," Steve whispers, cursing, but King's on it.

"We'll take questions after the panel has presented all its findings," he says, standing, his voice going to bass levels, unruffled, confident. He sits back down and throws his crew a tired, I-was-expecting-this look. The hand goes back down and the murmuring stops.

Warren hustles to the podium, the crowd a great hushed mass, like some breathing sea creature. "The bones and coprolite have a larger site context that is important to detail," he starts. "My colleague, Steve McLean, will delineate implications of larger-scale settlement pattern data which we feel also play a role, but for now I want to stick to the site." He nods at John and he takes down a blow-up of the coprolite (they could not resist that one) and puts up a map and photo of the kiva with its roof beams collapsed and present. "The kiva, as you see here, did not have either roof-burning or removal of beams for use elsewhere, as is usually the pattern. Rather, it appears to have collapsed after abandonment, unscathed, and abandonment itself appears abrupt. Metates," he breathes, "pots, stone ornaments, and other items were found whole and still usable. The typical pattern of structure abandonment involves removal of virtually all artifacts and materials of value, and this is clearly not the case here." He pauses a minute, then moves on to the pollen analysis, which amounts to a damning declaration of abject failure in the realm of horticulture production. ("The only remains of cultigens were two maize glume fragments from the fill of a puki on the floor and a single, charred maize cupule from the ash dump south of the hearth in one room of the Pueblo above and to the east of the kiva.") He suggests that "the combination of taxa represented in the assemblage suggests that gathering occurred in early spring, which would have been a time of relative food scarcity even under normal conditions." He blinks his wide Irish eyes. Finally, he mentions the high prevalence of red pottery from the Chuska region to the south, and wonders if these people had not moved up from there.

Steve is standing up even before Warren is finished, to quell any chance that the sea creature, still relatively hushed, will stick its tentacles up in the air again. "If the site itself is suggestive of stressful situations with a possibly abrupt and violent end, the data from that time period in the region resonates clearly with it," he says. John exchanges the kiva photo for the Four Corners map again, replete with other dots representing nearby sites. Steve points to them and runs through statistics about how many other structures within a ten-mile radius from Tin Cup had bashed-in bodies at 1150, the fact that the area was abandoned more often than it was occupied, and the implication that, along with soil analysis he has barely begun ("I intend to focus my dissertation on analysis of differential soil production zones"), this was one crappy place to try and make a living.

He sits down and John stands up. The litany of bone breakage, the vivid descriptions of the kiva with its roof beams still prevalent along with many of its artifacts, the Japanese dead – all swirl in John. *What is the definition of evil? What?* But the sea creature is shifting and a twinge of anxiety forces his mouth open. "In conclusion," he says, "while we have no specific explanation for the flare-up of seemingly cannibalistic violence at the end of Pueblo II times in the Four Corners region, we can safely say, about our site, that such violence was preceded by crop failure, occurred during a drought, probably took place in early spring – which is a stressful time in the Southwest even in better years – and that the violence effectively brought on the abandonment of the site." He breathes. It comes to him: *The definition of evil is the utter destruction of another being's dignity. What for, why, how that destruction happens – does it matter? And what small and big evils do we do to ourselves by destroying our own hopes and dreams?* He falters, nearly choking on a remembered sliver, the San Diego State catalog, dog-eared at the history offerings, in his father's trash.

He stares at his text. Someone coughs and the implied restlessness sends more awkward words out of him, though the text is, thank God, scripted in bolded, double-spaced, 20-point font. If not for that he would never get past the marbles in his mouth, the murky despair in his head. He nearly buckles into sad laughter, thinking that the disabilities seemed the least of it at the moment. All that shame *(your own self-hate)*, taken care of by big print he has learned to read by rote. "We speculate—" he stops, tangled, hopeless, breathing hard – "we speculate, based on the high presence of Chuska ceramics, that perhaps these people were relatively new to the region and thus more prone to scapegoating or predatory action by those already 'native' to the area." *Okay. Keep going.* "At any rate, there appears to be an intense 'burst' of it around 1150, at this site and others, and then not again, even though 150 years later drought hit once more, other forms of violence escalated, and the area was effectively abandoned." John dares to look up at the crowd, and lets out a pile of held-in air. "Thank you."

A brief moment of utterly confusing silence sets in. For a second or two people wait for one of them to stand up again, quickly, and quell their questions. But it doesn't happen. Freed of any more information overload, fifty hands shoot up in the air, and a competitive chatter ensues. John and Warren and Steve and King are immobilized by the activity, their chests rearing back as if someone had poked fingers into them. "Shit. I feel like I'm the president at a news conference," Steve mutters.

"Hey," Warren says. "If the president can handle it, so can we. Bush was dumber than hammered owl shit, after all."

"Hammered *owl* shit?" Mellars whispers, delighted and appalled.

But King, the adult, takes over, his chest straight and unruffled. He points to a small man in a wool crusher that in John's mind has seen far too many field seasons and probably smells like a wet sheep after rain.

"How do you know the coprolite is not coyote or some other animal?" Crusher Man asks, looking at Mellars.

Mellars comes to his senses and beams. "Ah. Just the question I would have hoped for. My lab assistant has been asking me that for months now. And I can only say this: The likelihood of a coyote, um, *squatting*, so to speak, in so precise a location seems farfetched. Also, the other proteins isolated in the coprolite are more consistent with human feed than coyote, including those associated with more run of the mill rectal bleeding and the like. A coyote is not likely to bleed human blood proteins from *his* intestines, in other words. He'll bleed coyote proteins, if he's distressed in that way. Also, the coprolite had no alluvium underneath it, suggesting later deposition, but was impinging directly upon ashes in the hearth. Whoever took the poop, in other words, did it prior to any abandonment, when the roof was still on the kiva. I have a hard time seeing a coyote navigating a kiva ladder."

A ripple of laughter runs through the tent and Crusher Man sits down, scowling. A flood of questions follows his dismissal.

"What about witchcraft?"

"How can you argue for cannibalism for certain outside this one coprolite?"

"How likely is it that an Anasazi coprolite has *no* vegetable matter in it?"

"How do we know this is not Toltec-style human sacrifice?"

And so they cascade onto them, question after question, some of the crew attempting to answer now and then, especially if the questions have more reasonable suppositions to them (e.g, "How does the 1150 data compare to later Pueblo III data?"). But John realizes, increasingly, that the crowd is in fact a mix of professional and amateur and, worse, newspaper reporters who know just enough to be dangerous. The noise begins to swell and John groans.

King seems to realize the facts about the crowd at the same

time John does. He stands up. "We do not –" he yells, above and beyond everyone else – "we do not condone sensationalist accounts or suppositions regarding our data." The crowd stops talking, some half-cocked in their seats. "Please. We ask that you respect our findings as much as any other, and that if you have serious scientific issues, to delineate those in answer to our article, which will be published in *American Antiquity* in the coming year. We have not laid out our case in the interest of sensationalism, but in the interest of respecting the history of a people on a landscape. Sometimes," he falters, wiping his face, "Sometimes that history is glorious. Other times it is brutal. But it is human, and I would be remiss if I didn't say that it has compelled me all my life and I should hope it has compelled everyone else here and that – that anything that compels you to such an extent has to have a touch of the holy to it."

Everyone stares at him, dead silent. People look down in their laps, sideways, anywhere but at each other. They'd never admit it, but in that moment John sees that King has reached into the most deeply private part of themselves, and he'd be willing to bet most of the people in that tent have perched on a ruin at 3 a.m. under a full moon in the hope that no one else saw them there, but that the gods themselves were listening, and listening hard.

The silence that follows is impossible. A collective breath swells the tent. John's brain goes lickety-split over tabloid-style notions that his boss has just introduced spirituality into a scientific discussion, that some hyper-rationalist nimrod will at any moment start expostulating on the absurdity of the very notion of holiness, that closet Born Agains, if there are any here, will start evangelizing in response. But the collective breath holds. None of them is used to this, and they do not know what to do.

Then, in the far back, a chair scrapes. A small Native American man stands up. He looks right at King and begins a slow, loud clap. "Thank you, sir," he says. "Thank you. That is all we could hope for from archeologists. Thank you for being so brave."

People turn to look at him, and the swell goes out of the tent in relief. King has received sanctuary from the only authority who could possibly grant it – a Native man whose historical wrath might just as easily have been loosed upon their findings. He smiles, King does, the corners of his mouth wobbling. John knows he is near tears. The urge to take his hand, as he wanted to take his father's, revisits him. He finds himself dropped-jawed inside – you want to do *what?* For your *boss?*

But in all this disbelief, this ferment of political correctness and incorrectness, of respect and sacred secularity, of his boss's emotions on raw display, his eyes stop at the woman sitting next to the Native man.

"My God," he croaks, and as Warren looks at John and King begins gathering up their display posters, John bolts out past the presentation table and into the crowded sea.

CHAPTER 13

I.

Do Not Lose Her. He keeps his eyes pegged on her, as she turns to collect a notebook left on her seat. He jostles elbows and issues vague apologies as he makes for the space between the side of the tent and the last column of chairs. Her chair is on the far left as he faces her, the very last seat in the very last row of the tent. Did she deliberately sit in a place where she could not be easily seen? Is she hiding from him or being polite, knowing that to see her in the open would kick him over into stuck silence? Will she run when he catches up to her? Being the lead on a scientific presentation is nothing compared to this. Nothing. This is Lanie saying goodbye in the phone booth in Flagstaff, this is his sergeant crawling up the ladder into his sniper tower, red paint all over him, this is Sister Teresa having the gall to ask him to read out loud before she realized he could not read at all.

Fuck.

"Meghan!" he calls.

She looks up, pales. Waits for him to come closer. "John," she says. She is neither friendly nor unfriendly. But she seems to be trying to suppress saying anything more. It is his turn to talk, is the message. His turn.

"Let's, uh, can we – can we go somewhere more quiet?" he asks. Her hair is shoulder length and strands of gray course through it.

She nods. A passel of children swirl near her as they exit the tent, and one boy – skinny, sandy haired, slate-blue eyes – comes up to her. John inspects him for signs of Jason, signs of himself. "Mom! Mom! Can I go to Angelica's camp? We want to build a fort!"

She smiles at him. "Sure. I'll be, um," and she looks around the far horizon. "I'll be in that clump of trees over there for a while, ok?" She points vaguely to the southwest, and he nods.

"See ya!" he says.

"Tell Angelica's mom I'll be there in a little bit!"

John doesn't know if he's heard her, but it doesn't matter. "That's your son? That's Nick?"

"Yes," she says. "Last time you saw him he was four months old."

It can't come out as anything but an accusatory truth, that statement, even though her voice is calm and even. He tries to get past this feeling, guilt washing over, then anger. He wants to defend what he has done even as he is trying to reverse it now.

"Why did you come?" he asks. "To Pecos? Do you still keep tabs on archeology?"

They start walking toward the clump of trees, her presence an awkwardness next to him. "Sure," she says. "I have friends who are giving talks here. I wanted to see what my feelings were, too, now that I'm a decade gone from it. I seem to be writing about those days, painting places I worked in the field. And this year the conference was close to home."

"Did you – did you know I'd be here?" That sounds egotistical beyond belief, but he doesn't know how else to ask it.

She laughs a little as if she knows how it sounds. "No. Not until I saw the program."

They stop at the trees.

"Do you even want to talk to me?" he asks. He is a little winded, aware of his too-big stomach taut over a plaid shirt. His heart pounds.

She gazes back at him and pain flits through the muscles in her face. For the first time John understands his cruelty at cutting off all communication; for the first time he lets someone else's pain gained at his expense course through him. He is awash in guilt and sin and faithlessness.

"I think maybe the question is more whether or not you want to talk to me," she says stoically, but her chin wobbles.

John takes her hand wordlessly and gently, the act of that a fall into terrible, gelatinous grace, and stumbles into the trees. He finds a flat shaded spot between a big juniper and a healthy pinon. She follows, not dropping his hand, and they sit, cross-legged, across from each other. The sun has come out and for the time being, anyway, the storms hold off. It must be after five.

"I'm sorry, Meghan," he says, his stomach in his legs and his fingers threading hers. He bounces both their hands up and down a little in nervousness. She swallows, waiting for more. John knows Meghan, knows she wants to talk on and on, knows she wants to fill in this awful silence with implications and reper-cussions and why why why and understanding and anger. But she is the one who said everything toward the end; he is the one who told her to leave him alone.

John swallows. "I'm not very good that this."

"I know. I just – I just – do you know how *cruel* it was that you never talked to me again?" She lets go of his hand and her fists ball and unball and her voice cracks, unable to help itself, and she juts her jaw at him. "I never got *any* closure. I had to do it all myself. That was so hard." Now she's openly crying and she blows her nose on a bandana she digs out of the little backpack she is carrying. "Shit. All the anger's back up. I haven't felt it for years and now here it is," she says. "Dammit. I don't want you to think I've spent the last nine years seething."

"I don't think that," he says. "You really loved me." He is watching her cry and feeling terrible.

She looks across at him. "Yes, you stupid shit. And I know you really loved me. And you never fucking *owned* it. That's all I wanted. Whether that meant we'd be with each other or honestly 'break up' it doesn't matter."

They look at each other. The evil feeling snakes around again, evasive, sideways, fearful of mirrors. "It was wrong of me to deny myself love," he says, trying to ignore the snake. He feels like he is in confession and that this is the hardest thing he has ever admitted to, but also the only true thing.

He is just like his father, he thinks, his shoulders curling in despair. And he repeats to himself what he said at his father's deathbed, what Meghan has just said: *You stupid, stupid shit.* That by keeping her – whatever she was to him – in the jeweled box, he denied himself love. All along he thought he was keeping it safe. *Sin,* the Bendectine monk comes back, *is not taking full account.* Shit.

"It is always wrong to deny yourself love," she says softly, echoing the monk in her own way. "A person who does that doesn't love himself."

He has to nod, but she goes on. "You wanted some little girl to protect. Made you feel like a big man. You wanted Smart Meghan to think you were smart, to praise you in spite of all your shit around school. But a funny thing happened, John." She looks straight at him. "I took all your love and protectiveness and I started to grow up. I *believed* your love. I believed you loved *me,* not my emotional state. Not my ability to prop you up in some closet in your heart where you could always go to feel good about yourself without ever having to do your own share of the work. And yet there was a place where we loved each other honestly and cleanly and enough to make for a marriage. We really *liked* each other. We both felt that, didn't we? That's what I was trying to tell you when I called you the last time and said I could be with you, that I would want that."

"But you were with Jason," he says, wanting her included in this.

She nods. "From the beginning, John, when I'd have, I don't know, visions of having a baby, or stability, or a home, that actually involved someone else, it was Jason. I think I felt you would never go there with me." She looks down at the ground, sad.

John is very still. "What if I had? Said, I'll divorce Sweeney and go with you?"

She looks at her fingernails now, then back at him. "I don't believe you ever would have. Not the John I knew. And that was just the point." She shakes her head. "Now that I have sixteen years on a partnership, now that thanks to a lot of good old girl therapists and the steady trust of a man whose trust I sometimes didn't deserve, I can hold subtlety and love and sex in my own home most of the time now – not always, but most of the time. That was always the deal with me, John, to turn home into a safe, uncontaminated place. I don't think that's what you have with Sweeney." She looks up. "I'm sorry. I don't mean to bring Sweeney into this. But I have wondered about you and her a lot. I could see that a man who had to keep his deepest love in a box was someone who would not be a good partner. I'd end up another Sweeney, carrying you along, if I went with you. I never had to carry Jason like that."

He hates her words. He hates the possibility of truth in them. Surely he is a better man than that? "But if I could have – would you have – ? If you didn't have to carry me? What about Jason?"

"It would have been hard. To make a choice. Really hard." She turns away and peers into the trees. "It can sound so romantic to say you had the love of two men. For a long time that fed that place where I'd been so unloved and left for dirt ugly for so long. I felt so beautiful around you." She stops and smiles a bittersweet smile at him that makes him buckle.

"You were beautiful. Are."

She blushes and goes on, shaking her head. "But it was really an agony. I told Jason about the truth of you at the point where I realized that to keep you lingering as even a potential lover was making for a split-off life, instead of healing old splits the way it was at first. And so, it was better the way it went."

"You honestly looked yourself in the mirror and said, 'I can't deceive myself over this anymore?'" He is flying by the seat of his pants, taking his cues from his earlier happenstance meeting.

"Yes."

"You looked yourself in the mirror and said you could let go of this thing with me? Let go of that love?"

"I didn't let go of the *love,* John. You do me wrong there. I said I would take it and give it to myself in my everyday life. Love like that does not die, but it can be transformed."

"And that didn't cause you pain?"

She snorts. "It caused me a lot of pain." She takes his hand back again. "I sometimes still look at the one or two photos I have of you. I dream of you, occasionally. You and my first therapist saved my life that first year when I fell apart and the world ended. I miss your flintknapping and your hands and your massages and the way you combed out my hair after a bath." She chokes up again. "I really miss those things. Those qualities Jason doesn't have as much. He has gentle hands and touch but he's not built like you, where the world is understood through texture and fingertips and bodily sensation and sound. I was so out of my body that it was perfect for me, to have that come back through you." She laughs a little. "Sometimes I think I gave you my head and you gave me your body and together we made a complete human being."

He lets his hand be held. If he wanted to he could feel the old passion, the old urges, but she's right – they seem built on a fantasy of protection and incompleteness, where one provides what the other doesn't have. But she's also right about a deeper love. He could never not love her, and his stomach turns in grief.

"Maybe," he says quietly, "the jeweled box started out to be a closet to keep you in. But I think it turned into something to keep because of what you just said."

They hold each other's gaze. He takes off his tinted glasses and leaves them off. She has crow's feet, now, around her eyes, but they are the same heartfelt eyes he has always known. "What do you mean?"

The shriek of children plays out through the air, far away. Campfires are starting up, the smoke wafting toward them. The shadows are long on the trees, but 5:30 or 6 in August is still a long way to sunset. The children's shouts waft in again. "I think," John scratches out, "that to let go of you was too hard. And Nick. Your child." But now the tears are spilling and he can't look at her. "Sometimes – you know, when we saw each other that time and you were only a month along – sometimes I've wondered –" God, he cannot say this, cannot admit this.

"You wondered if he was your child?" she says, very softly.

He only nods, the lump in his throat large, his eyes downcast.

"You wanted a baby with me?" she asks, amazed, crying now too.

"Yes," he wheezes, and puts his hands to his face. How much he has blown it has never been clearer.

Meghan reaches for him and hugs him to her.

"I'm sorry," he mewls, into her hair. "I am so sorry."

II.

"That was brilliant, Mark, brilliant," Shayla Greer is saying as John approaches the campsite. "Shut everyone right up." King is beaming and a bustle of people swarm the camp. Their crew seems to be the talk of the tent, so to speak, with Mellars holding court with more biochemically minded sorts off the one side and Steve throwing out words like "loser clans" and "Chaco" and "differential access" to another bunch of cronies. Beer bottles abound, and a fire has been started.

Meghan and John have parted ways fifty feet from camp. He has her email address, she his. He doesn't know what else they have, but they have that. Only Warren seems to see him, and steps out of the throng a little bit, a stocky near-shadow in the sharp light of evening. John wishes at that moment that they were at his place in Salt Lake and Warren were cooking him breakfast. All the kindness that he is remembers itself in John's bones, and he takes off his glasses, wipes his eyes, and holds his gaze to Warren's.

"Oh, man," he says, seeing John's face in its entirety, perhaps for the first time in his life. "You look like shit."

"I know."

"Want a beer and some food?" he asks, clasping his shoulder as they turn to walk toward the others.

"Yes," he says, and they both know they don't need say anything else.

PART SEVEN

CHAPTER 14

I.

If someone were to ask him how he survived the chatter of that evening, or the ride home to Salt Lake, he is not sure he could tell them. He managed to eat and then slip away into his tent the moment darkness fell, and there he slept the sleep of the exhausted. He felt as if blankets he had carried all his life were no longer weighing down his shoulders, but had slipped off in tattered fragments all around him, and that if he died that night his body would be found, a shriveled, done-in, nude thing amongst a scatter of shredded Pendletons and moth-eaten buffalo hides. Warren has to shake his tent to get him to wake up the next morning, or he would have slept through the day. He stumbles to pack up, say a few good-byes, and occupy his seat in the back of the Suburban. Steve they drop off in Santa Fe, King telling him he has a crew chief job with him anytime. Steve grins his dopey, wide-mouthed grin, but his eyes are shy and he throws John a look somewhere between gratitude and respect. John, surprised, salutes, ever so slightly, letting the irony of the ingrained Marine Corps in him play in a smile that almost reveals itself. Steve smirks back and John feels, obscurely, gratefully, that Steve and Warren and even King and Mellars – not to mention George – have somehow begun to save his life. In that dim haze he listens as Mellars, Warren, and King make small talk as they wind out of the Rio Grande basin and back up the Chama Valley. John dozes in and out, snatches of dreams and places coming to him and then fading out again. He is recording a hogan in Kana'a Wash half a mile back of Wukoki Ruin at Wupatki. He is finding a basket, nine hundred years old, stuffed in a cleft in Mule Canyon, southeastern Utah. Sweeney smiles at him from under blonde bangs as she knaps a Desert Side-Notched point in the eastern Oregon dusk. Someone feeds him pasta. Coco meows.

Nina sands a piece of driftwood into the shape of an owl. Surf thunders and he is sucked into a sea cave to delighted seals.

They camp again, this time up Kane Creek outside of Moab, red dirt underneath them and a sheer red canyon drop-off immediately to the north. While John is realizing their entire campsite is a giant lithic scatter full of white chert, King offers him a job.

"What?" he says, not quite hearing King as he is fishing for a place to lay his bag down without disturbing too much ground. "I can't believe the BLM would designate a campsite on top of such an obvious scatter."

"The Bureau of Lonely Men knows no bounds when it comes to stupidity sometimes," King says. "Now, I asked you if you needed employment."

"Yes," he says. He looks directly at him too. Fuck Sweeney, he thinks. Not Sweeney Sweeney, but Sweeney the Coattail. He rolls his eyes at himself, at his torn-apart life. "That'd be great." Then he remembers George and frowns.

"What is it?" King asks.

"I promised my Makah friends that I'd teach them some traditional technologies in preparation for their whale hunt this fall."

"You can do what I'd like you to do from there. It's just lithic analysis. From two of Warren's old projects that're taking forever to wrap up. I'll have another project for you next summer if my bids go through, but I can get you through the winter."

John stops playing with his bag and folds it over his arms. "You mean that?"

He grins. "You still look like death warmed over from yesterday, but yeah."

"Thanks," he says, and realizes King and Warren had taken a little walk into City Market together in Moab not an hour ago, to buy steaks and firewood. He wonders what Warren has told him. "You trust me, I take it," John says as King turns to go.

King stops. Ruffles his hair in what seems to be the same

wonderment as John possesses around this issue of trust. "Well,
yes, I guess I do. I guess," he says, looking at Mellars laughing as
Warren tries to start a fire and fails, "I trust the lot of you. I've
never seen people work so well together."

"My life's a pig sty at the moment," John blurts. He wants him
to know exactly what he's getting, in sort of a pre-emptive self-
protection. He doesn't want him disappointed in him later on. "I
don't know if I'm married or not, I don't know what home is.
Beyond your offer I have nothing. And I will always read with a
ruler."

King nods and squints. "Warren told me."

"And you're okay with that?"

He chuckles. "The ruler is the least of it, isn't it? Just the
symptom of a whole lot of other garbage, eh? The set up for it."
He nods to himself. "Been there with my own version of that,
man, you can be sure. So you'll be a fine worker, given all that
necessary diligence, won't you?" And he skips off into the red-
flushed twilight of canyon country, beauty, as the Navajo would
say, all around him.

II.

The sea's a nasty shade of gray, as is the sky. They are pretty much
the same shade, and waves crash into Neah Bay. "Are you sure
you want to whale in this?" John yells at George, through the rain
and wind. They stand, with matching yellow rain slicks, on the
pier.

George nods. "It'll abate tomorrow."

John waits a heartbeat and then says, "After this I have to go
back to Salt Lake."

"I know."

"So you still haven't told me who you killed in your car
accident."

"Jeez, bro." George turns to him.

John looks at him. "You're the diver," John says, simply. They've spent the last three months flintknapping, making cedar bark cord, and bladders out of sewn-up seal skins. Peter and Howard have even sat in the same circle as George, begrudgingly, making twine. Nina, though, has melted all of them, chattering as she whacks off chert with an ease it takes most mortals years to learn. Howard and Nina smile at each other now and then, a subtle, great love ebbing and flowing between father and daughter. John sees this and sends what he supposes he'd call a prayer, for lack of a better term, out into the great Pacific, where he is certain the seals in San Diego are paying attention. *Maybe one father and one offspring can get it right this time. Maybe this will turn the planet around.* Thanks to her driftwood sales, which are gaining a certain cachet as collectibles and are therefore arcing upward in price, Howard has to leave less and less for shitty pay doing construction in Port Angeles, or Bremerton, or Seattle. John thinks of his role in this as perhaps the one product of good – like a beautiful piece of wood floating in from the sea – he has managed to wring from his failures.

George is nodding into the spray of wind and rain. "I am the diver. That's true."

"So…"

"Saw your final edits," he says. "Your proofs." They seem to be talking past each other.

John sighs. "You did?"

"Sure. Disabilities Lady showed me. Melinda Weeks."

"So?"

"Pretty good. Even I could read it."

"Thanks."

"But you got rid of Wayne. On the title page."

"You mean my name?"

"Yeah." The wind's howling and John can't believe they're talking like this, but then again, if the wind weren't there, they wouldn't be talking at all.

"I think that died with my dad," John says.

"John Gregory Thompson, then. No Wayne."

"Yes. Do you like it?"

He smiles. "I'll have to call you John Gregory-bro now."

"Only if you tell me who you killed."

He turns, heavy, the rain dripping down over the lip of his hood. "Let's go back to the shack, man. I'll tell you there."

So they go to the shack and George reveals everything. If Sweeney is a swirling agony from John's mistaken past, a voice in the phone call he makes twice a week to hold desperately to some last strings of a status quo he knows he no longer wants but does not know how to change into something else, then so is one Rowena Newall to George. George's face withers, a large brown prune, as he explains the ex-fiancé who once carried a baby in her and who once had a brother who was George's best friend.

"I killed them both," he says. "The baby, and my friend, I mean."

John can't look at him. He stares into the fire, its pop and hiss and the rain outside the only noise. "I don't know what to say to that."

George half-snorts. "I don't either, bro. Not after a year, even. Not after twenty lifetimes."

"You have Nina, though. She adores you."

"Yeah. You have Nina too, you know."

John smiles. Nina-cum-Mehgan at her most childish. Nina the little girl whom he has helped but who stands quite well on her own. "Thanks," he says.

"I maybe got my friend back, too, a little, through you," he says wanly, as if he knows how feeble this is, because people you love are not replaceable.

"So that explains your behavior," John says, trying for a light touch.

"You mean why I told you you had had to come back, asshole?"

"Yeah. That."

"Well, there you go."

"What about Rowena?" John asks.

George shakes his head. "She's more of a ghost than Sweeney is to you, since after the crash she moved away."

. "Do you ever see her?" John asks, after a respectful silence where they sip instant coffee around his sputtering wood stove.

George shakes his head again. It is clear he can't talk about it without his chin wavering and tears spilling out of him. "I really fucked up. She married some guy in Vancouver. Teaches up there on one of the rezes."

"Was that your baby she lost in the accident?"

A sob finally barks out of him. "Yeah, man, what do you think?"

"Sorry. I am so sorry, George."

Silence again.

"I could have had a baby, too," John says, after a time.

He looks at him. "What do you mean?"

"I mean, I mean –." What does he mean? That if he'd lived an entirely different life he would have been a proud father of a couple of kids, with a clean lover who helped him make those kids? Well, yeah. "I mean I didn't know I wanted that, maybe, until now."

George swallows. "Did Sweeney ever want kids?"

John wags his head no. "She, uh," he breathes heavily, as if to clear words stuck in his chest, "she never did. And made it so she couldn't early on."

"Wow," says George. "Well, You could divorce Sweeney and find someone else. Or get you and her to adopt."

"Yeah," John snorts, "and you could forget Rowena and move right along and do the same thing."

He snorts back. "Not likely, eh?"

"No. Not easily, anyway."

"How come life isn't like the movies?" And then he hyenas

the old George hyena laugh. John smiles and stands up as George does.

"Gotta go?" he asks.

"Yeah. Prepare for tomorrow. I gotta whale to redeem."

"Good luck," he says.

"You'll be there on the beach when we get back?"

"You bet. I want to see if my equipment held up."

III.

The sea is uneasy the whole time. John works in spurts, a half hour here or there, on lithics. Or he goes to the library and attends to emails regarding the final draft on Tin Cup Wash. The proofs are back from *American Antiquity*, along with peer reviews. The journal editors grumbled about how long it took, but none of the comments were a surprise. Someone will write a rebuttal about witchcraft; another letter will come in insisting the turd was just coyote crap all along. The arguments are tireless and often simply for the sake of themselves. He can focus for a time on such minutiae but then he wonders if the crew is not coming into view; if their slender, elegant wooden canoes are not rowing in, the rain lashing all around them. George gave up on grease and went for a wet suit. The November weather has been nothing less than atrocious. But the whales had been scouted. It was time.

For three days John wanders out of his shack, to the library, back to the gas station for instant cocoa, out to the pier. Elderly women pat his hand, beaming that their grandsons are out to sea in some of the most treacherous weather John has seen yet. Nina proudly announces to anyone who will hear that her uncle is the diver. Old men sit under dripping eaves and tip their chairs back, their eyes looking to the same sea as John's do. Four days. Five. A week. The old ladies, still beaming, exhibit creases along their brow. The men chew tobacco and jerky a little uneasily. Sweeney asks him when he will be home. He asks if he has a home. She asks if he wants one with her, if she is the woman he wants. And he would say yes but when he thinks about the baby he lurches inside because then it is never her baby. He doesn't know if this is because he has never conceived of her carrying one, knowing her tubes to be tied, or if it really is because she would not be the person to do that with. He is fifty years old. Isn't he past baby age anyway? What kind of man dumps his wife and marries some young thing, just to procreate? And that wasn't the point anyway, was it? Just like the ruler was symptomatic of a whole lot of garbage, as King said. As Colleen Jensen tried to point out to him years ago. You can handle a disability if you accept its presence in your life, just as you can handle a childless marriage if you accept the marriage.

Meghan used to say that men had a cow path going between right and left brain, women a super-highway. The super-highway allowed for processing of such difficult questions with relative ease. The cow path stupefies John. Meghan would be happy, he thinks, that he is even able to ask the questions at all.

Maybe this is just a tale of regrets, of mid-life reckoning. Don't we all do that? He asks. He stumbles on an out-of-date self-help book in the library that suggests just that. But after two pages he finds himself stereotyped, labeled, and cajoled into that acceptance, and he is not ready for it yet. He writes both Lindsay and Meghan tentatively, little tentacles of restoration that are terrified and half-assed. And there is a reason why he has returned to such rainy country, aside from George. Why he is not ready for the desert canyons just yet.

That will come. King is still pleased with him and is bidding on a contract for Grand Gulch country that Warren and John would co-direct come summer. It is odd, to be gaining footing he has yearned for all his life at such an old age. He will never be a famous academic. Louis Leakey is not in his sights. But perhaps a stand-alone career is. Perhaps he does not have to leave everything to Sweeney. And that leaves her, by herself, in a field devoid of anything but grass and wind, unprotected, all the cross hairs of love and familiarity and uncertainty blowing by like the hair on her head, every which way.

Shit.

"Hey!" A shout.

"I see them!"

A great wave of yelling goes through the village. John is buying Slim Jims at the station and runs out the door without even paying for them. The rain is a merciful mist at the moment, and in the oncoming dusk a canoe curls in on the waves. Then another, and another.

The third has something, they can tell. It is slower, and has a dragline of white ocean water streaming behind it.

"They caught one!" Nina shrieks, dancing around him. "They caught one!"

John doesn't know that you "catch" a whale, but he smiles at her. "Looks like it."

It must take a long time for the canoes to beach, for their smooth prows, like the sharp heads of knowing animals, to slide onto the sand, but it seems less than that. Bonfires have been lit, drums out, celebrations begun. The men in the boats shout their triumphs and at last John sees George, hopping out by the third canoe, the whale lolling in the surf. The crew in the canoe waits for bigger surf and positions it so that it rides forward onto the sand on the wave.

John can barely see.

"John! John Gregory-bro," George shouts above the roar of surf and the cackle of people-talk and bonfires, looking for him.

John spits forward from behind the fires. "Here! I'm here! Congratulations." George's face is wet, with rain or tears or ocean water John cannot tell, but he looks happier than he has ever seen him. George is shaking with cold as he hugs him.

He slides something into John's hand as he pulls away. "Now

cut!"

"What is this?" he asks. But as soon as he looks down he knows what it is.

"The Folsom. The point you gave me a long time ago, bro, in exchange for the salmon. Remember?"

"I do."

He gestures toward the whale's mouth. They walk up to it, that enormous black-gray carcass. The mouth slopes down to the beach, superbly barnacled. The other end curves right to the whale's eye. It is sealed by stitches George has sewn in deep ocean.

"Look at it," he says. "Look at it and cut."

John wavers. "Are you sure – shouldn't you do that? Isn't this really for a Makah?"

He shakes his head vehemently. "It's for you."

And so he takes the Folsom, the knife point he made, sharpened, he sees, to precision, and crouches down in front of the whale's nose. He sees the stitches but first he leans over onto that slimy, barnacled, black mass and puts his ear to it. The whale is cold on his skin, but he does not care. He lets his ear sink into the wet beast and listens like a man sounding a river, his fingers under the cedar twine. The entire tribe might be watching, but he does not care about that either. His father, Sweeney, Warren, King, and most proudly of all, Colleen and Meghan. They might be watching too. But he is sounding now, listening. Sounding.

"Goddamn it, cut!" George is impatient.

He hears, he thinks, one last sigh from deep within the whale. And takes the blade and cuts.

THE END

BOOKS

O is a symbol of the world, of oneness and unity. In different cultures it also means the "eye," symbolizing knowledge and insight. We aim to publish books that are accessible, constructive and that challenge accepted opinion, both that of academia and the "moral majority."

Our books are available in all good English language bookstores worldwide. If you don't see the book on the shelves ask the bookstore to order it for you, quoting the ISBN number and title. Alternatively you can order online (all major online retail sites carry our titles) or contact the distributor in the relevant country, listed on the copyright page.

See our website www.o-books.net for a full list of over 500 titles, growing by 100 a year.

And tune in to myspiritradio.com for our book review radio show, hosted by June-Elleni Laine, where you can listen to the authors discussing their books.

mySpiritRadio